AMATEUR NIGHT

Jane da Silva novels by K. K. Beck

Amateur Night
A Hopeless Case

K.K.BECK

AMATEUR NIGHT

THE MYSTERIOUS PRESS

Published by Warner Books

A Time Warner Company

Mysterious Press books are published by Warner Books, Inc., 1271 Avenue of the Americas, New York, NY 10020.

W A Time Warner Company

The Mysterious Press name and logo are registered trademarks of Warner Books, Inc.

Printed in the United States of America

First printing: July 1993

10 9 8 7 6 5 4 3 2 1

Library of Congress Cataloging-in-Publication Data

Beck, K. K.
    Amateur night / K.K. Beck.
        p.   cm.
    ISBN 0-89296-480-4
    I. Title.
PS3552.E248A43   1993
813'.54—dc20   92-56769
                                                         CIP

For Fernando

Chapter 1

Jane da Silva had been making a concerted effort to cheer herself up with a low budget shopping fling at a place she thought of affectionately as the teen tart store. And while Jane knew she shouldn't really be spending any money on clothes right now, and conversely, that if she was, she certainly deserved to do it somewhere better than this place, she had managed to assemble a collection of cotton knit items in bright colors that sort of worked because they didn't pretend to be expensive. She also thought she could carry them off reasonably well through sheer force of personality. And the things she'd chosen were basic enough so that it didn't really matter that, at thirty-seven, she was about twenty years older than the store's target market.

It was too bad, however, that she had to run into Bucky Montcrieff, of all people, as she was coming out of the place laden down with big, crinkling white shopping bags of cheap chic.

Bucky Montcrieff, the ultimate consumer and devotee of perfect tailoring and natural fabrics, didn't even bother to look anything but horrified and embarrassed for her. But then Bucky, tall, handsome, mid-thirties and not without a certain oozy charm, wasn't a particularly nice person.

He peered past her and into the store, over the electronic gate meant to catch shoplifted merchandise with buzzers and alarms. At the counter, a teenage girl in black wrinkled rayon, with hennaed hair and a Morticia Addams complexion, slouched sullenly. Grunge rock, a Seattle specialty, droned away. Jane thought she could smell the oily, chemical scent of polyester wafting out of the place.

"Did you buy something in there?" he said tactlessly.

"Sometimes I think too much good taste can be a vulgar thing, don't you?" she said with a big smile. Unfortunately, Bucky was someone she had to be nice to.

Bucky worked in his uncle's law firm, Carlson, Throckmorton, Osgood, Stubbins, etc., which happened to be the law firm that had drawn up Uncle Harold's eccentric will.

"I'm really sorry the trustees didn't give you your uncle's money," he said. "I've been thinking about you."

It had been a couple of weeks since Jane had appealed to the board of trustees of Uncle Harold's quaintly named Foundation for Righting Wrongs. The way the will was set up, Jane had to find some hopeless case to solve as a kind of nonprofit detective before she could cash in on her inheritance. The trustees, a group of querulous old men, cronies of Uncle Harold, had bounced her first effort on a technicality.

"I thought I'd give it another try," she said, trying to sound brave and cheerful and insouciant. She was determined that Bucky, elegant, handsome, well-heeled, overperfumed and overconfident Bucky, wouldn't feel sorry for her.

"I know, but you really tried so hard, and you got beat up and everything," he said. "You must be pretty discouraged. I feel sorry for you." A look that closely resembled sympathy passed over his smooth brow.

"I'm fine, really," she lied, wondering if Bucky wanted her to start sniffling a little and collapse on his shoulder. She wouldn't give him the satisfaction. She deflected his halfhearted offer of coffee, and tried not to let the encounter unsettle her. When he'd first met her, and it looked like she was coming into a fortune, he'd been extremely attentive. Bucky was clearly one of those smug people who don't like to be around failure, she thought. They were often the same people who'd made it with a great deal of help from their relatives.

Well, Uncle Harold had tried to help her. It was out of respect for him, she felt, that the board had given her a few thousand dollars to tide her over, but it had occurred to her she might have to get some kind of job if another suitable hopeless case didn't come up soon. She imagined herself holding a sheaf of oversized menus and saying, "Smoking or non?" in a dignified voice to restaurant patrons. Which wouldn't be the end of the world. As long as she didn't have to do it forever. Jane was plagued by habitual restlessness.

She went back home—home being Uncle Harold's gloomy old house on Capitol Hill. The board let her live there for now. It was an asset of the foundation. If Jane found a case the board liked, she planned to completely redo the place. Refinish the nice wood details, now covered in dark varnish; prune the overgrown camellias and let in some light; get rid of the pink Formica counters in the kitchen.

On the porch, she heard the phone ring, and managed to get inside and pick it up in about three rings. "Jane? Calvin Mason here."

"Oh," she said breathlessly.

Her adrenaline was still pumping from the experience of standing on the porch shifting packages and jamming the key into the lock while the phone rang within the house.

"You still looking for a hopeless case?"

"Desperately," she said. She didn't have to put on an act for Calvin like she did for Bucky.

"There might be some new evidence in a case of mine. I represented this guy who was convicted and now a juror says we all overlooked something."

"Sounds wonderful," she said.

"Maybe. You want to know what I feel? Deep in my heart? Speaking as the guy's attorney, and as a human being? There's no doubt in my mind. My client is clearly guilty as hell." He cleared his throat. "To tell you the truth, I guess I used the case as an excuse to call just to see how you were doing."

"I'm doing okay," she said. "And you don't need an excuse. But you know I'd like to come up with another little project for those trustees. Tell me more about the juror."

"I got a phone call from her this morning. She said she'd been thinking about the case. Happens all the time. They think you want to rehash everything, when all you want to do is try and collect a fee and get on to something else. Something hopefully a little more profitable."

"So what did she say?"

"She wants to come in and talk to me tomorrow. Like I say, she thinks everybody overlooked something. I thought you might like to be there. It might be something you can do something with. Because there's no way I'm going to devote any time to this lousy case."

"What kind of case was it?"

"It was," said Calvin, sighing audibly over the phone, "my one and only murder case. So I feel obligated to listen to what juror number ten has to say, even though I can't imagine anything she'd say that would change my mind about Kevin.

"A lot of jurors hate to convict," he continued. "They

look hard to find some reason not to. I remember her. A sweet-looking older woman with a big soft face. I pegged her for a bleeding-heart type the minute I clapped eyes on her." He paused, and said casually, and Jane thought a little shyly, "If you want me to brief you on the case, why don't you come by for a beer later? Maybe a pizza or something?"

"Okay," said Jane. Calvin Mason was one of the handful of people in town who knew what she was doing here in Seattle in the first place. She could relax around him. She didn't have to come up with some story about her life, which, on the surface of it, seemed rather blank just now. And she liked Calvin, a lawyer with a scruffy little practice who made an extra buck here and there as an investigator for more well-heeled lawyers—like Bucky.

Jane felt a certain kinship with Calvin Mason. They both lived a little bit on the edge. And he'd been sweet to her during her last attempt to get her hands on Uncle Harold's money. Of course, she'd said she'd pay him when she cashed in, but she never did cash in, and he seemed to take it pretty well. Failing to collect money was, she had gathered, a lifelong habit of his. It was something else she had in common with him, but she was determined to get tougher about her life. She'd made a vow not to be broke anymore after forty. If Calvin's case panned out, she could live a respectable life, forget about the teen tart store and get herself some cashmere sweaters for fall.

• • •

Calvin Mason's office, in the Fremont district, was actually unit number three in the Compton Apartments, a twenties brick building that he also managed. The living room had some comfortable old upholstered pieces and a large battered desk flanked by twin army surplus file cabinets. It was a comfortable room, not as grim as Bucky had once described it to Jane ("a pathetic little office with a Murphy bed and a degree from Matchbook U"), especially as it had recently been painted.

Calvin Mason was in his thirties, with thick curly dark hair, horn-rimmed glasses and a somewhat bearlike quality. He had an intelligent, watchful face that also looked as if it could be transformed fairly easily into amusement.

"Pizza's on its way," he said when she arrived, popping open a can of Rainier beer for himself and pouring one for her into a prefrosted glass, a hospitable touch she found charming. He ripped open the top of a bag of Chee-tos. "Hors d'oeuvres," he said, pouring it into a salad bowl and setting it down on the coffee table. Then he flung himself into a big easy chair, swallowed some beer, leaned back and closed his eyes. "I mean, the guy was good for it. I knew that from the word go. Everybody knew it, except him." He opened his eyes and looked at her. "Been shopping?"

Jane was sitting forward on the sofa. She had changed into bright yellow pants and a large dark turquoise T-shirt. The shirt still had the store folds in it.

She was a little embarrassed that he'd figured out she'd been shopping, because of the money she still owed him from her last aborted case.

"Ten-dollar sale," she said airily. Actually, while the shirt had been ten dollars, the pants were $19.95—still undeniably cheap. Anyway, she did intend to take care of him as soon as she could, and she'd already told him so, so there didn't seem any point in saying it again. Jane believed constant apologizing just irritated people.

Calvin Mason didn't seem to have connected her shopping with his lack of payment. "You look nice," he said, with a shiny-eyed look of wistful appreciation. Jane hadn't

decided whether Calvin was actually attracted to her—
there were flickers of it, like just now—or whether he was
just one of those appealing men who seem to be slightly
in love with all women.

He closed his eyes again. "Anyway, Kevin was all messed
up on drugs. As usual. He was a drug pig. Uppers,
downers, never quite getting the dosage right. That's why
he was knocking over a pharmacy in the first place. He
says he can't remember what happened between the time
he sauntered into the place and the time he dropped his
gun in plain view with his fingerprints on it right in the
middle of the store. The cops came and found him sitting
on a curb a few blocks away with a bad case of the shakes.
We're not talking about a criminal mastermind here."

"Sounds good and hopeless," Jane said.

"It's hopeless, all right," he said. "Even his mom swears
he's guilty, for God's sake. I delicately suggested she take
out a second mortgage on her house to finance an appeal, but she said there wasn't any point in it." He
grabbed a handful of Chee-tos and shrugged. "I had to
agree with her."

"Poor guy," said Jane.

"Who? Me or my client?"

"Well he's the one in the slammer. What was the
sentence?"

"Twenty to life. He's in Monroe."

"That part sounds good and hopeless," she said. Springing someone from a grim penal institution. Surely the
board would be touched by that. "But I'm a little un-
nerved by the fact that his lawyer and his mother have
abandoned all hope. Tell me exactly what happened."

Calvin sighed. "He went into this little mom-and-pop
pharmacy on First Hill. Pop was in the back room, mixing
up a batch of something. Mom was at the counter typing
a prescription label. He went in and tried to get some

drugs. He displayed a weapon. Mom had been through it all before. She pulled out a big old Colt .45 from behind the counter. I guess he didn't look scary enough. He's a weasely little guy, and, like I said, he had the shakes."

"That should have scared her," said Jane.

"The lady fired a shot into the ceiling, but she got one from him right in the forehead. Then my guy panicked and ran off, dropping the gun on his way out. The husband ran in and found his wife dead and the weapon on the floor."

"And there were no witnesses? Was this broad daylight?"

"That's right. It's not a big modern drugstore. Just a little hole in the wall that depends on prescriptions from nearby doctors' offices. They just have a prescription counter and a few odds and ends at the register. Key chains, candy bars, magazines."

Jane remembered that First Hill was full of hospitals and medical offices. Its nickname was Pill Hill. In fact, she'd been born there, at Swedish Hospital.

"But anyone could have walked in while he was holding up the place," she said.

"That's right. Like I say, Kevin isn't exactly your criminal genius. I've been defending him for years. Ever since he racked up enough points as a juvenile to get into serious trouble. Meter picking was his specialty. But Kevin is nineteen now."

The doorbell rang and Calvin went to answer it. Jane dug in her purse for some cash. If she could afford new clothes and owed him money, the least she could do was spring for the pizza. He brushed her cash aside. "Never mind," he said.

"Anyway," he continued, arranging the pizza in front of her on the coffee table and gently tearing apart the triangles, "I told him a million times as he got toward his eighteenth birthday that the stuff that was no big deal for a juvenile could be a big-time felony after his birthday. So what does he do? Goes out and kills an old lady." He bit the point of a slice of pizza and paused for a second to savor the taste. "Hopeless enough for you?"

Jane handed him a napkin and helped herself to pizza. "Definitely. What kind of a defense did you mount?"

"Well, the results would indicate that it was a crummy defense," said Calvin. "Not that I had much to work with. Kevin's story was that he blacked out. But he had some low-life friends waiting for him around the corner in a car. I hinted that perhaps they came in and did the deed. No one ever found them. I hammered away on that." Calvin took on a Clarence Darrow pose and demanded indignantly, "'Why haven't we seen my client's companions in court here today?'" He sighed. "I intimated that when we'd tried to get the cops to find them, they'd thrown out the paperwork. Which was basically true."

The pizza was terrific. She realized she'd forgotten to eat lunch today. "Did you look for them?"

"It was a little hard. Kevin hardly knew them. That's the kind of jerk he is. One white female, one white male. In their teens. He just knew them as Dorothy and Sean. Druggers. They provided the gun and said they'd wait for him at the corner. When they heard the shot, they must have taken off. Perfectly reasonable thing to do. So he sat there at the curb waiting for them, but the police found him instead."

Calvin polished off his first slice of pizza, then dived at the cardboard box for number two. "Then I carried on about the absence of powder burns. The prosecution clouded it all up with technical testimony and then speculated that he'd worn gloves and ditched them. It was very cold that day. In fact, it snowed that day.

"I said if he'd had gloves, why were his prints on the gun, but they said he'd handled the gun before coming to rob the place. So I said, okay, he handled it, but that doesn't mean he fired it. I thought if anything would get him off, it would be the lack of powder burns.

"Then we tried out the concept that because his shadowy companions had provided him with the gun, he didn't necessarily know it was loaded. The prosecutor chewed me up and spat me out. He said there wasn't any proof these people even existed, and certainly no testimony to indicate Kevin didn't know the gun was loaded. I knew I'd lost the jury when he pointed out that if Kevin thought it was empty, there wasn't much point in his pulling the trigger. They actually nodded. With self-righteous looks on their faces. Always a bad sign."

Jane clicked her tongue with sympathy. "Where did the gun come from?"

"A residential burglary. It was registered to a law-abiding dentist on Capitol Hill, and had disappeared along with his VCR and the stereo sometime previously."

"How did they find Kevin? You say he was sitting on a curb in a daze."

Calvin rolled his eyes to the ceiling. "It hardly ever snows in Seattle, right? But it snowed that day. Kevin left a big muddy footprint on the floor. And one right outside in the snow that pointed east. Inspector Clouseau could have found him. He just kept going east for about five blocks."

"It sounds pretty awful," said Jane. "But I'd still like to hear what your juror has to say."

"You're hell-bent on this hopeless case thing, aren't you," said Calvin with a sigh.

"We've been over this before," said Jane. "I may as well give it a try. What have I got to lose?"

"I don't know. Your dignity? Jane, excuse me if I'm getting too personal, but you're a class act. You don't have to do this stupid stuff."

"I think," said Jane, feeling herself stiffen defensively, "that I'm good at it."

"So what? It's still a stupid way to make a living. And believe me, Kevin is a loser. He started out just stupid when I first represented him, at fourteen or so. But now he's worse than stupid. He's a real hard case. And still a loser."

"Losers are supposed to be my specialty. That was Uncle Harold's whole idea."

"Your Uncle Harold had bags of money," said Calvin, his voice rising a little. "It was a hobby." He leaned over for some more pizza.

"No, I think it was more than that to him," she said. She thought about the letter he'd left for her to read after his death. She had it memorized. After all, it was sort of a plan for her life, delivered posthumously by Uncle Harold. In an uncertain world, a plan for one's life, especially one with built-in financing, was something to be carefully considered.

It said:

> Since childhood, you have displayed a natural altruism with a native cleverness, and these qualities can be brought together to good purpose if you carry on the work of the Foundation for Righting Wrongs.
>
> My instructions to the trustees are very specific. The tasks you undertake must be difficult ones, for there is no real satisfaction, I have discovered, in anything that is too easy.
>
> I have chosen to indulge your love of luxury, another of your traits, Jane, and perhaps a less commendable one, in order that you will choose to take on the work; so that you will not be

distracted from it by the need to earn a living; and because of my affection for you.

I have no doubt that you will earn every cent of it, and, that if you discharge your duties faithfully, someday we may both be reunited in a world in which there is no Wrong, only Right.

Love, Uncle Harold.

If Kevin was a real hard case, so be it. She knew what Calvin meant, but she felt there might be a double meaning there. Hadn't Uncle Harold said there was no satisfaction in whatever was too easy?

"I want to meet your juror," she said.

Chapter 2

Juror number ten turned out to be a retired librarian in her late sixties or early seventies named Caroline Marquardt. Jane liked her immediately. She had fine, light brown hair, which looked too monochromatic to be real. It was arranged in a wreath of tight curls around her face, a sort of serviceable perm intended not to flatter but to keep the hair looking neat. Her rather snubby round face had a kind expression, and was made up neatly with lipstick, rouge and too much orangey powder.

She looked like a sweet, utterly conventional woman, except for a kind of bristly energy and a shrewdness in her blue-green eyes. And her voice. Miss Marquardt's voice was a surprisingly tough, gravelly voice. Jane could see her in her youth. A wisecracking career gal, the female lead's best friend. Maybe played by Eve Arden or Ann Sothern.

Miss Marquardt was now installed on the sofa in Calvin Mason's living-room-turned-office, in her powder blue polyester pants and tunic, sitting with her legs crossed, bouncing the top leg a little, a large handbag on her lap.

For this morning's meeting, the pizza boxes had been cleared away, the Venetian blinds adjusted to cast businesslike bars of shadow and light across everything. The pillows were plumped up and the cat had been put out.

Calvin himself, sitting behind his desk in a tweed coat and tie, was listening to her with a little frown of concentration. Jane sat to one side.

Miss Marquardt hadn't registered surprise at Jane's presence. ("Mrs. da Silva, who sometimes assists us," Calvin had said vaguely. Jane had assumed a businesslike Della Street air.) The juror had also taken the unconventional-looking office in stride, and was launched well into her tale.

"I couldn't really put my finger on it," she was saying. "Something just kept nagging at me. I tried to stall with the jury. I said, 'Well, just to be sure, let's go over all the evidence, bit by bit.' I was hoping it would come to me. I wanted to know what it was that got me thinking there was something wrong." Miss Marquardt laughed a gravelly laugh. "I bet they all thought I was senile. Finally, they hammered me down. After all, the evidence was pretty bad for that young fellow."

She paused expectantly, as if wanting Calvin to confirm her last remark, but he just cleared his throat.

"Anyway," she continued, "last week I was over at my niece's house. She has a baby, an adorable little girl. That baby, who, by the way, is named after me—isn't that sweet?—is just at that grabby stage. Pulls herself up and grabs things, from coffee tables and so forth, then gives you a real defiant look. It's so cute, it's hard not to laugh."

She fiddled with the clasp of her purse. Calvin watched the gesture with alarm. Jane figured he was afraid he'd be expected to admire baby pictures, but Miss Marquardt continued.

"Well, little Caroline, she tottered over to the magazine rack and pulled out all the magazines and pitched 'em all over the floor. And when I was picking them all back up, it occurred to me. That's what the thing was that was bothering me so much." She stopped triumphantly.

Jane glanced over at Calvin. He looked politely attentive, but slightly glazed over. Jane felt confident that Caroline Marquardt would come to the point eventually. She just had a rambling style of conversation. Probably because she lived alone and didn't talk to other people as much as she would like. Jane could relate to that. Lately, she'd had to check her own tendency to strike up pointless conversations with sales clerks.

"It was those photographs," continued Miss Marquardt. "The ones of the crime scene. And that awful gun on the floor and all that? Well, there was one detail that didn't make sense. There was the prescription counter, and a few feet in front of it, the gun. But in the corner of the picture there was a chair—well just the legs of it, actually, and a magazine, *Elle* magazine, facedown on the floor next to it."

"Yes?" said Calvin, looking puzzled. "What's your point, exactly?"

"Who was reading that magazine?" said Miss Marquardt. "There was no sign of any struggle or anything. What was the magazine doing there next to the chair?"

She leaned forward and narrowed her eyes. "After the trial I went by that pharmacy. Someone else runs it now, of course. Poor Mr. Cox didn't have the heart, I guess, to keep on. Can't say I blame him."

She sat back again. "Anyway, I saw the chair. It's there for people to sit in while their prescriptions are being filled. And it's a tiny little place. There's a stand with magazines on it against the wall. I imagine that someone was sitting there, waiting for a prescription, reading a magazine. Mr. Mason, I think that there might have been a witness. A witness who dropped that magazine and fled.

It seemed like a loose end. Something that should be accounted for."

"I'll have to take a look at the pictures of the scene again," said Calvin. "But even if there were a witness, I'm not sure just what difference—"

"It would be very easy to find out who the witness was," continued Miss Marquardt.

"Of course it would," said Jane, smiling happily at juror number ten. "Because the victim was typing a prescription label at the time."

"Exactly," said Miss Marquardt. She looked over at Jane with the satisfaction of having found an ally.

"Yes," said Calvin Mason thoughtfully. "Well, I'll look into it." He rose. "I really appreciate your coming by. I'm sure my client will as well. But I'm afraid it doesn't look too hopeful for him. He seems resigned to his situation." He cleared his throat. "In fact, I understand he's become quite religious up there at Monroe."

Miss Marquardt waved her hand. "They all do, don't they? You always read about serial killers and Savings and Loan crooks getting Christ once they've been stopped. Maybe they're sincere, but you've got to wonder. Your client didn't strike me as a particularly savory young man. But don't you think you should try to find that woman? I'm assuming it's a woman because of the magazine."

"Well actually, as I recall, um, I'm pretty sure we did get in touch with the party whose name was being typed on that prescription label," said Calvin. "Seems to me she'd phoned in that prescription and she was planning to come by for it later." He shrugged. "I'll have to review that."

"I don't believe it," said Miss Marquardt firmly. "That little pharmacy looked quite orderly. And it was very small. A magazine lying on the floor like that, it would have stuck out like a sore thumb. And Mrs. Cox would have put it back in the magazine stand." Jane noted that Miss Marquardt assumed the female half of the team would do the straightening up. Probably not a bad guess.

"Hmm," said Calvin noncommittally.

"We'll let you know what we find out," added Jane. It was clear to her the juror wouldn't soon forget her discovery. Miss Marquardt looked grateful and a little excited.

After Calvin had seen her out, adding that he would be glad to help her if she ever needed a lawyer herself someday, he flung himself into his easy chair and loosened his tie.

"Well," said Jane. "What do you think?"

"Kevin can't afford an investigator to check this out. It should have been done before the trial, in any case. If I had the slightest suspicion he wasn't guilty as sin of blowing away a perfectly innocent citizen—"

"What did the woman on the prescription label say, exactly?" said Jane. She got up, feeling restless and a little excited, just like Miss Marquardt. She discharged her energy pacing along the velvety blue border of Calvin's faded Chinese carpet.

"Nothing," said Calvin. "I never talked to her."

"Did anybody?" Jane reached a file cabinet and turned around, retracing her steps. The carpet had smudgy beige pagodas in the corners.

"Maybe the police. I can't remember."

Jane stopped and stared at him instead of the carpet. "You mean you lied to poor Miss Marquardt?"

Calvin sighed heavily. "First of all, if I'd said I hadn't done anything, she would have thought I was a sloppy lawyer. You never know, maybe the old girl needs a will or something."

"That's terrible," said Jane, who felt that you should

only lie when you really had to. And certainly not to prevent people from thinking you were incompetent.

"Secondly," said Calvin, "it's clear to me that she thinks this is real exciting. Like a detective story or something. She probably read a lot of Nancy Drew when she was a kid. The last thing we need is her rummaging around investigating it herself."

"I read a lot of Nancy Drew when I was a kid," said Jane firmly, just in case he was sneering at Miss Marquardt's juvenile taste in literature.

"Why doesn't that surprise me?" said Calvin with a superior little smirk.

She ignored the smirk. "I want to check this out," said Jane. "Can I be working for you? Can I tell people that?"

He shrugged. "Okay. I did pitch this to you as a potentially hopeless case. And our old deal still stands, right? A finder's fee if it works out?"

"Deal," said Jane, who'd paced to the other end of the carpet and sat back down.

"But listen," he said. "Try not to use my name if you talk to the cops or anybody official, okay?"

"Are you afraid I'll embarrass you by my amateur investigatory techniques?" said Jane with a little smile.

Calvin smiled back. "Yes," he said. "If you need anything like that, let me know. I have the contacts."

"Okay," said Jane, with some relief. The only Seattle police officer she knew was Detective John Cameron, who, as far as she knew, was working hard at reconciling with the wife who'd left him for her kid's softball coach. She and John had told each other their problems and indulged in a little erotic grappling on the sofa in Uncle Harold's living room. It didn't seem fair to bug him when he was trying to do the noble thing. Not that he would still be tempted. That, she realized, was the irksome part.

"Maybe I should get an investigator's license," said Jane.

"To flash at people. There isn't a test or anything, is there?"

"Forget it. The legislature just made it real complicated. A pretty hard test. Lots of red tape. Just say you're working for me, I guess. If it comes up."

Jane smiled. "You're very helpful," she said.

"I just hope we're not opening up some kind of can of worms here," said Calvin.

Jane, of course, hoped that was just what they were doing. "And," she added, "can you arrange for me to meet your client?"

He looked thoughtful. "Kevin? I could probably get you into Monroe with me to see him. I can't say I'd look forward to a little reunion."

"Please?" said Jane.

"Oh, okay," he said, sounding reluctant but resigned.

•   •   •

She began that afternoon by visiting the pharmacy on First Hill where Mrs. Cox had been killed.

It was a small cubbyhole of a place on the first floor of a big medical building on Madison Street. She could see that it would make a good place to knock over. The entrance, which logically should have been from the building lobby, was on the outside of the building, off a courtyard. Leaving meant you could be out on the street instantly. There were no storefronts on either side—just smooth marble facade forming the base of the building.

You couldn't see inside very easily either. There were two small windows and they were filled with stuff—crutches and hot water bottles and stacks of Ace bandage boxes— all very utilitarian. The kind of thing you'd want to buy after a visit to the doctor's office.

Jane checked the address. It was no longer called the Cox Pharmacy. Now it was the Nguyen Pharmacy.

Inside, there was an Indochinese man in his mid-twenties in a white coat behind the register, which was set just at the end of the prescription counter. He was handing over a paper bag to an elderly man. "Don't forget to take it on an empty stomach," he said in unaccented English. He had the slightly beefed-up look, the direct eye contact and the American social smile of the assimilated Asian.

Jane glanced over to the magazine stand on the opposite wall, and to the plastic chair whose spiky metal feet had alerted Miss Marquardt to the possibility of a witness. The layout seemed to indicate that someone waiting for a prescription had been reading that magazine. If you were just browsing, you'd stand over by the rack. Not that this was the kind of place you'd spend much time browsing. Jane figured that the odds and ends on display here—a few stuffed animals, chocolate bars and, always a mover in Seattle, small fold-up umbrellas—were primarily there as impulse items for the people who were waiting. There was only a small rack of patent medicines—Alka-Seltzer, Kaopectate, Tylenol, aspirin.

"Mr. Nguyen?" said Jane, who noticed the man wore a name badge that said MIKE.

"Yes?"

"I'm an investigator for the lawyer for Kevin Shea. The man who was convicted of murdering Mrs. Cox."

"Yeah?" He looked slightly wary.

"We're checking out the possibility that there was a witness to the crime. I don't know how much you know about it."

"The little creep came in and shot the poor lady in cold blood," said Mike. "Look, no offense, but I'm not real sympathetic, okay?"

"I understand," said Jane, sighing. "It was a terrible thing."

"She was a real hardworking lady," said Mike. "Never bothered anybody."

"You knew her?"

"Yeah. I did an internship here when I was at the University of Washington a couple of years ago. And then I helped out the Coxes part-time during the school year on and off. They were glad to have the help. They didn't have any kids or anything." Despite his Americanization, Mike still seemed to think an ideal business was a family affair.

Jane looked around the small area, wondering why they needed any help. The place seemed tiny. "It gets pretty busy sometimes," he said, understanding her gesture. "They had a couple of good nursing home accounts. And even though Mrs. Cox was a workaholic, George liked to go fishing once in a while."

He shook his head. "They should have taken more time off. They could have afforded it. It wasn't like they were just starting out. But they never knew what would happen. Who would have guessed it?"

Jane nodded. She had to get him off the tragedy.

"So you bought the business then?" she said.

"That's right." Jane thought he looked a little uncomfortable. As if he were ashamed to have profited by the Coxes' bad fortune.

"Kevin Shea's lawyer had recently considered the possibility that there might have been a witness here. I wonder if you remember, or if you ever knew, what prescription label she was typing the day she was shot."

"I couldn't tell you that," said Mike. "That is, I could, I suppose. It might be in the records. But I'd have to have Mr. Cox's permission, and to tell you the truth, I'd hate to bother him. He'd just like to forget. Is this punk planning an appeal?" He frowned. Jane figured he wouldn't ask Mr. Cox. She'd have to do it herself.

"How do I get in touch with Mr. Cox?" she said.

"I'll ask him to contact you. If he wants to," said Mike. "You can leave a card."

Jane took one of Calvin's cards out of her purse and placed it up on the counter. She didn't think they'd hear from him. She'd probably have to go after the grieving widower herself, and she didn't relish the task.

Chapter 3

The next morning it only took a minute, in the periodicals room of the downtown public library, to read the account of the crime in the *Seattle Times*. The murder of Betty Cox wasn't front-page news. FLORIDA CRASH KILLS SEVENTY read the headline. FIRST HILL PHARMACIST SLAIN had been on page one of the local news section, and there wasn't much here Jane didn't know. She skimmed the highlights. "An apparently bungled robbery attempt... suspect in custody." At the end, though, there were a few personal comments about the victim.

"The whole building's in shock," ran a quote from a Carol Vandermeer, a receptionist in the medical center, who had talked to a reporter from the paper. "All our patients knew Betty. She was a permanent fixture." And Mike Nguyen, described as "a recent University of Washington pharmacy graduate," was quoted too. "I can't believe this. Mrs. Cox was a real help to me when I was in school. This is a horrible thing." Nguyen had apparently showed up for work only to find the police carrying out Mrs. Cox's dead body. He hadn't mentioned that when they'd talked.

Yes, it was horrible. Someone just snuffed out so randomly, and to no purpose. The whole thing seemed so open-and-shut. And it seemed as if earthly justice, in its rough, lumbering way, had been done. The only loose end was a magazine on the floor.

Jane returned the microfiche to the desk and went up onto the library's outdoor terrace. It was a little chilly for May, but the view was good. Water and boats, and hanging baskets of geraniums and lobelia. And, as everywhere else in Seattle, there was good espresso. Jane had a double tall latte.

Drinking her coffee, looking over at the seagull who sat on the balcony railing and eyed her beadily, Jane decided she had better throw herself into this full-time. After all, if there was something in it, she may as well have a running start. If there wasn't, she would have shown God or Uncle Harold or whoever was monitoring her that she was acting in good faith. Then, maybe, a genuine hopeless case would be sent her way. Having made this tentative deal with fate, she approached her task with some relish. She realized she wanted this case to work out, not just so she could get her hands on Uncle Harold's lovely money, but also so she could have something to do.

During the trial, Calvin Mason's attempts to cast suspicion on Kevin's shadowy companions, Sean and Dorothy, seemed reasonable. The only trouble was, no one had ever found them. Jane figured now was as good a time as any to start looking.

Finishing up her coffee, she went back into the library and found a pay phone. She called Calvin Mason.

"How hard did you look for Sean and Dorothy?" she said.

"There wasn't too much I could do," he answered. "It's a little tough without last names, dates of birth or good descriptions."

"Of course," said Jane sympathetically, trying to indicate she hadn't meant he'd been slack. "What exactly *do* we know about them?"

She could hear Calvin sigh over the phone. "Just that they were in their teens. Kevin couldn't describe them too well. Just average everything. But they do exist. Mrs. Shea saw them. They came by her house earlier that day, looking for Kevin."

"So they aren't just figments of Kevin's imagination?"

"Oh, no," said Calvin, "Mrs. Shea is credible. Two people named Sean and Dorothy exist. Whether they had anything to do with this crime is debatable. Criminals always cast around for someone else to blame. Why not a couple of untraceable people, maybe the last people you saw before you did the crime, and the first people on your mind when you got caught?"

An irritable-looking man was waiting for the phone. Jane gave him an apologetic smile and a wide-eyed gesture of helplessness, as if she wanted to get off the phone but couldn't. He gave her a begrudging smile back.

To Calvin she said, "Mind if I talk to Mrs. Shea?"

He thought for a second. "I suppose not. You are trying to help her son. But Jane, don't be shocked if she's less than supportive. The poor woman has been through the mill with that kid. Don't bother trying to provide any false hope. She's past all that."

Jane turned around so she didn't have to face the man who was waiting for the phone. "You mean some mothers give up?"

"Some mothers have to," said Calvin. "I'll get you her number. She works nights, for a janitorial service, so don't bug her too early in the morning." There was a click on the line. "Hang on," said Calvin. "I've got another call."

After what seemed like two minutes, during which Jane suffered an attack of anxiety and guilt about the man waiting for the phone, and just as she was about to hang up and give it to him, Calvin came back on.

"Guess who that was?" he said. "Mr. Cox. And he wasn't too happy with us. Said some woman was snooping around the pharmacy, and he didn't like it, and he wanted to make sure Kevin never got out."

This sounded less than promising. "I suppose he doesn't want to see me," she said.

"No. I suggested that, but he said if it was so god-damned important, why wasn't I speaking to him person-ally. I made an appointment to see him tomorrow afternoon."

"Can I come?"

"Not a good idea. To tell you the truth, all he wants is an opportunity to ream me out. As far as working out his grief goes, he's still in the anger stage. Can you blame him?"

Jane sighed. "Give me Mrs. Shea's number, will you?" In this sordid drama, Jane was just as glad she was dealing with the participant who had become resigned to her tragedy.

• • •

Jane called from home that afternoon, and identified herself as being with Calvin Mason's office. She paused nervously. She hoped that despite what Calvin had said about her giving up on Kevin, the boy's mother didn't still harbor some resentment that he'd lost the case.

"I've been paying him regularly," said Mrs. Shea firmly.

"Oh, it's not that at all," said Jane. "It's just that he, well, I, um, we're thinking maybe there's still something that can be done for Kevin. I wondered if I could come and talk to you about Sean and Dorothy."

"How come?" There wasn't suspicion in her voice, so much as honest surprise.

"Well, it looks like there might have been a witness. It's a very slim chance."

"You got that right," said Mrs. Shea.

"Would you mind talking to me? It shouldn't take long." Jane reflected on the absurdity of her pleading with this woman to try and do something for her son.

The woman sighed heavily. "What the heck," she said. "Why not?"

Her house was in a scruffy but honest-looking neighborhood in the South End—a small white bungalow with peeling white paint and turquoise trim. A row of Christmas lights was tacked along the roof line. If Mrs. Shea waited just a little while longer, it would be closer to next Christmas than last. Although, who knows, maybe they'd been there for years.

A less depressing touch was the line of marigolds in the front flower bed. There were also some tomato plants, small and vulnerable-looking, sitting hopefully inside huge wire tomato cages. Jane made a wish that by August the cages would be smothered in vines heavy with fruit. Mrs. Shea, she had decided, deserved at least that.

Kevin's mother was a well-worn fifty or so, with a thick head of dyed red hair in the opulent style of a country and western singer. Her face was the face of a woman who was tired but tough and undefeated—lined and jowly, with shrewd, sensible eyes and a firm little no-nonsense mouth.

She had one of those bodies that are all shoulders and bosom and stomach, tapering off into squarish hips and skinny legs, and she wore a big pink sweatshirt with butterflies on it over shiny black stirrup pants and black flats.

"Well, come on in," she said philosophically. "Let's hear what you've got to say."

Very briefly, Jane told her about the possibility there

had been a witness at the drugstore a year and a half ago when Kevin had come in and tried to rob the place.

"So you think maybe he did just drop that gun and get out of there like he said at first," she said flatly.

"I don't know," said Jane. "But I want to find out."

Mrs. Shea led Jane into a living room and gestured toward a big reclining chair in gold plush.

There were little crocheted doilies everywhere—on the maple coffee table, and the side tables with spiral legs, on the backs and arms of the chairs and the sofa, on a big sideboard with glass doors revealing rows of bone china teacups in various floral patterns.

"This isn't going to cost me anything, is it?" Mrs. Shea sat on the matching gold plush sofa and fiddled with one of the doilies, smoothing it out with big, capable hands.

"No," said Jane. "Don't worry about that. This is strictly voluntary on my part."

Mrs. Shea looked a little puzzled. "Well, okay," she said. Jane was sorry she'd said "strictly voluntary." She hoped it didn't sound patronizing.

"You said 'at first' just now," Jane began. "Talking about what Kevin said happened. I'm sorry, I wasn't around during the trial. Did his story change? What did he say later?"

"Later, after he was incarcerated and got his head cleared up from all the drugs, he said he couldn't remember. That he was too messed up to know what happened. He thought maybe he did kill that woman."

She said it unflinchingly, as if challenging Jane. Jane didn't flinch either.

"I understand you met these two people Kevin claims were with him. Sean and Dorothy."

"That's right."

"Could you describe them?"

"Well the boy was real slick. A real good-looking kid,

real well spoken. About seventeen or eighteen maybe. I didn't like the looks of him at all. Dark hair. Can't remember much else. He had good teeth, though. Movie star teeth. Like they'd been fixed. And he had a real nice leather jacket on. Not like a biker's jacket, more like one of those aviator jackets, you know. Brown. I figure he stole it somewhere from some guy who worked hard to make a few bucks to buy himself that jacket."

"I can just imagine the type," said Jane. "Sounds like a creep, all right." Letting someone know you agreed with their impressions always kept the confidences flowing freely, Jane knew.

Mrs. Shea nodded. "Definitely. I'm pretty sure he knocked up that girl that was with him, and he acted like he didn't give a shit."

"She was pregnant?"

"That's right. Just starting to show. She looked bad. Kind of rough skin, long light brown hair that looked damaged, you know." Mrs. Shea fluffed up her own luxuriant hair. Jane wondered if it was a wig, inspected the part that revealed real-looking scalp, and decided it was her own.

"I asked the girl about it. I said, 'Honey, are you taking care of yourself and that baby?' 'cause I figured she might be on drugs or something." Mrs. Shea shook her head in disgust. "She looked ashamed, but the boy just kind of smirked."

"How far along do you think she was?" said Jane.

"Three, maybe four months. Just starting to show, like I said, but there was something about the eyes. Pregnant women have a special look in their eyes—kind of steely."

"I know what you mean. Do you remember what they were driving?" Jane doubted they could be traced from a sketchy description of a car, but she wanted all the detail she could get.

"No. I stood there at the door talking to them. I didn't want them inside. They'd probably try to rip me off if they were friends of Kevin's. That's who they rip off, you know. People they know. Their parents' friends, their friends' parents."

Jane nodded. It made sense. Why would kids out of control bother to do their marauding far away?

"I just told them he wasn't home. But I kind of wanted the girl to stay. I would have called her mother for her, or whatever. She looked like she'd been running wild. She seemed younger. Maybe fifteen or sixteen."

"Do you think they were good friends of Kevin's?"

Mrs. Shea waved her hand disparagingly. "No. He hardly knew their names. They told me to tell him Sean and Dorothy came by, and when I did, later, he seemed kind of vague. He didn't have any real friends. When you're an addict, you only have one friend and that's drugs. And that's no real friend either."

She leaned across the coffee table intently. "If you haven't lived with it, you can't possibly understand," she said with finality. "You can't even love that person anymore. Because that person is gone. Buried, like under a thick, heavy veil." She sat back and looked stubborn, as if expecting Jane to argue for never giving up hope, for holding out forever for redemption.

Jane just nodded solemnly.

"I blamed myself," continued Mrs. Shea. "I blamed the fact that his dad took off years ago. I blamed the fact that I raised three other kids, and when it came around to Kevin, who was the youngest, I was just plain tired. I blamed the fact that I worked nights and I was asleep when he came home from school even though I needed the shift differential."

She sighed. "Finally, my other kids told me, 'Mom, just let it go.'" Her big hands rose from her lap like two birds released from a cage. "He was stealing me blind. I had to hide my purse in my own house. Then he got ahold of my checks and forged my signature. I found out when my own checks started to bounce. It was just one damn thing after another. Finally he got my bank machine card, and he twisted my arm behind my back until I told him the number. Then he totally cleaned me out." She shook her head, as if disbelieving that this horrible thing had actually happened to her, that a child had turned on her.

Jane nodded to let the woman know she was with her, and made sure she didn't look shocked. She wanted her to keep going.

Mrs. Shea obliged. "You see, what keeps you hanging in there is little pieces of the real kid show through once in a while. You think you see what he's like underneath it all. In the way he smiles or if he helps you carry in a bag of groceries or something. Or you remember him when he was a little kid or a baby—you look at his face and you remember how he looked when he was three or four. But what's left, it's not the real kid. That kid is gone."

"I'm so sorry," said Jane. "I really am. You seem like a nice person. You didn't deserve this."

"Knowing he's in prison, I can relax for the first time in years," said Mrs. Shea. "I can go to sleep at night, knowing he isn't going to get into some kind of trouble. Kevin killed that woman. And he probably could have killed me, just as easy. It's a horrible thing to say, but it's the truth." She stopped and shook her head. "I still pray for him once in a while," she said. "But I'm doing it for myself. It's just a way of putting it out of my hands."

Jane got up and went over to a row of highly colored portraits of people in their twenties, all looking vaguely alike with dark hair and blue eyes. There was a baby picture tucked into the corner of one of the frames. "Are these your other kids?"

Mrs. Shea beamed. The mood in the room changed. "That's right." She went over to Jane's side and wiped some dust off the tops of the frames. "Here's Lisa and Dennis and Mark." She held up the frames one by one and set them back down on their doilies. "And this is my grandson. Joshua.

"Lisa's at home with her baby now. Her husband's got a real good job at Boeing, and they got a house near here. Dennis is in the service. He's married but they don't have kids yet. And Mark's working at Pizza Hut, and he's learning refrigeration."

"They look real nice," said Jane.

"That baby is a real joy," said Mrs. Shea. "All the fun, and none of the worries. It gives you a real shot in the arm, a new person like that, coming into your life."

"How old is he?" said Jane.

"Eighteen months," said Mrs. Shea. Which meant, Jane reflected, after she'd thanked Mrs. Shea and walked out to the car, he'd been born about the time his uncle Kevin had been arrested. She counted on her fingers. And made him about six months older than Dorothy's baby was about now. There had to be a record of its birth somewhere.

And something else Mrs. Shea had said had given Jane an idea. She had to get the name of the dentist who'd owned that gun.

Chapter 4

When George Cox had called, Calvin had treated him gently and respectfully, just as he had in court when the widower had described discovering his wife's blood-soaked body. In court, Cox had seemed rather numb, answering monosyllabically. Calvin had asked him only a few questions to establish that he hadn't been an eyewitness, and in fact had never seen Kevin until that day in court. His main goal had been to get him off the stand and out of sight of the jury as soon as possible.

But on the phone, when Mr. Cox called yesterday, another George Cox had made himself evident. He was very angry.

"I don't appreciate your sneaking around, sending some woman to talk to Mike, trying to get evidence to get that little bastard out of jail," he said.

"I'm sorry," said Calvin, trying to disassociate himself from the whole thing. "Mrs. da Silva is a friend of the family, and naturally they want to do what they can to help the boy."

"It's just ridiculous. What do they think? That he didn't do it?"

"It appears," said Calvin, "there may have been a witness."

"A witness! That's ridiculous. Why didn't they come forward? The coward went in there and killed my wife."

"I'm sorry to upset you. In fact"—Calvin congratulated himself on his diplomacy here—"it was because we didn't want to disturb you that we didn't approach you directly."

Cox snorted. "Don't you think I have a right to know what's going on? If you're fooling around opening this all up again, I want to know about it. We need to sit down and have a little talk."

"Um, all right. Perhaps I can come by. I don't want to inconvenience you, Mr. Cox." Calvin also didn't particularly want Mr. Cox to find out his office was his living room. Which was why he found himself sitting on a large leather sofa, across a burnished metal coffee table, staring into the face of a scowling George Cox.

Calvin wasn't quite prepared for Mr. Cox's apartment. He had imagined a cozy little boxy house somewhere in Ballard or the North End, with a crocheted afghan draped over the sofa, with maybe a little dog, and AstroTurf on the patio.

Instead, George Cox had a big apartment on Queen Anne Hill with a fabulous view of downtown, a cluster of black and silvery high rises, and the water of Puget Sound beyond, backed by low forested islands softened by mist.

The rooms in the apartment were full of new furniture—big square pieces, and there were no feminine touches. Sitting on a twin sofa opposite him, George Cox looked more like a man in a waiting room than the man who lived here.

It was clear Mr. Cox had started his life from scratch. Calvin had an aunt who'd done the same thing when her husband died. Sold up everything and moved into a condominium in Arizona.

The only personal touch was a mounted sailfish hanging over a massive black marble fireplace.

"Thank you for meeting with me," Calvin said. "I am very sorry about your wife, Mr. Cox, and I really appreciate your taking the time with me now." The leather felt cold.

Mr. Cox nodded impatiently. He was around sixty, with a narrow, pale face, glasses, and a few strands of thinning sandy hair. He wore a carefully ironed plaid shirt and a pair of khaki trousers with neat creases.

Pharmacists, thought Calvin, always seemed to look neat. He couldn't remember ever having seen a sloppy one. They had to be meticulous and careful about detail, after all. One wrong drop and they could kill someone. And get sued, thought Calvin, with a lawyer's concern for liability overriding any regret over a pointless death. He decided meticulousness was something he could use.

"It may seem odd to you that we're pursuing something so carefully, and well after the trial," he said. "But we have to be sure of every detail, and make sure we've given our clients our best shot."

"Yeah," said Mr. Cox in a brusque, get-to-the-point way. He seemed a little calmer than when he'd called. "But I warn you, there's certainly no doubt in my mind what happened to Betty."

"Yes, I understand," said Calvin. He decided to launch right into it. "Your pharmacy was small, wasn't it?"

"Yes." He seemed somewhat surprised at the question. "But it was very profitable, let me assure you. We had a lot of business from the medical building."

Calvin hadn't meant to cast aspersions on his business. "Of course," he said.

"In fact, Mike should make a pretty good living out of it," added Cox.

"I'm sure that's true," Calvin said. "What I meant was,

it was a small area, so it must have been easy to keep straightened up."

"It was always straightened up. In the pharmacy business, everything has to be organized. A place for everything and everything in its place." Cox crossed his arms and legs, sat back and looked quizzical.

"Naturally, Mr. Cox. That's why we were surprised to see a magazine on the floor in one of the photographs used at the trial."

"Photographs?" Now Mr. Cox looked slightly alarmed. Calvin was afraid he was thinking about the photographs taken of his dead wife at the crime scene.

"Of the weapon," Calvin said quickly. "On the floor, where it was dropped. You see, there was a magazine there, facedown on the floor. Next to the chair where someone might wait for a prescription."

"Customers would often read a magazine while they were waiting," he said. "It annoyed Betty no end." He chuckled fondly. "She always watched the nickels and dimes, and she wanted them to buy the magazine."

"Still, didn't they usually put them back in the rack afterward?"

"Oh, sure. Once in a while they might forget and leave it by the register, I suppose. I don't quite see what you're getting at."

"We were wondering," said Calvin, who had begun to think he looked like a jerk and that he'd come on a fool's errand, "whether or not there'd been someone in that chair when all this happened. Maybe they were frightened and ran out of the store, leaving the magazine there on the floor."

"I don't think so," said Mr. Cox. "Wouldn't they have called the police? That's it? That's your big breakthrough?"

"Well, it is a possibility we'd like to check out," said Calvin, feeling more and more foolish. "I was wondering if you knew whose prescription label Mrs. Cox was typing at the time."

"I haven't a clue," said Mr. Cox. He was getting testy again. "After everything that happened, it was the last thing on my mind."

"Naturally," said Calvin, wondering how he could end the interview and get out of the apartment. "But would there be any record of it?"

"I don't know," said Mr. Cox.

"Maybe Mr. Nguyen has the records," said Calvin. "It's all on computers, isn't it?"

"Well he has all the records, naturally," said Mr. Cox. "But I don't see the point, really."

"Could I ask him?" said Calvin.

"I'd rather you didn't," said Mr. Cox mildly. "To be quite honest, I don't really see why I should help the man who killed Betty. It's been over a year now. I want to put it all behind me, get on with my life. And there's the whole area of confidentiality."

"I would think that you'd like to be absolutely sure," said Calvin.

"I *am* sure," said Mr. Cox. "There's no doubt in my mind."

Calvin frowned. Perversely, he was becoming a little irritated with Mr. Cox. The advocate in him swelled up in his chest. What made Cox so sure? What if that little slime Kevin were innocent? Calvin didn't believe it for a minute, but he thought Cox should cooperate, on the off chance an innocent man was serving a long sentence for the murder of his wife. But then he reminded himself that Cox was behaving like every other relative of a victim he'd met. They wanted it all over with, and they wanted the perpetrator to be punished. They wanted finality, not loose ends.

"Well maybe the name on that prescription label is in the police report," said Calvin.

"I wouldn't know about that," said Mr. Cox.

Calvin rose and gazed over at the fish mounted on the wall. Cox followed his gaze. His face broke into a smile. "Isn't that a beauty? Eighty pounds. Got that down in Cabo San Lucas."

It was incredibly blue. Calvin tried, without much success, to imagine Mr. Cox engaged in a Hemingwayesque battle with a fierce fish.

At the door, Mr. Cox's manner softened. "You know," he said, "pharmacists live with holdups. There's always the possibility some thug or addict will shoot you. That's why we had the gun. It made Betty feel safer. But I always thought if it happened, it would happen to me. Not Betty." He shook his head sadly.

"I'm sorry," said Calvin, who again felt pretty lousy for having disturbed the guy.

"I'm getting used to it," Cox said. "We met in pharmacy school, you know. We worked side by side for over thirty years." He shook his head. "If Betty'd had her way we would have been at it for fifty. She never wanted to retire."

Calvin nodded sympathetically.

"But there was no way I could go on without her. We had all our little routines down pat. I sold it to Mike for nothing down, just to get out of it. I couldn't do it without her."

He bent his head down a little and rubbed his forehead. "I thought I'd go in and help Mike out a few days a week, just to get him up and rolling. Turns out I couldn't even bear to do that."

"Very understandable," said Calvin, who wished Cox would shut up and let him go. He felt more comfortable around the nasty Cox than the grieving one.

"My life changed overnight. And after the trial, and them sending that kid to prison, it felt like the last bad part was over too. That's why I don't want to help you." He shook his head. "That's what you have to go on? That there was a magazine on the floor? Is there anything else?"

"No," said Calvin. "It could well be there's nothing to it at all. We just want to make sure."

"Seems pretty thin to me," said Mr. Cox, with another shake of his head. "I'd appreciate it if you called off this woman. I don't want her bothering Mike or any of my old customers. What did you say her name was?"

"Jane da Silva," said Calvin. Right now, he was mad at her himself. Just because of her, he'd been up here bothering this old man.

Chapter 5

Jane blessed Dorothy's parents for naming her Dorothy. There weren't that many of them giving birth in Seattle a year ago. Most Dorothys were probably well beyond ovulation. She must have been named after someone—a grandmother maybe. Or after Dorothy in Oz. After eliminating a Dorothy Chang, who had a little girl at Swedish Hospital, there was just one in the births column of the *Seattle Times*.

Jane was back in the periodicals room, becoming a regular like a couple of disreputable old men smelling of tobacco, sour wine and urine who sat at long tables reading day-old newspapers, while Jane worked a few feet away with the microfiches.

Working on the assumption Dorothy was in bad physical shape, and a good candidate to give birth prematurely, she'd started at what Mrs. Shea had estimated to be the girl's seventh month. In a way, Jane felt relieved the baby hadn't arrived early, even though it meant going through more newspapers. She had already begun to worry about Dorothy. She liked her name, for one thing. In fact, she found herself absurdly happy when she found the announcement. A Dorothy Fletcher gave birth on June 10 of the previous year. A boy. No father's name. Northwest Hospital.

Getting the birth certificate was easy. She walked a few blocks south down to the Public Safety Building and paid eleven dollars. There was Dorothy's address, her age (fifteen) and her address in the Wallingford neighborhood. The baby's name was Charles. The father's name was Sean Carlisle.

She went to the pay phones by the main entrance to call Calvin Mason. His machine was on. "I think I found Dorothy of Sean and Dorothy," she said, with an ebullient feeling of being involved with a project that was moving forward. To keep it going, she added, "Could you find out the name of the dentist who'd had his gun stolen? The gun that killed Betty Cox?" Something Mrs. Shea had said had made it seem worth following up. She waited a little while to see if he was really there, lurking behind his machine.

Her ebullience vanished. It was too bad not to be able to tell someone she might have found Sean and Dorothy, and gloat a little that she had succeeded where Calvin, and presumably the police, if they cared, had failed. Now she felt rather lonely.

And maybe it was silly anyway. What if she had found them? There was nothing to guarantee they knew anything about the murder of Mrs. Cox.

A dead end, she realized, would be pretty disheartening. She needed a hopeless case if she wasn't going to continue to be one herself. The trustees had given her five thousand dollars to live on and to take care of any expenses involved with finding a case to pursue. Thank God she'd managed to negotiate Uncle Harold's old Chevy out of them too. Even if she confined her shopping binges to the teen tart store, the money wouldn't last too much longer.

She decided to stop by the video store on the way home. She'd get herself a nice classic—maybe a French one. The Algerian who ran the place had a lot of classic French films. Something with Jean Gabin.

As she approached the store, it occurred to her that renting a VCR every time she needed a movie fix was becoming a false economy. Uncle Harold's house was too old-fashioned to have one. His stereo system only played LPs and the corners of the refrigerator were gently rounded.

The best thing to do, she decided, would be to get herself a VCR. They couldn't cost that much. And so what if her money ran out a week earlier that way? At least she'd have the luxury of plenty of cozy old movies in the meantime.

She proceeded to a discount electronics store and bought the model that happened to be on special, paying for it with cash. Uncle Harold, she imagined, if he'd ever gotten around to getting himself a VCR, would have spent a few hours at the library with back issues of *Consumer Reports* before doing anything so rash.

Ever since she had come back to Seattle, she'd developed an irritating habit of wondering whether or not Uncle Harold would approve of her actions. It had started with her attempts to carry on his work. Now it was creeping into the rest of her life. Thank God he hadn't been hovering in her mind when she'd decided to buy all those frivolous shorts and T-shirts.

As the hyper young man who'd sold her the VCR crammed it into the trunk of her car, it occurred to her for the first time that maybe she should pack it in. Get a real job. Never mind that she had frittered away her youth on a lot of fun jobs with no future, and had somehow found herself pushing forty without noticing it. The thought of a résumé was horrifying. "Last position: mediocre cabaret singer with limited range."

There was simply nothing to do but run by the video

store and get a nice cozy old movie. Maybe a few chocolate eclairs were called for as well. Jane felt that carefully modulated self-indulgence was the best way to ward off depression.

•   •   •

Calvin Mason envied the detectives in books and on TV who had terrific sources in the police department. They never had any trouble finding out what the cops were up to. Even in real life, lots of investigators were ex-cops who had buddies on the force to tell them whatever they needed to know.

Sure, in the books and the movies the helpful cops were always threatening to yank the detectives' licenses or arrest them or something, but they always caved in and handed over juicy files or even let the detectives tag along on an investigation because they actually liked them.

Calvin Mason wasn't an ex-cop. He was a lawyer who beefed up his income a little with other ventures like collections, apartment management and investigations for more successful lawyers.

In his rare appearances in court on criminal matters, he was a defense attorney, so he didn't have that nice clubby relationship he could have developed with the cops if he was a prosecutor. There was no getting around the fact that he'd spent some time attempting to trip up police officers on the witness stand and implying to juries that they were lying brutes who beat confessions out of defendants in elevators. It wasn't so much that he'd made enemies of the police officers he knew. It was more that in his dealings with them Calvin sensed they thought he was a jerk. The nicest thing they'd ever done for him was run a gratuitous warrant check on him.

Which was why he was having lunch with Carol, a

civilian employee of the Seattle police who was his not so confidential and definitely low level source in the department. Fortunately, Carol didn't ever expect a very expensive lunch. She had other needs.

They were sitting in a corner table at Denny's. Calvin was eating the Patty Melt and Carol had a chef's salad, which she was saturating with Thousand Island dressing. "I hope you can make it to Raymond's game this week," she said in a voice that managed to sound pathetic yet demanding at the same time.

"Be glad to," said Calvin heartily. "How's he doing this season?" A Little League game was better than a science project.

Carol sighed. "I'm worried about his self-esteem," she said. "He's spent a lot of time on the bench this season."

Calvin shrugged. "There are lessons in life to be learned on the bench," he said philosophically. Then, because he figured women always wanted everyone to be happy, and didn't understand the whole point of sports anyway, which was to kick ass, he added, "But those Little League coaches should give everyone a chance to play. It's supposed to be fun."

"It's not easy being a single mom," said Carol. "He needs a man to play catch with him." She looked up at Calvin hopefully.

Damn, he thought. Watching a bunch of goofy kids floundering around the field was bad enough, because it meant having to sit on the bench listening to Carol whine about this and that so he couldn't even concentrate on the game. Now she wanted him to toss a ball around with her uninspiring kid and be a male role model. He'd heard her whole routine before. Calvin was sick of all this male role model stuff. He couldn't remember his own father or any other adult male playing catch with him. As Calvin remembered it, his father just came home from work, fired up a Lucky Strike, read the paper, and yelled, "Ruth, can't you get these kids to pipe down?" once in a while.

"So how have you been? You're such a good mother, but you've got to be good to yourself too," said Calvin, hating himself for pandering blatantly with the kind of stuff Carol ate up.

She shrugged. "I don't know. There don't seem to be any decent men around." Calvin nodded sympathetically. Carol was one of those women who didn't really like men very much but wanted one anyway. Fortunately, she'd never given any indication she wanted him, so presumably he was just another indecent one. Just in case Carol felt she was ready to scrape the bottom of the barrel, Calvin came up with a hasty move to deflect her.

"Well, at least you've got that nice steady job, working for the city. You'll get a good pension and all that. This being self-employed isn't what it's cracked up to be. I'm trying to find a few thousand to throw in an IRA or something." He paused. "In fact, my life is getting shabbier and shabbier." That ought to do the trick. Calvin Mason was convinced that shaky finances were a big turnoff for most women, just as money and power could draw them like flies to some charmless, hideous toad of a man.

Carol gave a sympathetic click of her tongue. "Yeah, work's okay, I guess," she said.

"That reminds me," said Calvin. "I was wondering if you could do me a favor."

"Sure," said Carol, "but before I forget, you know how you fixed the garbage disposal before?" Carol tilted her head sideways the way women did when they wanted you to do something for them. "It's making the same noise it did before it crapped out last time."

"Mmmm," said Calvin. He'd told Carol not to put

celery and stuff down there. Last time he'd found a chewed-up twist tie and a rubber band in the disposal. No wonder her husband had bailed out.

Calvin thought again about Jane da Silva. He never should have told her about that juror.

He had only done it, he realized, because he liked her company. And because there was something mysterious about her. He was still trying to figure her out. What had she done in Europe for all those years, for instance. A hopeless case seemed the only thing he had that she needed. Why couldn't she just have had a broken garbage disposal?

Now, because of her, he had to fix one anyway. When he got there, Carol would no doubt have rounded up a collection of broken small appliances. Then she'd throw a ladder against the side of the house and send him up to clear out the gutters, and if there was any time left over she'd probably ask him to have a man-to-man talk with Raymond about the importance of condoms. "I'll come over tonight and take a look at it," he said. "I'll bring the plunger and the snake."

Chapter 6

Dorothy's age, and her address in Wallingford, had given Jane the impression that she lived with her parents. It was a well-established neighborhood of older single-family homes, near Green Lake, in the North End of town.

She had absolutely no idea what she would do when she got there, but she figured she could tell something about the situation just from looking the place over.

The house, on Sunnyside, was a small cottage-looking place, set back from the street with an untidy garden in front. Jane cruised by slowly, then parked under a shady tree across the street, just out of view of the windows.

The houses in this neighborhood, built in the teens and twenties, had undergone many cycles of renovation over the past eighty years or so. When Jane was a little girl, it was a slightly scruffy neighborhood of working-class whites, people who couldn't afford to move to the suburbs with the upwardly mobile of the fifties and sixties. Later, because of its proximity to the university, it had taken on a bohemian tinge, and groups of students had lived in some of these houses. Now it had become gentrified, populated by the kind of people who'd grown up in the suburbs themselves and found them boring. The neighborhood was shared by representatives of each demographic wave, and it showed in the way the houses and gardens were kept.

The old blue-collar element, on in years now, had favored vinyl siding and updating with aluminum windows and wrought iron railings. The new arrivals had encrusted their old houses, some of them architecturally quite simple, with lots of lattice, ripped off the fake siding and replaced it with cedar, and picked out the details of window trim and gables with interesting color combinations. They'd also enclosed their gardens with fences, a reaction, no doubt, to the boundless contiguous front lawns of their suburban childhoods.

Their gardens went beyond the standard Seattle collection of ornamental cedars and rhododendrons with some clumps of heather. They favored clematis and standard roses and containers full of pansies.

Dorothy's house looked as if it had been renovated in the seventies. For one thing, it was looking shabby. For another, it was painted olive green with mustard trim, and the numbers on the house were neither the slanted black plastic hardware store functional numbers of the old guard nor the prim brass numerals of the new wave. They were big, balloonish seventies numbers carved out of natural wood. There was also a dilapidated deck hanging from one end. Jane was thrilled to see a stroller sitting on that deck.

She saw some movement within the house, shadows behind the Pier One bamboo blinds in the front window. Jane mulled over how she might get in the house. "Your baby is so beautiful, we'd like to use him in a commercial" appealed to her, but she thought it was a little cruel, getting some mother's hopes up.

She circled the block, trying to get a glimpse of the rear of the house. There was an alley and a garage and not much else. But she did notice a FOR SALE sign on a house on the corner, which gave her the inspiration she needed.

She parked in front of that house, and, just in case someone was watching, stood and looked thoughtfully at it. Then she walked around the block to Dorothy's house and went up the walk.

From within the house, she heard raised voices. She went onto the porch and waited a second before knocking.

"What are you going to do all day?" said an exasperated woman's voice.

"Take care of the baby," said an adolescent shout in reply.

"Please. Please clean up the house today. When I get back from work my heart sinks when I walk in here and it's a mess."

"Mo-om." Adolescent exasperation.

Mom's reply was softer now. Fury under tight rein. "Dorothy, don't push me."

Jane had a hard time hearing. Frustrated, she leaned closer to the screen door.

Dorothy's yelling reply, however, was easy to hear.

"When we get Sean's fucking money, I'll move out, okay?"

"You can stay here as long as you need to, honey." Mom actually sounded a little tender here.

"I still want the damn money," yelled Dorothy.

Jane couldn't believe her luck. Overhearing this remarkable conversation, which answered a few important questions about Dorothy, was incredibly fortuitous. But was it? Probably, Dorothy and her long-suffering mother had this high-decibel conversation or one like it every morning. It did have the stale ring of a long-running play.

Jane had a story ready. "I'm thinking of buying that house around the corner and I couldn't help but notice your stroller, and I wanted to find out what kind of a neighborhood this is for kids." She had already developed an instant persona. A nervous, older mother from Chicago. Her husband was a professor who just got a nice tenured position at the university.

It occurred to her now, however, that a more direct approach might yield some results. After all, if she was the professor's wife, she'd be stuck with that role. She could never come back as Jane. Which might come in handy sometime.

She stood on the porch, trying to decide what to do, staring down at the doorbell. There was a piece of adhesive tape above it, with writing in ballpoint pen that said, DOESN'T WORK. PLEASE KNOCK.

Before she had a chance to do that, however, the door opened, and she was looking through the screen door at a startled woman in her mid-forties with a big pouf of dark curly hair, and big dark eyes.

"I was just about to knock," Jane said, trying not to look like a Jehovah's Witness or an Avon lady.

The woman was wearing a sexy knit dress in big red and white stripes and big white beachy-looking earrings. She carried a briefcase in one hand and a coffee mug with a heavy base, the kind designed for use in a car, in the other. Jane liked her looks. The woman looked at her with curiosity, but she smiled.

"My name is Jane da Silva, and I work for an attorney in town. We're looking for Sean Carlisle."

"So are we!" said the woman with feeling. "Come on in. I've got to get to work, but I've got a minute or two."

Inside the living room there was more olive green—this time in worn carpeting. In an apparent attempt at updating, there was a cheap but attractive oriental laid over it. The furniture was rattan with tropical cushions, and there were some luxuriant plants around. It had a brave, festive-on-a-budget look to it. So did Mrs. Fletcher, thought Jane. As if she might sit in this room after work drinking a margarita and singing along with the stereo. There were a couple of rows of bookshelves and a big framed poster of poppies in a vase.

"This is my daughter, Dorothy," said the woman. Jane looked at her with interest. She was a sulky-looking girl, with fluffed-out sandy hair down to her shoulders. Her skin looked clear and young. Jane was glad to see that Dorothy looked a lot better than the way Mrs. Shea had described her a year and a half before. She had a big soft face, and suspicious-looking hazel eyes. She was wearing rolled-up cutoffs that showed off thick but firm-looking white thighs, and a T-shirt that said HARD ROCK CAFE, although Jane doubted the girl had much nightlife going for her lately.

In the corner of the room, one hand poised on the coffee table, the other gracefully extended for balance, stood a solid-looking baby with big round eyes and curly dark hair. He was staring at Jane, blinking slowly. Then he broke into a big smile, showing off some tiny disclike white teeth.

"What an adorable child," said Jane.

Both women's faces softened into proud smiles.

"That's Charlie," said Dorothy, gazing at him rapturously.

"Is Sean in some kind of trouble?" said Mrs. Fletcher, throwing her briefcase on the sofa and sitting down. "Dorothy, honey, get some coffee for"—she turned back to Jane—"what did you say your name was?"

"Jane. That would be lovely." She gave Dorothy a nice smile to counter any possible sulks from her mother's having sent her summarily into the kitchen.

Dorothy got up and slouched off. "Take anything in it?" she yelled over her shoulder. She was tall, taller than her mother.

"Black, please," said Jane.

"Maybe you know," said Mrs. Fletcher, apparently eager to get into it and sipping her own coffee, looking at Jane over the rim with her big brown eyes. "We're going to get a paternity suit going against the little shit. He's only a kid, of course, but he'll be eighteen soon, and all grown up in the eyes of the law. And his family's loaded."

"Have you got a good address on him," said Jane, opening her purse and hoping there was something official-looking in there to write on.

"That sleazebag father of his won't give it to us," said Mrs. Fletcher indignantly. "Says the boy's away at college. Out of state. Which will make it a big hassle for us, as you can well imagine. College. Right. Give me a break."

"Doesn't Dorothy know where he is?" said Jane.

Dorothy came into the room, handed Jane a cup of coffee, took a swig out of her morning Diet Coke and sat down on the floor, legs crossed. "No," she said sarcastically. "Dorothy doesn't know."

"I'm sorry. I didn't mean to talk about you as if you weren't here," said Jane, giving her a level gaze. "I didn't know you'd come back in."

Dorothy shrugged, and Jane considered her apology accepted.

"The thing is," said Mrs. Fletcher eagerly, "even if the little worm doesn't have any money now, we want to get a judgment against him. That way if he comes into any-thing later, we can grab it."

Jane turned to Dorothy. Dorothy was why she was here. "Has he met Charlie?" she said.

"Nope. Says he isn't his." Dorothy flicked her hair back, and tried unsuccessfully to look tough. The baby tottered over to her side and buried his face in her shoulder, then peeked up at Jane flirtatiously. All three women paused to smile at him and admire him.

"You can prove all this nowadays with blood tests," said Mrs. Fletcher, with the eagerness of a litigant on the rampage. "We've got to get a blood sample out of him, but he's dodging us."

"He can only do that for so long," said Jane.

"What do *you* want Sean for?" asked Dorothy. It was a good question. One her mother, in her eagerness to outline her own case, had neglected to ask.

"We think he may be a witness. In a criminal matter." She watched Dorothy carefully. Dorothy just shrugged again. Jane didn't get, couldn't get, a reading.

"It wouldn't surprise me a bit," said Mrs. Fletcher. "He's into drugs, or at least he was, and ripping people off and everything. It's really disgusting." She shot a look of irritation over at her daughter, who gave her a sullen look back.

Jane wondered if by the time Charlie knew what she was talking about—namely his father—she'd shut up. She doubted it. Still, it was hard not to like Mrs. Fletcher. She had spirit.

"So what's his father's address," said Jane, who now had a pencil poised over the back of her checkbook.

"Dorothy'll give it you," said Mrs. Fletcher, now looking in panic at her red plastic watch. "Excuse me, but I've got to run. Listen, can we stay in touch? In case you find him?"

"Of course," said Jane, wishing she had a business card.

"Dorothy, sweetie, get her phone number and stuff, will you? So nice to meet you," said Mrs. Fletcher as she gathered up her briefcase.

Jane made as if she were just about to leave herself, walking into the kitchen with her coffee cup. The refrigerator was plastered with pictures of Charlie in various stages of development. Dorothy, holding the child's hand, followed her in.

"Is Sean in some kind of trouble?" she said off-handedly.

"Maybe," said Jane, turning to face Dorothy, crossing

her arms and leaning against the counter. "Something to do with a drugstore robbery."

This time, Dorothy flinched. Jane leaned closer to her. "I didn't want to talk about it in front of your mother," she said.

Dorothy looked frightened but grateful.

"I figured if you're old enough to be a mother yourself, you're old enough to talk to me about this without your own mother there," Jane added.

Dorothy's face instantly took on a more mature cast. "Sit down," she said, indicating the kitchen table. "Would you like more coffee?"

"No thanks." Jane paused for effect, while Dorothy squirmed a little in her chair, finally setting the child down. He began to crawl around under the table. "Dorothy, there might have been a witness at that robbery. You know what I'm talking about, don't you? The day you and Sean went to look for Kevin Shea."

"Kevin. Kevin went to prison," Dorothy said. "I heard about it."

"That's right. But he said you and Sean were with him. Were waiting around the corner."

"So? Even if we were, how were we supposed to know what he'd do? All I know is what was in the newspaper." Dorothy flipped her hair over her shoulder in an angry little gesture.

"Dorothy," said Jane. "I don't think you had anything to do with all this. But if it was Sean, it could be important."

She shrugged. "I don't know, I haven't hardly spoken to Sean all this time." She was avoiding Jane's eye.

"It wouldn't be fair to Charlie, would it?" said Jane. "If anything happened to you because of this. Not if it's Sean's fault."

Dorothy looked directly at Jane now. "I don't get it," said Dorothy, her voice rising a little. "Who are you? The whole thing is all settled. Kevin was found guilty and he's in jail."

"I work for Kevin's lawyer," said Jane. "But we don't have to tell your mother that right now if you don't want her to worry." Or, thought Jane, if you don't want her to yell at you for hanging around with a bunch of lowlifes. "I'd like to keep you out of it. But I need your help."

"What do you want me to do?" said Dorothy, sounding wary.

"Tell me what happened. Tell me the truth."

She sighed a big sigh, then launched into it. "Kevin asked us to wait for him around the corner. He said he was going to buy some Percodan. That he had a fake prescription for Percodan. We waited, then we heard the shots, and Sean took off. That's all I know. The whole thing about me and Sean being involved in any armed robbery is totally stupid." She dismissed the whole affair with a wave of her hand.

Dorothy obviously wasn't interested in the story she told. It meant nothing to her. The fact that Betty Cox died that day hadn't penetrated any corner of her soul. Either she was a cold-blooded psychopath, or she didn't really know what happened. Or she was protecting Sean. She had blazed through that story quickly, almost as if by rote.

Now Dorothy changed tack and got on to what really interested her. "I haven't seen Sean for a long time," she said. "Do you think he's really in college like his dad says?" She looked up at Jane with a hungry look. Jane wondered if she hadn't just made a big mistake telling Dorothy who she was.

Chapter 7

On the drive out to the Monroe State Reformatory, Calvin told Jane about his interview with Mr. Cox. "And so," he summed up, "the guy says he doesn't want either of us to bother him. You can't hardly blame him."

"What did you tell him about me?" asked Jane. She was leaning back in the passenger seat watching the suburbs and pretty wooded areas—clumps of alders and firs—from below partly closed eyelids. She looked lazy and contented. Calvin felt the little rush he sometimes felt when heading out on a road trip, even though Monroe was only an hour or so out of Seattle.

"I told him your name. But I said you were a friend of the family." Calvin didn't add that he'd said that to establish some distance between Jane and himself. He remembered in a sort of bemused way that he'd been embarrassed and vaguely irritated with her up there in the pharmacist's apartment.

Now, driving through the countryside with her at his side, he wondered why he'd been so irritated. He turned and looked at her profile—a nice straight nose, he thought, and he realized he hadn't seen her from this angle before.

"But don't worry," he said, in a manner that was purposely offhand and casual. "We don't really need Mr. Cox. I got a source working on getting us that police report."

Jane turned and smiled at him, a nice big grateful smile. "Fantastic," she said.

Once they got to Monroe, Calvin reflected that it didn't really look so grim, at least not from the outside. With its brick facade and white columns, sitting on a hill with sweeping green lawns and trees in front, it looked kind of like an old-fashioned high school. Until you noticed that the scale was all wrong. The building was a lot bigger than most high schools and the windows were a lot smaller than most windows.

He drove up the hill and looked at Jane. She didn't seem nervous. A lot of people got nervous just at the idea of visiting a prison.

"It doesn't look so bad," she said. "But I guess it's pretty horrible. I mean I guess they all terrorize one another in there, right?"

"That's the kind of guys they are," he said. "There's no way I can think of where you get a bunch of mean sons of bitches together and expect them all to treat one another like gentlemen. It's medium security, so it's not nearly as bad as Walla Walla, though."

"Will they search us?"

"They run us through the metal detector. It's pretty sensitive. They tell me an underwire bra will kick it off." His gaze drifted involuntarily over to her chest for a second as he said the last.

Jane was looking at her chest too, as if trying to remember what her underwear was like. She was wearing a white blouse and a black knit skirt. "I thought they used plastic nowadays. If bells go off, will some burly matron strip search me?"

"They'll keep at it until they figure out what's setting off the machine. They might figure you for one of those crazed women who fall in love with cons. I had a client like that once. An ex-nun. These guys like to have someone on the outside to run errands for them and send them money, and I guess the women like the idea of knowing where the guy is all the time. Anyway, I told them you were my investigator, and they didn't pursue it further, thank God. Just let me do all the talking."

"I don't think my penchant for unsuitable men extends to the incarcerated," she said. "Do they wear denim uniforms?"

"No. They wear regular stuff in here. They look like a bunch of convenience store clerks or rock band roadies, and they can be pleasant enough. Especially to women. But most of them belong here."

"Including Kevin?"

"Including Kevin. I wish I could tell you different."

"I don't want to get his hopes up," said Jane.

"I don't want to get your hopes up," said Calvin. "One of the reasons I said I'd take you here is so you can't accuse me of leading you on with what I consider a very dubious proposition. A look at Kevin might be a good reality check."

They parked and went inside and upstairs, where they stashed everything—car keys, pocket change, Jane's purse—in a tiny locker, and went through the metal detector. Calvin had to go back and remove his belt and shoes, but Jane made it through. Then they heard metal clang behind them, spent a moment between two locked doors, emerged into the cafeteria, had their hands stamped ("Like a high school dance," said Jane, intrigued) and went into the small client-attorney room. More clanging metal signaled Kevin's arrival by a separate door.

The prisoner scraped a chair across the floor, and sat down looking at both of them from behind a screen of long blond hair. He leaned back in his chair with his chin slightly raised, like a troublemaker in the back row of a high school classroom. Calvin watched Jane check the details—a tight yellow T-shirt, a pair of newish-looking jeans, scruffy tennis shoes.

Calvin introduced her perfunctorily. "This is my assistant," said Calvin, not bothering to give her name. Next thing he knew, Kevin would be calling her collect. Kevin stared at Jane with interest. She smiled a businesslike smile and crossed her legs. Kevin watched her cross them. She seemed to notice but she didn't act uncomfortable, gazing back at him without revealing any emotion.

Kevin Shea had been working out since Calvin had seen him last. Once a skinny kid with a caved-in chest, he now looked like a giant torso with a little head on top and a couple of barrels for arms. Sitting here in the attorney's room, Kevin didn't seem to know where to put those new arms. They were propped in his lap at awkward angles like a couple of foreign objects.

Those massive arms were also sporting a complicated canvas of Escher-like tattoos—surreal landscapes incorporating some hearts and flowers and skulls, all in slate blue. Kevin had apparently fit right in to prison culture.

"Don't go below the wrists with those tattoos," Calvin said, pointing to Kevin's hands as he sat down in the beat-up wooden chair. "That way, if you're sorry later, you can wear long-sleeved shirts. You know, you might get a straight job or something someday."

Kevin looked blank.

"Seriously," said Calvin. "Most people regret it later."

Kevin shrugged, and Calvin wondered why he was bothering. It now occurred to him Kevin Shea looked stoned, not an unusual state for inmates here.

"How's it going?" Calvin said.

Kevin shrugged again. "I keep busy. I'm in anger management and leather tooling."

"What about that prayer group?"

"I kind of got out of that. I'm going to get my GED,

though. A lot of these guys in here are pretty dumb, but I think I'll get my GED."

"Listen," said Calvin. "I'll get right to the point, but I don't want to get your hopes up. We've been doing a little checking into your case."

Now Kevin looked wary, and as if he were trying to get his wits about him and maintain them. "Yeah?"

"Seems like there might have been a witness to that holdup attempt. We're trying to find them. The fact is, no one actually saw you kill anybody."

"I don't think I did kill anybody," said Kevin.

"That's not what you said last time," said Calvin.

"I know. 'Cause I didn't remember. And those prayer guys got me all messed up there for a while. They made you feel better if you'd fucked up big-time, so you could feel real bad about it, and impress God. Course, it's better to be in here on murder than on something like a skin beef or something, you know?"

Calvin cringed at the prison term for a sex offender. He was glad he didn't do too much criminal work. It was the class of people you met.

Kevin's glassy-eyed stare drifted around the interview room. "But now I figure if I did kill someone, I would have remembered. I would have remembered the sound of the gun or something, wouldn't I have?"

"I don't know," said Calvin. "I came to find out if you had any thoughts on the matter."

"What kind of a witness?" said Kevin.

"I don't know. You tell me," said Calvin.

"Seems like there might have been." Kevin looked thoughtful. "Shit, a witness, and nobody found 'em. The cops didn't. You didn't. I'm rotting in here and no one found that witness." Kevin managed to look indignant.

"Well it would have helped if you'd told us about a witness," said Calvin, trying not to sound too peevish.

"Would it be like a man. Or like a woman?" said Kevin thoughtfully.

"Like one or the other, I imagine," said Calvin. "Or maybe even an actual man or woman." It wasn't necessary to keep sarcasm out of your voice when you were talking to this jerk, he thought.

"Does Mom know about this?" said Kevin.

Calvin nodded.

"Do you talk to her? Think she could send me some shoes? I want Nikes. Air Jordans with the pump. High tops."

"I'll mention it."

"Tell her I'm making her a wallet."

Calvin nodded. "Okay, you're making her a wallet. Aren't you going to ask why we think there was a witness?"

Kevin frowned and his eyes came momentarily into focus. "Come to think of it, I think there was someone there."

"Oh really?" said Calvin. It was amazing how these guys seized on whatever they could and managed to convince themselves that they were somehow the victim of a terrible injustice. He'd seen it time and time again. The self-righteous protestations of innocence; the slow, steady twisting of the facts in their minds until they were right and everyone else was wrong.

Kevin smiled and managed to look like a charming little kid. "Pretty stupid of me to hold up the place with someone in there like that, huh? I was pretty messed up." After a pause, he added, "But, there coulda been someone there, now that I think about it. Maybe reading a magazine or something."

Calvin looked over at Jane. He expected her to lean forward. To burst out that he was on the right track, to give him some clues so he could fabricate a story. She just blinked slowly.

But later, in the car, she grabbed his sleeve. "You heard him. He said a magazine. It's there somewhere in his subconscious. I know it! Can't we hypnotize him or something?"

"No," said Calvin. "We can't do anything like that. It'll just cause problems for us in court. The guy's mind is fried. He's a terrible witness. He doesn't know what happened."

"But he said that about the magazine," said Jane. "Didn't that give you a thrill?" She was bouncing in her seat.

"Hell, maybe he noticed the magazine in that photograph like juror number ten did, and some little synapses in his brain clicked in. I noticed you stayed calm in there when he came up with the word 'magazine.'"

She stopped bouncing. "I didn't want to give him false hope, like I said. And I didn't want to encourage him to make something up."

"Which he would. He's completely unreliable. A shifty little con artist. If you want to get him out of there—"

"Before he tattoos his hands," said Jane thoughtfully.

"—then you'll have to prove he's innocent."

"I need to find the witness," said Jane.

Calvin felt a stab of guilt. He was leading her on. She was seizing at Kevin's ramblings, and she'd knock herself out trying to make a case out of nothing. She seemed cool and self-possessed and capable, but every once in a while it occurred to Calvin that someone should take care of her.

But he suppressed that thought right away. She'd taken pretty good care of herself until now. He didn't want to get suckered into worrying about her. "Are you going to buy me lunch?" he said.

Chapter 8

The next morning, Jane slept in, then forced herself up, into the shower, into clothes. So far, she had nothing on the day's agenda other than returning her tapes. If she had died during the night, she mused, the only way anyone would ever know is when the Algerian from Ace Video came breaking down the door looking for *Philadelphia Story.*

Everything was on hold until Calvin told her what the police report said. She made herself a cup of tea and stood at the kitchen window, looking out at the garden. It was raining steadily, the steady rhythm of raindrops on leaves making that familiar sound of her childhood.

Funny, when she'd lived in warm places, like the South of France, the sound and smell and feel of occasional rain made her nostalgic for home. Now that she was back here she found it depressing.

The phone rang. She went into the hall to answer it, noting how the gloom from outside seemed to penetrate all the rooms of the house.

It was Calvin Mason. "Hi!" he said cheerfully. "I got the name of that dentist for you. It was all in the police report. One of your more thorough examples, thank God. The guy's name was Carlisle. William James Carlisle. A dentist like I said. Here's his address."

Jane felt a shot of adrenaline at the name Carlisle—the same name that appeared on baby Charlie's birth certificate in the space marked FATHER. Mrs. Shea had said rotten kids like hers stole from their parents' friends sometimes. She'd wondered if she could somehow track down Sean through the dentist.

But she hadn't expected this. Just like Kevin, Sean had stolen from his parents. But presumably he'd made it look like a regular burglary. A little slicker than Kevin's rough stuff, twisting his poor mother's arm to get her bank machine code. Although Sean could be a nephew or something, she supposed.

"Wow," she said. "Thanks."

"And that's not all," said Calvin, sounding very proud of himself. "I found something else in the police report. Well, actually, it was in the detective's notes. The name on that prescription label juror number ten thinks will lead us to a missing witness."

"Terrific," said Jane.

"The customer's name was Jennifer Gilbert." He gave her an address in the University District.

"Fantastic," said Jane.

"That ought to get you started," he said.

Jane began to tell him she'd already started. In fact, it almost looked as if she'd wrapped it up. She'd found Sean and Dorothy, and almost tied the gun to Sean. If Jennifer Gilbert was able to cast any doubt on the prosecution's version, there might be a chance to clear Kevin. She thought of him up at Monroe, carefully lacing together a wallet.

But she decided to wait until after she talked to Jennifer Gilbert to report on her progress. Then she might be able to bring Calvin a nice, neat package. And if he could go anywhere with it, and get Kevin out of Monroe, she could present the board with a nice, neat package. A hopeless case, an injustice remedied. What could be a more appropriate endeavor for a nonprofit detective than saving some poor guy from the penitentiary who couldn't afford decent investigative help to get himself cleared of a false charge?

She wondered if Kevin had to be actually innocent to satisfy the board. What if she was able to get him a new trial that hinged on reasonable doubt? Jane didn't know what it took to get a new trial. In the movies, it always seemed to happen quickly, the great wheels of injustice coming to a screeching halt, then cranking into reverse. Something told her that in real life it wouldn't be quite so simple.

But she was getting ahead of herself. What she had to do now was find Jennifer Gilbert. It wasn't too hard. She was right there in the phone book. Under initial J, at the same address Calvin had found for her. Which probably meant she was single.

Jane called her. Of course, there was no answer. She was probably at work. Instead, she called the office of William James Carlisle, DDS. She left her name and number and said very firmly, "It concerns a legal matter." She wanted to get a look at him, talk to him, gauge whether or not he knew his son was involved. Maybe try to find out where his son was hiding. The Fletchers had made him sound like a monster. She didn't want to let him know she was looking for Sean. She'd probably already gone too far with Dorothy.

Jane already felt a little sorry for Dr. Carlisle. After talking to the mothers of Kevin and Dorothy, Jane felt pity for the parents of rotten adolescents, and she also felt some of the terror and dread that must accompany being a parent. Once you had a child, Jane thought, your vulnerability to heartbreak became unfathomable—part of a big gamble you took that also increased your capacity for joy.

Presumably, Sean had a mother too. She wasn't in the phone book, though. There was just the two listings for Dr. Carlisle, office and residence, and Jane had called his office assuming he was at work.

He called her back within half an hour. He had a firm, amiable voice.

"Dr. Carlisle," she said, "My name is Jane da Silva, and I'm working for an attorney named Calvin Mason."

"This doesn't have anything to do with the Fletchers, does it?" demanded the doctor with irritation.

Bingo, thought Jane. "No," she said, managing to sound puzzled. "Mr. Mason represents a young man who was convicted of murder, using a weapon stolen from your home."

"Oh yes, of course," the dentist sighed.

"We're doing some investigation for a possible appeal," she said, "and I wonder if I could come and ask you just a few questions about the weapon."

"Well, I could give you maybe fifteen minutes between patients," he said dubiously. "But I went over all that with the police."

"Fine," said Jane, mowing right over his ambivalence. "How does this afternoon look?"

•   •   •

Dr. Carlisle's was the only name on the door, but his offices were huge. There seemed to be a half dozen patients being worked on simultaneously, their chairs arranged throughout a suite of rooms that flowed into each other. Attractive young women, hygienists, presumably, were bent over them, murmuring cheerfully as chamber music piped through the area.

Jane met Dr. Carlisle in a small office at the very back. He turned out to be a very handsome man with the devastating combination of a tanned, boyish face and dark hair with gray at the temples. He had a quick, wide smile and a long-lashed appraising squint that was almost flirtatious. If Sean was as charming as his father, poor Dorothy hadn't stood a chance.

"So what's the problem," he said, indicating a guest chair, and flopping down casually behind a small desk. He was wearing an aqua-colored uniform that looked like something a surgeon might wear in the operating room, all cotton, just a little crinkly. Much sexier than the traditional white coat. Jane bet he knew it too.

"You know, I never did get that gun back." He acted like it was her fault, but teasing. He was good, all right. She tried to enjoy it without getting sucked in.

She smiled. "I'm sure your insurance company compensated you for it. And the stereo and the VCR."

"Yeah. I was just kidding."

"I came to ask you if you ever had any idea who might have stolen that gun."

"Nope," he said. "I have to assume it was the kid that used it to kill that woman on First Hill."

Jane was struck by the fact that he didn't seem to feel bad that his gun had killed a woman. She knew just what he'd say if someone brought that up: "Hey, I didn't steal it. I didn't pull the trigger." The Dr. Carlisles of this world were supremely confident. It's what made them attractive.

"This was a standard burglary?" she said, wondering what that meant. "You came home and found out you were ripped off?"

"That's right. My wife and I were out of town actually. At a cosmetic dentistry conference in San Francisco. The kids were at school. The burglary was a daylight thing. It was the first time we'd left them alone. Kind of scary. My wife was pretty upset."

"Most residential burglaries are committed by teenagers," she said, vaguely remembering having read something like this somewhere and wondering if it were true. "A lot of them actually have some connection to the victim. They're parents of friends or something." She'd learned that from Mrs. Shea. "We'd like to ascertain if Kevin Shea, our client, really did steal that gun. Do you think anyone your children knew could be involved?" Not for the first time, she wondered what the hell she was doing here bothering people with stupid questions. What was he supposed to say?

She glanced over behind him. There was a family grouping. A pretty wife, kind of shy and soft-looking, and two teenage children, a boy and a girl. The girl looked soft and pretty like her mother, but with a little more backbone. The boy, presumably Sean, was handsome and a little cocky-looking. As Mrs. Shea had said, he had great teeth. Of course, his father was a dentist.

He followed her gaze. "I have teenage kids, but they're not exactly hanging out with thugs and losers. I got great kids."

"They look very nice," said Jane. "How old are they?"

"Melissa is fifteen, and Sean's seventeen."

"You don't think they might have had a party or something while you were gone? Maybe this Kevin was involved somehow. Kids do stuff like that," she said.

"Not my kids," he said with satisfaction. "I never had any trouble with them."

Outside of that troublesome paternity matter, thought Jane. "That's wonderful," she said. She leaned over confidentially. "In my work, I run into a lot of parents who can't say that."

Dr. Carlisle preened a little. "I set limits and I stick to

them," he said. "Of course, they're almost grown up now. Sean's away at college."

"And he's only seventeen."

"He skipped a grade," said the dentist. "He wasn't being challenged. He got bored."

"I see. Where's he going to school?"

He looked slightly uncomfortable. His confidence slipped a notch, and to Jane's amazement, he lost his charm instantly. Suddenly he looked a little ferrety around the eyes, and his scrub suit looked silly. "The University of the Pacific. In Stockton, California," he said.

Jane nodded, and thanked him for his time. On her way out, she passed his framed undergraduate diploma. It was from the University of the Pacific, in Stockton, California. Either Sean really was attending his father's alma mater, or this was the first place that popped into his head.

That evening, around seven, Jane tried Jennifer Gilbert's number again. This time, there was an answer.

Jane introduced herself, and established that she was indeed talking to Jennifer Gilbert. The voice was one of those constricted, mincing female voices, typical of a certain kind of resolutely middle-class, genteel, self-effacing woman. It was a childlike voice coming from the head, through the nose, without any air in it at all, as if the head and the body were severed. It sounded tight and timid. Jane had seen plenty of attractive women (all Americans, for this particular quirk of speech seemed to afflict no other nationality) who, upon opening their mouths and coming out with that constricted little voice, lost their appeal instantly.

Jane launched right into her pitch in a confident, superior sort of way, emboldened by the implied passivity of that voice.

"I'd hoped to be able to come and see you," she said.

"I'm working for a lawyer, representing a young man convicted of murder."

Jennifer produced a Minnie-esque squeak.

"Maybe you know about this case," said Jane, with the air of someone who was in the habit of juggling a half dozen murder cases. "A pharmacist named Betty Cox was shot."

"Yes?" said Jennifer.

"And while she was shot, she was typing a label for a prescription."

"It wasn't mine," said Jennifer.

"What?" said Jane sharply.

"I mean, I wasn't there," said Jennifer. "The police called me a long time ago. I've already told them. I phoned it in. Why is this coming up again?"

There was a click on the line. "Just a second," said Jennifer. "I've got another call." She came back after what seemed like three minutes. "I'm really busy now," she said. "I'm advertising for a roommate and I'm getting a lot of calls. I can't talk to you anymore."

"Can I come by and ask you a few questions?" said Jane, trying now to sound gentler.

"No! Please, I don't want to get involved. I don't know anything about this."

"Well, an innocent man may have been wrongly convicted," said Jane, trying to sound dramatic and succeeding a little too well, she thought. "If I could just ask you a few questions—"

"I can't," said Jennifer. "You guys have to stop bugging me." Then Jane heard a gasp that sounded like a sob. "I can't help you." She hung up.

Chapter 9

Fortunately, that click on the line had offered her an opening wedge. Jennifer was advertising for a roommate. The next day, Jane took a long, drizzly walk down to Broadway and picked up a *Seattle Weekly*. That, she figured, was the most logical place to look for her ad. And even though she had the address and phone number, reading the ad would provide some verisimilitude.

She stopped to read some of the other ads, which presented a bleak picture of urban life—lonely hearts ads from self-described paragons yearning for sex, love or affection; support groups forming for survivors of a variety of psychic batterings and social ills; clerical jobs for artsy organizations at insultingly low salaries, hinting at the compensatory glamour.

It was there, all right, under WANTED TO SHARE. Jane recognized the phone number. In her lengthy ad, Jennifer described herself as a "Quiet professional woman," her apartment as "a spacious U District apartment in charming, historic building, close to campus and bus lines" and her ideal roommate as "a responsible, female, non-smoker, friendly and open to communication. Cats okay." Jennifer volunteered the use of her car, and the rent was three hundred dollars, including utilities. Jennifer seemed eager to please, and, it seemed, wanted a friend as much as a roommate.

Jane didn't dare call. Her voice would give her away. But she counted on the fact that when you talked to someone on the phone you invariably created a physical appearance to go with it, and in Jane's experience it never matched the real person at all. If Jane showed up in person, with some story about having heard about the apartment from someone on the bus, but not having the phone number, she bet she could worm her way in.

She might even sign up as Jennifer's roommate if she thought it would help. It wouldn't take long to get the truth out of her. Jane was slightly horrified at the thought of going through Jennifer's things, but she knew she could do it if she thought it would help.

Uncle Harold, she reflected, would never have stooped to such subterfuge, but damn it, he'd been rich. It wasn't her fault he'd made a desperate woman out of her by dangling a fortune in front of her.

That evening, she went to Jennifer Gilbert's building in the University District. It was fabulous, a Moorish pile from the twenties, all beige stucco and curly red roof tiles, with big terra-cotta pots of fan palms and geraniums at the entrance. Jane had driven by and admired it many times.

The structure, which looked as if it had been flown up from Southern California, was flanked on either side by dull tall apartment buildings.

There was a line of door buttons, and she found J. GILBERT and pushed it. Even the buttons looked original—black Bakelite plastic. Initial J. Gilbert, combined with the architecture of the building, made her think of John Gilbert, the twenties movie star. She peered through the glass doors, trimmed with wrought iron, into a lobby lined with orange and blue tiles.

Neither Jennifer Gilbert nor John Gilbert responded. She stood there in silence for a moment more and finally decided that it was probably better to wait a day so her voice wouldn't be fresh in Jennifer's memory. She'd come back tomorrow.

She spent the next day trying to find Sean Carlisle. The registrar's office at the University of the Pacific in Stockton said he wasn't registered there. Jane was almost disappointed, because she'd come up with an elaborate lie about confirming a student loan, intended to weasel an address out of them, but on reflection, finding out he wasn't there at all was progress. Dr. Carlisle was lying about his son's whereabouts.

Assuming that he'd be at work, drifting congenially among the many chairs in his office like someone mingling at a cocktail party, Jane decided she could easily swing by his house for a look around.

It was a big square turn-of-the-century house on Capitol Hill, cheery pale yellow, with white trim and white columns on the porch, not far from Uncle Harold's house. It was a nice-looking house, the kind of thing you could imagine on a Christmas card with a wreath on the door and about a foot of snow glistening on the roof.

Once she pulled up in front, she realized there wasn't much she could do. In the movies, she'd sit out in front with a newspaper all day, watching the household's comings and goings, which sounded excruciatingly boring and conspicuous too.

Instead, she went over to a deli on Fifteenth Avenue, bought herself a double tall latte and used the pay phone. "Is Sean Carlisle there?" she said to the young female voice that answered.

"No," it replied, sounding disappointed the call wasn't for her.

"I found his wallet," said Jane, "and I want to make

sure it's the right place. His address is on the driver's license."

"He's not here. He won't be for weeks," she said. "I thought his wallet was here. He won't need a driver's license where he's going." There was a sisterly sneer in this last.

Jane tried to keep the eagerness out of her voice, and attempted to phrase the next question carefully, in hopes of finding out exactly where the hell the little bastard was. She heard an older female voice in the background. "It's someone for Sean. They found his wallet," hollered the young girl.

She came back on the line. "Here's my mom."

There was a rustling noise as the receiver was passed over. "Can I help you?" said a frosty little voice.

"I found a wallet that I think belongs to Sean Carlisle," said Jane.

"There's some mistake," said the woman sharply. "Who is this?"

"Then he's not here?"

"No!" said the woman. "May I ask who's calling?"

"I must have made a mistake," said Jane hanging up. She didn't care particularly what the Carlisles thought about this odd phone call. She'd figured that they'd assume it was Dorothy and her mother after them, or maybe the outraged relative of some other young female, seduced and abandoned.

Maybe Sean was in jail. Where else wouldn't you need a driver's license? She put in a call to Calvin Mason and left a message on his tape. "Could you pretend to be an ambulance-chasing lawyer—big stretch, I know—and call the jail and see if Sean Carlisle is in it?" she said into the machine. She wasn't sure if Sean was a minor or not, or if there was a city jail and a county jail or what, but she assumed Calvin would figure it all out.

It wasn't until much later, when she was in bed reading, that he called back. "He's not in jail," said Calvin. "Or if he is, he isn't in King, Snohomish or Pierce counties. Is this Kevin's old pal Sean, the one I wasn't sure existed?"

"I think so," said Jane. "He fits Kevin's mother's description. And, interestingly enough, his father's gun killed Mrs. Cox." She tried to keep the smugness out of her voice.

There was a pause. "Damn," said Calvin. "I didn't find him. If I had, I could have used that fact in my defense. Not that I don't still think Kevin did it, but still..."

"Don't feel bad. I found him because he knocked up his girlfriend, Mrs. Shea noticed, and I traced her through the birth certificate."

"Go over that again?"

Jane explained what she'd done. "So you see, I couldn't have found him the way I did until Dorothy had little Charlie."

"But you haven't found him yet," said Calvin.

Chapter 10

The next day, Jane went back to Jennifer Gilbert's apartment house, leaned on the buzzer for a while, and stood, frustrated, reading the other names in the row. To her surprise, the bottom button read A. NAZIMOVA, MANAGER.

It had to be some kind of a joke. Alla Nazimova, an old movie vamp, had owned and operated the Garden of Alla in Los Angeles, the classic Hollywood apartment complex that had tenants like Robert Benchley and Humphrey Bogart and F. Scott Fitzgerald. Jane had never seen the old place before it was torn down, but it too, she knew, had Moorish architecture, like this place.

She couldn't resist. She pushed the button, wondering if she'd be buzzed in by the old girl herself, kohl-rimmed eyes and all.

Instead, a nasal male voice crackled out of the intercom. "Yes?"

"I'm here looking for Jennifer Gilbert," she said, wondering whether she should be coming up with some story to explain why she was bothering the manager.

"Oh my God," said the voice dramatically. "Come right in."

She leaned on the door while the buzzer droned on for what seemed like a minute, and half fell into the lobby.

A minute later, a thin, elegant man of indeterminate age appeared. His silver hair was short and parted with geometric precision. He wore a cream-colored polo shirt and gray flannel trousers with pleats and cuffs. Instead of a belt, he had a necktie threaded through the belt loops, a style Jane knew Fred Astaire had made popular. To complete the retro look, he was wearing spectator shoes in black and tan.

"I was expecting Alla Nazimova," she said with a smile.

He smiled back. "A silly little joke of mine," he said.

"The Garden of Alla."

"Exactly. Hardly anyone gets it. Just us antiquarians."

"Those who know we missed the elegance of a superior era," said Jane, who, although she was an antiquarian herself, and had in fact made a sort of a living singing old Gershwin and Jerome Kern and Cole Porter songs, had never set out to live in the past as completely as the individual now before her.

"Exactly!" he said again. "My name is really Arthur." Before she had a chance to introduce herself, he came up to her and took her hand, holding it as he peered into her face. "Are you the one who called from Jennifer's office? Maybe you're right, maybe we should check."

Jane paused for just a flicker, wondering whether to assume the persona of a co-worker. It was too risky. She didn't even know what Jennifer did for a living or what the woman from the office had said over the phone, or if she'd left her name.

"I had an appointment with her," she said simply. "Is something the matter?"

Arthur looked clearly worried. "Her office called. She didn't come to work today. They were really astounded because she never misses a day, doesn't even take sick leave, and they were worried about her. I told them there wasn't anything I could do. I went and banged on the door, but she doesn't seem to be there. But if she had an appointment with you—"

"Well sort of," said Jane, lying through her teeth. "That is, she was expecting me." She'd have to make up some variation on this story if Jennifer was home. "She was looking for a roommate."

"That's right," said Arthur. "My God, what shall we do?"

Jane seized on the "we" and started to take charge. "Well, if it's out of character for her to just disappear, maybe we should check," she said briskly.

"I'll get the passkey," he said, apparently glad to have a witness. "I've never done this before. It's not really my style, barging in on people. I mean, maybe she just had a terrible hangover or something." Jane followed him to his apartment door.

"Come in, come," he said with a welcoming little gesture. She glanced furtively around at the decor. It was a museum of the twenties and thirties. Art deco cigarette boxes, a statue of an alabaster flat-chested female nude embracing a crescent moon, a big vase of calla lilies.

The man Jane had thought of as Arthur Nazimova, although she had presumed he had another last name, now became rechristened in her mind. Arthur, Art for short, Deco dug around in a desk drawer. "Really a quiet girl, not exactly the type to go on a bender or anything," he said.

Jane stared around the apartment in awe. "What a fabulous collection," she said.

He beamed. "I started years ago, when nobody wanted any of this stuff," he said. "*Those* days are over. Last week I saw an adorable little chrome toaster for fifty bucks. Fifty bucks! Can you imagine? I used to pick up really nice cocktail shakers for five."

How many cocktail shakers could one person use, she

wondered. Her eye ran over a matching onyx letter opener, inkstand and blotter on the desk. And who would use an ink stand or a blotter these days? Art Deco apparently. There was a handsome fountain pen lying nearby.

"All good design this century happened before Pearl Harbor," declared Art Deco emphatically, his search for the key momentarily forgotten. "There's no need to go any further."

"And the popular music was so wonderful," said Jane, humming a phrase from "Embraceable You," swaying a little and looking around her some more. While she shared his love of the period, there was something a little creepy about living so totally in the past. The telephone was a gangster-style Bakelite plastic model, and a cunning little space heater with a stylized floral grille hardly looked UL-approved, with its frayed fabric cord. In fact, there was nothing of the modern time period at all, anywhere in view.

"Do you have a VCR?" she asked. Then thinking this was impertinent she added hastily, "You'd need one to study the set decoration in old movies."

"Exactly," said Art, moving over to an old radio cabinet—walnut with brass fittings—and opening it to reveal late-twentieth-century examples of Japanese electronics. He shuddered a little at the ugliness of it and closed the door firmly. "A necessary evil," he said.

"Yes," said Jane. "How did we live without them? Now you can look at all those great old Carole Lombard pictures whenever you want to." Her body fell into Carole Lombard's debutante slouch, whether unconsciously or not, she wasn't quite sure. Jane feared her years as a stylized sort of vocalist had seriously impaired her ability to behave naturally.

"You belong in this building," said Art Deco firmly.

"I know I'd be happy here," she said. "But first we have to find Jennifer, don't we?" It was clear to Jane he had forgotten entirely about Jennifer, and was in danger of having his astral body drift off to some parallel Ernst Lubitsch universe.

"Oh, yes. Jennifer." He frowned and dug around for the keys some more. "To be perfectly frank, she's never really appreciated this building, or what I'm trying to do here. I mean, she's a sweetie and all that, but I'm afraid she doesn't have much sensitivity to good design." He held up a key with a smile of triumph. "You'll see what I mean," he said in a confidential tone. "Those ceramic geese with those blue ribbons around their necks, and fridge magnets with inspirational messages." He rolled his eyes as much in pity as disgust and made a discreet gagging gesture.

Jane followed him up the hall and around a dog leg to her apartment door. Art Deco banged on it for a while, then called out "Jenn-i-fer" as he inserted the key and they went inside.

There was no answer, just the heavy stillness of somebody's empty house. They went past the small tiled entry hall into the living room. It was the lighting that made it clear at once there was something terribly wrong. A big lamp lay on its side on the rug, casting a huge yellow circle of light, broken by the shapes of a table and chairs, against one wall, and casting the rest of the room into ominous darkness.

Art Deco gasped a little, and Jane looked around the room. There was a small desk by the French doors, and the drawer had been pulled out and placed on the top of the desk, the contents all jumbled up as if two big paws had been stirring them up.

"This does not look good," said Art with a solemnity

Jane hadn't imagined he possessed. "I suppose we'd better check the other rooms. God, I hope she's all right."

Jane went into a bedroom off the living room. Jennifer
was not all right. She lay on her back across the bed, her
eyes and mouth wide open, her face purple. The fluttery
ends of an orange silk scarf seemed to come out of her
neck. Jane realized that the rest of the scarf was drawn so
tightly around her throat that it was embedded, hidden
by puffy, dead flesh.

Chapter 11

The woman's face was an empty mask of flesh. She was gone. Jane forced herself, nevertheless, to put two fingertips on Jennifer's calf, just on principle, just to be absolutely sure there was nothing to be done. The flesh was cold. Jane drew back quickly and stared down at the body.

Arthur rushed from the room, and Jane could hear what sounded like a medicine cabinet door being slammed shut and the sounds of retching coming from the bathroom they'd passed on their way in here.

Jane didn't want to look at her face too long, but she managed to take in other details. Jennifer had a stiff, wavy, brassy blond coiffure that looked matronly. She was wearing a dark green sweater and a challis skirt in a dark green and orange print, an orange picked up exactly by the scarf twisted around her throat. She had a big, squarish body and sturdy legs. One foot was bare—the other had on a bright red fuzzy slipper.

Jane backed out of the room slowly, registering the flowered bedspread, the bedside stand with a remote control for the TV and a copy of *Cosmopolitan*, the bureau—a big oak thing like you might find in a hotel. Its surface was covered with spray bottles of cologne and knickknacks—a ceramic owl, an earthenware vase with dried flowers, a metal tree in a lapis-colored shell tub, on which a dozen rings were hanging, a little brass and copper box that Jane bet held earrings.

"We've got to call the police," said Jane over her shoulder.

There was the sound of running water. "Jesus Christ," said Arthur from the bathroom. "I just threw up."

"Maybe you should call from your apartment," said Jane. "Fingerprints and all that." She reflected that just a few minutes ago he was pretending to gag at her fridge magnets. Reluctantly, she left the bedroom. She was, she realized in a numb way, repelled yet fascinated by the scene, by the corpse sprawled unceremoniously across that floral bedspread in that banal room. It was all so out of place, so outrageous, so horribly wrong. Dizziness started to overcome her. She tried to fight it back.

She found Arthur again in the hall. There was a fine haze of sweat over his forehead and he looked pale.

"Sit down," said Jane. "Just sit down." She led him back into the living room, and sat him down on the sofa. She knew they should leave right away, preserve the scene, call the cops. But Art looked faint.

"If you think you're going to pass out, or anything," she said, "put your head down." Somehow, trying to help Arthur kept the horror at bay.

"I'll be all right," he said shakily. Instead of putting his head down, he leaned it against the back of the sofa. "God, the poor thing. The poor wretched thing," he said.

Jane knew she wouldn't get to see the apartment again. While he was talking she scanned the living room. All of the objects of the dead woman's life seemed horribly pathetic and pointless.

It was a big apartment, with white stucco walls, and all the authentic period details that gave Arthur such joy: moldings of shiny dark wood, light fixtures of wrought iron, a row of bright orange and blue tiles in front of the rounded fireplace.

On a mantel there was a small ceramic unicorn with a gilt horn and hooves, and an oak-framed mirror with a border of poppies etched into the glass. But there were no books and no pictures. Their absence gave the room a bleak, transitory look.

The furniture was simple and modern-looking. Large stuffed pieces in gray tweed with some vaguely colonial coffee tables that looked like they might have been recycled from Mom and Dad's house. There was a big, Danish-looking striped cotton rug—yellow and gray. It was slightly scrunched up near the entrance to the hall and the bedroom. In the center of it was another red fuzzy slipper. She felt suddenly cold.

"He dragged her into the bedroom," said Jane. "He strangled her here, then dragged her into the bedroom. Look at the slipper."

"Oh, my God," said Arthur. He gazed at the slipper for a moment. "It happened in the building." He turned his head toward the desk.

"Then he looked for something," she continued, following his gaze to that jumbled drawer. Next to it was the telephone.

"I'll call," said Arthur, staggering up.

Whoever fished through that drawer must have found what he wanted. Nothing else had been disturbed.

Arthur had evidently seen a few detective movies in his time. He was holding the receiver in a linen handkerchief. "Christ! It's busy. 911 is busy, can you believe that?" He slammed down the phone, picked it up again and jabbed furiously at the buttons. This time, apparently, he got through. "There's a dead body in my building!" he said. "A woman's been killed."

Jane walked slowly into the entry hall and looked at the door, which was open a few inches. The varnish around the lock was immaculate. There was also a small wrought iron spyhole. If he came in this way, she let him in. She turned back to the living room where Arthur was saying, "I'm the building owner. Yes, yes, I'll be here. I have the key. All right, all right."

There was a small table in the hall with an empty letter tray. There was an umbrella leaning in the corner, and on the wall nearby, a grouping of framed photographs. She thought she recognized Jennifer herself in a stiff studio family shot. There was a mother and father, both wearing glasses, a young man in a suit with too much mousse in his hair and, perched precariously on the arm of the love seat where the other three sat, there was Jennifer, recognizable by her stiff, blond hair. She had a round face, a lot like her mother's, and a pleasant smile. Somewhere, that family was going about its business, thinking that Jennifer was all right.

The other pictures were snapshots. An old lady sitting in a wheelchair surrounded by baskets of flowers and looking vaguely pleased. Jennifer again, in a sweater, hugging a cat, and another of Jennifer with a female friend about the same age, standing stiffly on a beach. There were three more snapshots of young women in their twenties, two of which seemed to have been taken in the apartment.

The grouping was asymmetrical. In the space where another picture should have hung, in order to give the composition balance, there was bare wall with a small brass picture hanger.

Arthur slammed down the phone. "I told them," he said. "I told them she was strangled. The police are on their way. They want us to wait in my apartment."

"Yes," said Jane.

"I told them you had an appointment with her, and that's why I went in," he said. "I guess they'll want to talk to you too."

He came over to her side. "There's a picture missing here," she said. "Do you know who it might be?"

He frowned. "No. Those older people are her family, I guess. They live in Spokane. I know she had a brother. And those are some of her old roommates." He pointed at the pictures.

"I guess she let him in," she said, pointing to the door.

He turned. "Unless he came in the French doors. Those locks are kind of flimsy, but I hated to change them. They were authentic." He looked suddenly ashamed. "I never dreamed anyone would..."

He went behind the desk and flapped at some long drapes.

"Don't touch anything," said Jane; then, thinking she sounded too bossy and sharp, she said, "that's what they always say in the movies."

"I know, I know. Jesus, it's open."

Jane went over to his side and slid behind the desk next to him. He smelled of some old-fashioned scent—chypre, she thought. The tall French door, with thick wavy glass in small panes, had a wrought iron handle. The door was open just a crack.

The door led to a small patio. There was a big glazed pot out there with some dehydrated-looking geraniums against a low white-brick wall topped with curly red tiles.

"God," said Arthur. "Let's get out of here."

"Yes," she said.

Still brandishing his handkerchief, Arthur led them out of the apartment and locked up. "I can't believe this is happening. My nerves are shot to hell. We need a cup of tea or something," he said as they went back down to his apartment. "Or maybe even a cocktail."

Could she tell this nice man she'd lied to him? Would he find out anyway? Would the police ask her questions in front of him? She felt sick and ashamed.

"Sit down," he said back in his apartment, practically pushing her into a small chair covered in silver satin. He began rattling over a black enamel drinks cart. "Brandy and soda for me," he said, wielding a silver siphon. "I've got everything."

"A little Scotch with some of that soda, please," she said.

"God, I feel horrible dragging *you* into this," he said, bustling into the kitchen and emerging with a silver ice bucket and tongs. "An innocent bystander and all. But to be honest, I'm glad I didn't find her all by myself."

He handed her a glass and patted her on the shoulder.

She took a sip. "What was she like?" she said.

"Poor Jennifer," he said, sipping his own brandy and closing his eyes for a second. "She was lonely. I could have been nicer." He sat down.

"We all could have been nicer to everyone," said Jane. "Don't be too hard on yourself."

"She was just a dull woman, a little too cheerful all the time. Transferred from her company's office in Spokane. She was an office manager for a company that sold something deadly dull. I forget what. Electrical wiring or something.

"I never figured why she lived here. I like to think," he said, "that my building attracts interesting people."

"Definitely," said Jane. "It's an interesting building."

"I think she took it over from someone at her office. It wasn't quite her. And then, at first, because it was so big, she got roommates in here. Actually, I think she got roommates in here because she was lonely. She went through them like Kleenex.

"Her roommates provided her with some social life. In fact, one of them told me that's why it didn't work out. Her roommate fell in love, and Jennifer was kind of clingy and jealous. She certainly never had any men of her own around."

He sat upright and his eyes widened. "Until last week."

"Oh?"

"A very attractive man showed up at her apartment. Late thirties, nice thick hair, cleft chin. The works."

"Really?"

"Yes, I was quite happy for her. Jesus, what if he strangled her? I ran into him in the lobby. I was grooming the plants. He was whistling, I remember, and he nodded at me and went over and knocked on her door, so I guess she'd buzzed him in.

"I was dying to know if she'd found a boyfriend. She could have been attractive, you know. She just never did anything with herself. Wore these horribly matronly print shirtwaist dresses that added years to her. She was about thirty I guess, but honestly, it's the kind of thing my mother used to wear to play bridge in. And she kind of slouched around."

"Did you ask her about this guy?"

"Well I hinted around, coyly. She just looked embarrassed and said he had something to do with insurance. I guess he was selling her a policy. But he didn't look like any insurance salesman I ever met."

"Oh," said Jane.

"She was one of those people," said Arthur, leaning back and looking pensive, "who never quite fit in. If you showed any interest, she'd glom on to you. I'm afraid I always gave her kind of a wide berth. I wanted to be nice, but I didn't want her hanging around too much, you know. Anyway, when she had one of her roommate break-ups, she was pretty upset. She came to me and wanted to talk about it. I should have listened to her."

"I understand, though," said Jane. "You have to protect yourself sometimes."

"Well, that's just it. I'm here all day. I can't have the tenants coming and crying on my shoulder all the time.

That's when I came up with my theory that she was really a dyke and hadn't admitted it to herself and was going all soft over Brenda. And I was impatient and thought to myself, 'Well if you aren't honest with yourself about your orientation, it's your problem.' But maybe she was just one of those asexual people—sort of an enviable way to be, really—and wanted a friend. God, life can be so pathetic."

He sighed. "I'll always feel guilty I wasn't nice to her that day. She looked as if she'd been crying. They'd had a big fight, she said. And she seemed to be feeling guilty about something. The trouble was, I was preoccupied myself. A dear friend of mine was flying to Key West that day, and there was a horrible plane crash in Florida, and I thought he might have been on it."

"That crash that killed seventy?" said Jane.

"Exactly." Arthur didn't notice that she knew the precise death toll. She remembered it from the newspaper she'd read at the library. The newspaper that had described the murder of Mrs. Cox. "Thank God he had taken an earlier flight."

"Thank God," said Jane. So Jennifer had been upset on the day Mrs. Cox died. Guilty and upset. Somehow it had blown up into a fight with her roommate Brenda.

"What was Brenda like?" said Jane.

"Brenda was kind of hard," said Arthur. "You had the feeling she was out for herself. But it was difficult not to like her."

Just then, they heard sirens outside. "About time," said Arthur huffily. He turned to Jane. "The police will call her family, won't they? They won't expect me to, will they?"

"I don't know," she said. With the sirens, a feeling of nausea had come over her. The sirens reminded her of another time, another murder, another hopeless case.

Chapter 12

As it turned out, Jane didn't have to lie. Unwittingly, Arthur did it for her. "Yes, I'm the owner," he said, "and this poor lady got involved entirely by accident." He explained that Jennifer had been looking for a roommate.

The policeman turned to Jane. He was a nice enough looking guy, florid and sleek. "So you never met Jennifer?" he said.

"No, I just spoke to her on the phone," said Jane.

"The detectives will be coming shortly," said the officer. "We're here to secure the scene. If you wouldn't mind waiting until they come—they'll probably have some questions."

Arthur handed over the apartment key, the police left for a while, and he made himself a second drink.

"I wonder what he took from her desk?" said Jane. "And from the wall."

"You know, now that I think about it, I think that might have been a picture of Brenda," he said. "She had one there, I know. At a party. Pathetic really. I can't imagine Brenda has a picture of her anywhere."

"You were telling me about Brenda," prodded Jane gently.

"Brenda was a Canadian," said Arthur. "She went back there. Vancouver Island."

"What was she like, besides being kind of hard," said Jane, who thought that if her picture had been taken, it was significant.

"A dancer," said Arthur. "She came here to study dance at Cornish, and she sort of worked part-time here and there. I don't know how much she worked or anything. In fact, I sometimes suspected she was leeching off Jennifer, but it wasn't my problem. The rent got paid. She was very pretty. White skin, black hair, blue eyes with thick lashes."

"Sounds Scottish or Irish," said Jane. "What was her name?"

"MacPherson," said Arthur. "Brenda MacPherson. She had a lot of style. But she was short. She went out on a lot of auditions and she always said she didn't get the job because she was short. You know the type, one of those short, spunky girls. Actually pushy is more apt."

Jane turned to Arthur. "Do you think that insurance guy killed her? The one with a cleft chin?"

"I don't know," said Arthur. "To be honest, I hope it was someone she knew. Some stranger getting into the building is even more frightening. And besides, I hate to think of someone getting killed so randomly. But if poor Jennifer, through some foolishness, left herself vulnerable somehow...oh God, this sounds awful, I know. Not that I want to blame the victim or anything."

"I know what you mean," said Jane, who spoke from personal experience, having dealt with two murders, one long ago, one in the recent past. "You want to think that life isn't completely random and cruel."

"That's it. That's it exactly," said Arthur. "I know it sounds strange," he said, "but I'm really glad you're here. I feel like I can talk to you, and this is such a horrible shock, I don't think I could have handled it alone."

But I came too late, thought Jane. She was turning over

in her mind the horrible possibility that her search for Jennifer might have caused her death.

• • •

Later that evening, Jane was sitting cross-legged on the sofa in Calvin Mason's apartment. He was leaning forward in his armchair. "I can't believe you weren't straight with the police," he said.

"I was going to be," she said. "But it never came up. They took my name and address, accepted Arthur's story, and let me go."

"You should have told them."

"I know. I meant to." She let her head fall forward into her hands. "I know it sounds ridiculous, but I didn't want that nice Arthur to know I'd lied to him."

"That *is* ridiculous."

"It's hard to explain. We had a nice rapport. He even took my name and address in case he had a vacancy. He said I belonged in the building."

"He does have a vacancy. You want to move into Jennifer's unit as soon as they vacuum up the fingerprint graphite?"

"I didn't think this would happen," said Jane, looking back up at him and pushing her hair back. "I was just trying to find out who was reading that magazine at the Cox Pharmacy. Don't you see? There's a chance that it's related. That somehow we've stumbled on to something."

"Your case. That's the real reason you weren't honest with the police," said Calvin. He frowned. "The way I see it you should either talk to the police or forget the whole thing. Probably forget the whole thing."

"How can you say that? It's your client at stake." She heard her voice sounding shrill. She told herself to relax.

Calvin sounded peevish and irritable. "I don't want you

to drag me into any mess, just so you can get your hands on all that money your uncle left."

"Calvin, you don't have to get involved. I'm going to look for her old roommate Brenda up in Canada."

"What? Why?" He pushed up his glasses.

"Because of what Arthur told me. She might know what happened that day. It was the same day they had their big fight. I know that because of the newspaper headline I read at the library—Mrs. Cox died the same day of that crash in Florida that upset Arthur. Brenda might remember whether or not Jennifer picked up her prescription."

Calvin appeared to flinch. "I wish you hadn't told me so much. Don't tell me another thing, okay?"

"I was working for you, remember? And the second reason I'm interested in Brenda is that her picture seems to be missing. Arthur thinks it is anyway.

"I was thinking you could maybe check a few things out while I was away," she continued. "Maybe you could find out if the police ever did question Jennifer Gilbert, and what she said." She was thoughtful for a second. "And that dentist. He sounds a little like the guy Arthur saw hanging around. The so-called insurance guy."

Calvin leaned forward. "It doesn't make sense. If the dentist's kid is involved, and if the dentist knew it and if Jennifer Gilbert knew it, and if he knew she knew it," he counted on his fingers, "that makes four jumbo ifs, well then why didn't he kill her before?"

Calvin had a point. Jane didn't answer, and he asked another question. "Look, are you going to tell the police why you were there or not? This could come back to haunt us. Correction, haunt me. I should call them, tell them you were checking something out for me and because you were an amateur and had read too many

Nancy Drews when you were a kid, you were evasive when they questioned you."

Jane knew, from his resigned tone, that he wouldn't do any such thing. "Maybe you can tell the police after I leave town," said Jane. "I don't know how long it will take to find Brenda MacPherson. Vancouver Island is a big place."

"As big as Portugal," said Calvin. "I remember reading that somewhere. Of course, I'm not really sure how big Portugal is."

"Do you want to tell the police I was working for you and that's why I was there?" said Jane.

"If you'd told them that at first it would have been fine, but now how are you going to explain why you lied?"

"Go ahead and tell them I was checking something out for you," said Jane. "Tell them that Jennifer Gilbert might have been a witness to that homicide."

Calvin frowned. "Hell, they have all that in their files. They should have been able to figure it out themselves. Which they won't of course, unless the same guy is working the case and he's got a good memory. Or unless my source remembers my asking about the case. I was careful, though. I managed to see the notes without saying exactly what I was looking for." He allowed himself a small smile of self-congratulation, which Jane found rather charming.

"God, you're good," she said in mock adulation.

He stopped for a moment and looked thoughtful, narrowing his eyes. Jane could practically hear the wheels clicking away in his brain. "There's some way I can get screwed here, I just know it. After it happens about a million times, you develop an instinct for these things."

"I just want a chance to find Brenda." Jane tried not to sound agitated. "If I talk to the police now, I won't be able to go do that right away. I feel responsible." She shook her head. "I don't quite understand it all, but I might have tipped off Dorothy, and she might have talked to Sean..."

"The unwed mother? By the way, did you get the impression they'd already hired an attorney on that paternity thing?"

"You can chase ambulances after we figure this all out," said Jane. "What's the best way to get to Vancouver Island?" She wanted to be *doing* something.

"With a car or without a car?" he said.

"With. I'll just have to come up with some budget motel money."

"I don't like it," said Calvin Mason. "For one thing, if any of this is related to your messing around, you're dealing with a killer."

Jane stretched out on the sofa. "Maybe it's just a coincidence that the witness I'm looking for is killed just before I find her. But it's quite a coincidence."

"Which is why you should tell the police," said Calvin. Jane knew he sounded perfectly sensible. She also knew that it was really his case she'd been investigating, and he had a perfect right to demand she tell the police and forget about going to Canada.

"Listen," she said. "This *is* your case. If Kevin didn't really kill Mrs. Cox—"

"I'm ninety-nine percent sure he did," interrupted Calvin.

"Okay," said Jane. "Probably you're right. But you don't even have a client anymore. Not really. Despite what he says, Kevin thinks he probably did it. His mother doesn't care. In fact, she sleeps better with him in the slammer. The only party interested in proving his innocence is me. And that's because—"

Calvin interrupted again. "Because you want Uncle Harold's money," he said.

"All right. I'll agree to that. So why shouldn't I go, find

this Brenda, and see if she remembered Jennifer saying anything about what happened the day she got that prescription filled at the Cox Pharmacy? If there's nothing there, we can all forget about it. If there is something there, well, then we go to the police."

"You have to stop saying you're acting on my behalf," said Calvin. "Because as my agent, you're acting against my instructions in withholding information from the police."

"All right," said Jane, feeling a little forlorn.

That said, Calvin made an abrupt about-face. "A good way for you to get there is to head up Interstate Five, cross the border at Blaine—there's about a million cars crossing there every day, so no one will remember you—then catch a British Columbia ferry from Tsawwassen and go over to Victoria. It's very simple. All you need is a driver's license, but they never even look at that. They'll just ask if you have a gun or mace, and if you're bringing anything in for anyone in Canada. You can be at the border in two and a half hours. And depending on when the next ferry leaves from Tsawwassen, you can be on Vancouver Island in another couple of hours. Keep in touch, will you?"

"I will," said Jane. She got up, suddenly anxious to leave. She hadn't been entirely truthful with Calvin, and that made her uncomfortable. She'd agreed with him when he'd said she was only in it for the money. But it wasn't just Uncle Harold's money that motivated her right now. It was also the horrifying thought that Jennifer Gilbert might still be alive if Jane hadn't stirred up the cold ashes of the old case.

"How are you going to find Brenda?" said Calvin.

"I'll see what I can do," she said. The truth was, she knew she should start here, working the phones, but the sooner she left, the more she lessened her chances of having to get involved with the police investigating Jennifer

Gilbert's death, telling them what she'd learned and turning over her precious hopeless case to them.

Calvin walked over to his desk. "Somewhere around here I have the name of a private investigator in Victoria. He called me once, wanted me to help him out with a case down here. Turns out I couldn't help him, but he seemed nice enough. Maybe he can do a quick check for you on Brenda MacPherson." He scrawled a name and number from his dog-eared Rolodex on a piece of paper and handed it to her. "Gas up at the border. They want a fortune for gas up there, and it's in liters, so you never know really how bad it is without using higher math."

There was something quite heady about leaving all by herself early the next morning; not knowing what she would find, not telling anyone exactly what she was up to, not knowing herself.

Chapter 13

The drive up went quickly—a little over two hours of good freeway through forest, farmland, the occasional town straggling off into junkyards and strip malls, then back into farmland.

Close to the border Jane was momentarily tempted by a discount shopping center in the middle of nowhere. Canadians, she knew, had for years flocked below the border to buy. Everything was more expensive north of the border and there was less selection.

The border itself brought back childhood memories of weekend trips to Vancouver. Peace Arch Park, a big and grassy expanse, dotted with the kind of formal English-style flower beds the Canadians did so well, surrounded a huge white monument, an arch right on the border itself, erected in 1918. CHILDREN OF A COMMON MOTHER it read across the top in gilt letters, a sentiment from a simpler time when both countries considered themselves firmly Anglo-Saxon. It had been put up right after both countries had fought together for the first time, in World War One, a time when a hunk of white plaster of heroic proportions didn't seem corny at all. People weren't afraid of sentiment then, and what's more, the people putting up monuments generally agreed about what constituted a noble sentiment.

On the Canadian side, there was a big rectangle of flower bed planted firmly in the shape of the Canadian maple leaf flag, with elaborate borders around it of dusty miller and lobelia. The American side wasn't so ambitious, but the flower beds were more labor-intensive and carefully maintained looking than most public landscaping in the States. They'd been shamed into it, she supposed, by the persnickety Canadians.

About forty-five minutes later, Jane was waiting in line for the BC ferry. She took out the scrap of paper Calvin Mason had given her. Gordon Trevellyan. She imagined a square-jawed retired Mountie.

During the two-hour crossing, she had a meal of fish and chips in the cafeteria (with the terrific malt vinegar that Americans too often forgot to provide), then took a walk on the deck. She noticed a framed picture of Queen Elizabeth, who was wearing a white ball gown, a blue sash and a pearl tiara.

The Queen's picture, the Canadian accents she heard aboard the ferry, the dollar bills in blue and red and green, all gave Jane a familiar and pleasant feeling of foreignness. She realized that she always felt more at home, more in control in some way, as a foreigner. And, although Jane knew the United States and Canada weren't terribly different, they were different enough to please her.

She'd always been able to tell English-speaking Canadians from Americans when she'd lived in Europe. It wasn't just that they were often bristling with maple leaf lapel pins in a blatant attempt not to be taken for Americans. It was their manner—less expansive, quieter, more courteous. And their characteristic speech patterns. Scottish-sounding vowels, more precise enunciation and cozy little turns of phrase.

And of course, the ubiquitous "eh," pronounced "ay,"

used instead of the American "huh" as a short version of "what?" (although Canadians were much more likely to say "pardon me?" if they hadn't caught what you said). "Eh" with a question mark was also added to the end of the sentence like the American "y'know?" to check that the listener was getting the drift. Without a question mark it served as a way to amplify a statement.

When the ferry arrived, she pulled over and went to a phone booth. Gordon Trevellyan had a bland English accent of no particular class, with an overlay of Canadian, and a friendly manner. He said he'd be glad to see her as soon as she wanted to come by, and gave her directions to his office on Pandora Street.

She distracted herself on the short drive from the ferry terminal at Swartz Bay into Victoria by looking for more evidence of Canadiana. McDonald's hamburger logos dressed up with maple leaves. Mileage given in kilometers. Stucco houses. For some reason Jane could never understand, British Columbia, covered with dense forests of cedar and fir, also had more than its share of houses in ugly, gritty stucco.

Gordon Trevellyan turned out to be a small grubby man of about fifty or so with a bristly yellowish gray moustache that looked as if it might be nicotine-stained. He wore a light tweed jacket, bulging out a little at the elbows, and managed to give the appearance of a man clinging without much success to respectability. There was a spot of what looked like egg yolk on his striped tie. Jane flicked her glance up from the spot after just a millisecond, but Mr. Trevellyan was apparently quite observant. He noticed her notice.

"Mmm," he said, looking down over his chins and scraping at the spot with his thumbnail. He coughed and turned his attention back to her. "The old regiment," he said.

"Oh, so you have a military background," she said. "I imagine most investigators have police backgrounds."

He cleared his throat. "Did my share of intelligence work in the military," he said. Jane, who was in the habit of creating biographies out of whole cloth for people she met, thought it more likely he'd been a military police-man. She imagined him twenty or thirty years ago, wielding a truncheon, breaking up a bar fight near some Allied base in Germany.

Maybe she would have done better out of the phone book, she thought to herself, glancing around his office, which seemed to be filled with dark Victorian furniture (where had it come from?) and smelled of Player's ciga-rettes. There was a cloudy-looking colored print of King Arthur pulling a sword out of a stone. Jane was reminded of Uncle Harold's Saint George and the dragon in her living room.

Gordon Trevellyan was making them both tea. He'd offered coffee or tea, but the jar of powdered instant she spotted on an old dark oak side table looked grim. She'd been spoiled by all that Seattle espresso. "Tea, please," she'd said. He fussed with an electric kettle and pulled some tea bags out of a box of Red Rose.

"Have you done any missing persons work?" she asked him.

"Plenty," he said with an unconvincing world-weary nod as he presented her with a mug of syrupy-looking brew. She glanced at it and decided she took milk.

"All I have is a name. Brenda MacPherson."

"It's a start, i'n't it," he said, sitting behind his desk, hunching over a yellow legal pad and jotting.

"And a general age. Late twenties." She tasted the tea. She found milky tea rather depressing. It reminded her of a visit she'd made to England in the mid-eighties to visit some London friends—and found them in poorly heated homes, everyone seemingly on the dole and all embittered and grumbling about Thatcher.

"No date of birth?" he asked.

She shrugged. "Sorry."

"Think she might have a criminal record?"

"I have no idea." Jane thought for a second. "I sort of doubt it."

"Married, single? Any kids?"

"Single as far as I know. And it's unlikely she has kids." Jane was struck with how little she knew about Brenda. Yet somehow she had an idea of what she was like.

"Citizenship?"

"Canadian. I'm pretty sure."

He nodded, pleased she'd known something at last. "Good. And you have any idea where she is?"

"Somewhere on Vancouver Island. Before that—about two years ago—she lived in Seattle."

"Got a picture? A general description?"

"No picture. She's short, with fair skin and dark hair. Probably in pretty good shape. Trained as a dancer."

Trevellyan poured milk and sugar into his tea and stirred it up vigorously, took a slurp, then made a few notes on a piece of paper. "Hmm. Well, if all else fails, you can stake me to a series of evenings in our famous Canadian stripper bars. A lot of dancers end up there." He wheezed happily at what she assumed was a joke.

"I didn't realized this was a hotbed of vice."

"Oh, no," he said, looking very serious. "It's all very legit. Clean operations. The Americans come up here, they can't believe it. It's all very classy." He gave Jane the impression he was a serious aficionado. "BC is famous for its stripper bars," he said with a touch of civic pride.

"I see," said Jane. "I haven't been here in years. I remember when I was a kid, gentlemen and ladies had to enter a pub through separate entrances, and it was against the law to open a grocery store on Sunday."

"That's right," he said. "Before my time, though. Things have loosened up considerably. This place is the California of Canada. Mind you, it's still fairly quiet. On the surface, anyways." He raised an eyebrow as if to suggest he was well acquainted with the seamy side of life. He offered her a Player's, lit one for himself, then got down to business. "Well, I can't tell you how long this will take. Could be pretty straightforward, could get complicated."

"I just want you to get me started," she said. "You don't have to actually find her. Or contact her. Just get me an address somewhere."

"Bound to be more than one Brenda MacPherson," he said.

"Fine. Give me any Brenda MacPhersons you can find in the approximate age range."

"Righto. How are you paying, love? Visa, Mastercard?"

"Cash," she said.

"All right. I charge you a hundred an hour."

Jane figured this was somewhere around eighty-five dollars U.S., depending on the exchange rate. "Okay. Would you like a deposit?"

"Sure." He sounded casual, but Jane thought she detected a gimlety little gleam in his eye as he exhaled cigarette smoke. "Two hundred'll get me started." She removed two Canadian hundreds from her wallet under his watchful gaze, glad that she'd exchanged money at the border. She had a feeling Gordon Trevellyan would have tried to chisel her on the exchange rate.

"What I'd like you to do," she said firmly, in case he planned to string her along with a lot of unnecessary charges, and try and dazzle her with the complexity of the task, "is check with a few of your usual sources. The phone company, maybe law enforcement, anyone with a big computer, and get me a couple of addresses. I'm assuming you've got some sources like that?"

"That's right," he said, looking a little wary.

"If it gets much more complicated than that, let me know."

"Where can I get in touch with you?" he said.

"I'm not sure. I'll call you in the morning, let you know."

"All right."

She rose to go, and he walked her to the door.

The essential snobbishness of the English culture seemed to guarantee that there was no sleaze quite like English sleaze. And nowhere better to find it than in some outpost of Empire like Victoria, British Columbia.

Jane was more than a little irritated. She imagined there were a good half dozen solid, professional investigative firms in Victoria, run by ex-RCMP with good contacts who knew the territory.

And Calvin steers her to a refugee from a Graham Greene novel! But then she brought herself up short. So what if he had egg on his tie and a shifty manner? She realized she was judging him by snobbish English standards. Maybe he'd do a perfectly fine job. After all, Calvin had told her about missing persons work. It was just as she'd described it to Gordon Trevellyan. A small bribe to someone with access to a computer somewhere. She didn't see how Gordon Trevellyan could screw it up.

Chapter 14

Jane spent the night in a grim little motel on the outskirts of Victoria, which she picked out of a tourist guide because of its low rates. It had a Ye Olde England theme, and was made of plywood plastered over and dressed up with some dark brown two-by-fours to look like Tudor architecture.

The War of the Roses was memorialized in the neon sign outside her room. The white rose of York shone brightly, but the red rose of Lancashire had a wicked flicker that penetrated the rather spongy curtains. That, and the valley of fatigue in the old mattress, made sleep difficult.

The next morning she gave herself a stern lecture about fortitude and being cheerful, but her resolve faded a little as she stepped into a tin shower cubicle that buckled under her weight with a metallic warping sound. She scrubbed at herself with some sort of carbolic soap, the kind she imagined prisoners might be issued to make sure they were properly deloused.

The hell with it, she told herself, as she slammed her possessions into her suitcase. From now on, no motel rooms that smelled of industrial disinfectant and were equipped with mildewing shower curtains and polyester towels. She looked around the room and sneered at the velvet painting of a knight in armor, tastefully attached to the wall by screws at each corner to make sure no one would steal it. On closer inspection she realized that as an additional security measure, a Phillips screwdriver would be required to remove the hideous thing from the wall. A mere dime wouldn't do the trick. Only the most persistent art lover could make it his own.

And from now on, she vowed, no motels without complimentary shampoo and conditioner, cable TV and opaque curtains that met in the center of the window. Surely Uncle Harold wouldn't have wanted her to live like this? A curmudgeonly phrase she had heard somewhere floated into her consciousness. "If you can't afford to travel, stay home."

But if she stayed home, and didn't pursue a hopeless case, she might never be able to travel. Even if this wasn't the right hopeless case, she was mindful of the bargain she'd made with God. She'd work hard and unquestioningly at whatever crumbs were thrown her, and she'd get a decent case one way or the other. Jane, while believing intellectually that it was theologically unsound to make deals with God, nevertheless did it all the time. She felt she might be getting too old now to break a lifelong habit.

She checked out, paying cash. When the little old overrouged lady at the counter asked her very sweetly how everything was, Jane merely said, "Just fine, thank you." What was the point of telling the poor thing that the place was enough to practically precipitate a clinical depression? After all, Jane could leave.

The little transaction seemed to put everything all back in perspective. Jane stopped feeling sorry for herself and drove back into Victoria in better spirits.

When she got there, she parked her car near the museum and set out toward the Empress Hotel. The Empress was opened in 1908 by the Canadian Pacific

Railway to give travelers a reason to go to Victoria, and it still dominated the harbor exuding all the confidence of the British Empire at the height of its powers.

The massive structure, looking like a French château, equaled in grandeur provincial parliament buildings nearby, and squarely faced the small harbor.

Like everything here, it was surrounded by perfectly kept gardens and lawns. A statue of the Empress herself, Victoria Regina, in her younger days, looked out at her corner of Empire with dignity, as tourists in tank tops and shorts, many of them from day boats from Seattle or from cruise ships, shuffled among the restored buildings of the harbor.

Jane found a rare parking spot nearby, locked the suitcase in the trunk, smoothed out her black dress, which she wore in an attempt to look like a traveler perhaps, but not a tourist, and went into the lobby of the Empress. They'd done a fabulous restoration since she'd been here last, and the old girl was looking pretty good, with soft carpets, gleaming carved wood and big, well-balanced spaces. Jane felt at home here. She often felt at home in surroundings she could not afford, and out of place in surroundings she could, as if some dreadful mistake had been made. She decided to eat breakfast here, damn the expense, but first she called Gordon Trevellyan.

"Where are you?" he said. "I should be able to get back to you with something this afternoon."

"I'll be downtown," she said. "You can leave a message for me at the Empress."

She went to the desk, explained that she wasn't a guest but that she might be expecting a message here, and tipped the desk clerk ten dollars. He took it with apparent squeamishness, but said he'd take care of it. She went to the newsstand and bought herself a *Times-Colonist*, then picked up a few brochures from the concierge's desk. She made a point of smiling nicely at the young woman there in a blue blazer, as if she were a guest who might need some help later.

In the restaurant, she settled into a corner table with a view of the room, and ordered eggs Benedict. She skimmed over the international news, which there wasn't too much of, and read about an ongoing dispute between local timber interests and environmentalists over clear cutting on the island.

There was also a story about some tourists from Quebec who'd been collecting hallucinogenic mushrooms on the Queen Charlotte Islands to the north. Some of the Haida natives had come upon them, and, resenting their intrusion on their land, held a gun to their heads and forced them to consume their entire sackful of mushrooms. The tourists had been flown by float plane to a medical clinic where they'd had their stomachs pumped.

Queen Victoria's little corner of Empire still had something of the untamed about it, Jane decided. These wild and woolly goings-on were interspersed with items about flower shows, pony clubs, ratepayers' meetings and movie and book reviews, all of which paled in her mind beside the story of the tourists from Quebec.

She imagined them babbling in hallucinogenic French in the little clinic in the bush, and wondered if they'd had those Gallic, Rousseau-like romantic notions of Indians living in harmony with nature. Until they'd found themselves on the wrong end of a gun.

She put the paper down, turned her attention to her eggs Benedict, and looked around the incredibly civilized room, quiet except for the chink of glasses and cutlery and low murmurs. At the table next to her sat a good-looking man in a dark suit, who appeared as if he were on a business trip. His thick brown hair was still a little wet above his collar from his morning shower, and he had an appealing, freshly shaved look.

Traveling and hotels brought out the libidinous in her, she thought to herself as she admired him. There was something romantic about the idea of strangers in transit, and the delicious sense she got when traveling of never knowing what might happen. Which was probably why she'd traveled so much.

He caught her gaze, smiled at her, and she found herself smiling back. She managed to finish her breakfast without resuming eye contact, but when she left she gave him another little smile over her shoulder.

Her spirits lifted by the brief encounter, she spent some time walking the historic streets, past cute little shops with tartans and bone china for the Americans, then went into the provincial museum and looked at Native art—dramatically lit massive totem poles in pale, bleached cedar. Stylized ravens, eagles, beavers, frogs, wolves, bears and killer whales transmogrified themselves into each other, faces sharing space with stomachs, wide eyes alert, with now and then blank-faced humans humbly intertwined in the composition, no match for the power of the thunderbird with his powerful wings. The exhibits were somewhat defensively labeled to indicate that the various chiefs had sold these works to the museum for reasonable amounts of cash back in the teens and twenties, and they hadn't been stolen by marauding colonial collectors.

In the afternoon, she went back to the lobby of the Empress. There was a message for her at the desk from Gordon Trevellyan. She found a pay phone and called him back, noticing that the Canadian quarter bore an out-of-date portrait of the Queen. It had been minted at least one chin ago.

"I've got what you want," said Trevellyan—a little

nervously, she thought. "A printout with Brenda Mac-Phersons from twenty-five to thirty years old. But there's been a bit of a wrinkle. How about if I come by your hotel and talk to you about it? I can be there in half a tic." They arranged to meet in the lobby.

He came in looking rumpled and seedy—the elegant surroundings made it even more apparent—and she shook his hand, catching the smell of tobacco and whiskey as he came toward her. "Let's go into the bar where we can talk quietly," he said. "The tourists'll be coming in for their damn tea in a sec." He looked at his watch and chewed a little at his yellowish moustache.

In the bar, tricked out like Rangoon in the days of the Raj with lots of potted palms and Indian brasses, he looked around with the air of a slightly eager regular, apprising himself of who was here. No one took any notice of him, and they sat down at a small table at the back.

"Got four of them," he said. "All over the map." He shoved a page across the table, fired up another Player's and hailed a waitress. There was a list of four addresses. One in Tofino, two in Victoria, one on Denman Island. There was a date of birth with each one. "That what you need?"

"Yes," she said. He'd mentioned a printout, but the information had obviously been transferred to this sheet. It had been typed on what looked like an old manual typewriter.

He ordered a large whiskey and soda, and she decided that teatime was late enough for a sherry.

"Forgive my asking, Mrs. da Silva," he said. "But was this a collection matter? I wasn't quite sure what your interest in this person was," he said, tilting his head sideways like a bird. "So I wasn't sure if you'd be interested in knowing about any other individuals who might be interested in this person."

"Someone else is looking for her?" said Jane.

"Very common in collection work as I'm sure you know. Maybe the two of you could get together?" He paused delicately. Jane imagined there'd be a fee involved. She'd love to know who else was looking for Brenda. What she didn't want was for the individual to know who she was and what she was doing.

"I hope I can count on your discretion," she said. "I'd just as soon no one knew I was looking for Brenda MacPherson."

"Fine," said Trevellyan. "Just thought I'd check."

"This person who's also looking for her? Is it a client of yours?" said Jane, trying to sound casual.

He cleared his throat and ground out his cigarette in the glass ashtray. "Not exactly."

Jane decided she was tired of fencing around with him. After all, didn't he work for her?

"Listen, Mr. Trevellyan," she said pleasantly but firmly. "Can we be very direct?"

He looked slightly alarmed.

She smiled and tried to reassure him. "I can't help it, really, being American. Any more than you can help being subtle, because you're English."

"I'm not English," he said with dignity. Damn. Now she'd offended him somehow, just when she was trying to be charming. He was probably a naturalized Canadian and was all prickly about the old country like some first-generation people could be.

"I'm Cornish," he said, sticking out his jaw resolutely.

"Cornish? From Cornwall?"

He looked defiant. "That's right. We're not really English, you know. The Anglos and Saxons and Normans and all that lot never really penetrated into Cornwall. We kept them at bay."

"Yes," said Jane, who vaguely remembered hearing something about Cornwall at some point. "The Cornish language is related to Breton French, isn't it."

"That's right," he said, with a gleam in his eye. "A Gaelic language."

"Do you speak it?" said Jane, fascinated. His English was certainly free of any colorful dialect.

"Well, no," said Mr. Trevellyan with irritation. "Di'n't have much chance now, did I? The English stamped it out along with most of our culture. But it was spoken up to the eighteenth century."

"It's wonderful that there are Cornishmen like you who haven't forgotten," she said stoutly. The picture of King Arthur on his office wall flashed into her memory. She remembered his castle was supposed to have been in Cornwall.

"King Arthur," she said dreamily. "Tintagel."

"That's right," he said, warming up to her now. "Perhaps you're familiar with the Cornish nationalist movement," he said rather breathlessly. "Some of us feel that what with the EC and that, there's no reason for us to be part of England anymore." All the craftiness had gone out of him. His blue eyes were rounded and betrayed the glaze of fanaticism.

She nodded solemnly, as if the idea were neither new nor eccentric to her, and their drinks arrived. He broke off when the waitress came to their table with their drinks. Maybe he thought she was an English spy.

Jane racked her brain for more Cornish lore. All she could come up with was that she'd once known a Marjorie Warmington who'd told her Warmington was a Cornish name. She felt she'd managed, nevertheless, to establish some fellow-feeling with Mr. Trevellyan, and seized the moment to get back on track. "What I was wondering, Mr. Trevellyan," she said, "is who else is looking for Brenda MacPherson, and why? And how you know about it. Could you tell me that?"

"Well there is a question of confidentiality," he began.

Jane smiled. "I'd be glad to reimburse you for any extra work the answers to my questions might have required."

"Well it's a little sticky," he said. "You see the source I used to get this information, well she's the one who told me someone else was looking for the same party. It made it awkward for her to run this name by the people on the Third Floor, that is, they wondered why there was so much interest in this person and it put my confidential source in an awkward spot."

"The Third Floor?"

He waved his hand dismissively. "My source was very keyed up about the whole thing. Had to do some fast talking. Claimed I put her in a bad spot."

"How much," said Jane, "would it require to put her more at ease?"

He smiled. "Another hundred might do the trick. As a token of our appreciation for any awkwardness she might have encountered."

"Fine," said Jane, reaching for her bag.

He looked a little more relaxed.

"Do you know who he is?" she said, sliding a bill across the table as discreetly as possible. Thank God the currency was color-coded. Hundreds had a kind of wine-colored ink. It made it much easier than if she'd had to root around in her wallet.

"Just that he's an American. And that he is staying at this hotel."

"That's it? That's all you know?" Jane looked at her hundred a little forlornly. Even with the exchange rate she felt it was too much for the skimpy information. She wasn't about to add to it.

She leaned across the table. "Mr. Trevellyan," she said, steadfastly maintaining eye contact as his hand darted out for the bill. "I wish you'd tell me everything you know. I feel I can count on you. As a Cornishman. You see, my maiden name was a Cornish name. Warmington."

"It was?"

"Yes. My grandfather told me wonderful things about the Cornwall where he grew up. He always told me we weren't English, we were Cornish." She fixed him in her gaze and looked as intent as possible.

He didn't say anything for a while, and she kept staring at him. Finally, he smiled a little and said, "Well, you're stubborn enough to be Cornish. My source works for a doctor. Every once in a while, as a favor to me, she calls up the people at BC Medical and gets some addresses. Some story about paperwork with the doctor she works for. They can run a search by name and approximate age. The addresses are right about seventy percent of the time. More if they're self-employed."

"I see," said Jane.

"Anyway, a day or so ago, some American got ahold of her name somehow and asked her for the same thing. I didn't realize she was doing this sort of thing for just anyone." He sounded peeved, as if he'd somehow been cuckolded. "She said she didn't want to call back and ask for the same information twice."

Jane's eyebrows rose. "So she didn't keep it?"

"No. Passed it on to this guy. Took me a while to convince her to run it all through again. She came up with some story for them about having lost the first run. But she didn't want to do it. Repeating it like that would bring attention to the whole thing."

"But you convinced her?"

He nodded and took a sip of his drink. Jane wondered how he'd convinced her. Subtle blackmail, perhaps? She couldn't imagine the authorities approved of medical personnel getting into people's medical records, even if it was just an address.

"And the upshot was the people there at 1515 Blanshard questioned her rather sharply about the whole thing. The poor thing was afraid the RCMP would be around to question her. I calmed her down."

"Good," said Jane. "And you managed to get out of her what you told me. An American, staying at the Empress. You didn't get a name?"

"No."

"You didn't, by any chance, give him mine?" said Jane.

"No!" he said, looking shocked. Jane wasn't sure she believed him.

Chapter 15

"But your source," said Jane, "she must have gotten a name."

"I presume so," he said, looking uncomfortable.

"Well you must have talked about him some. After all, she told you he was staying at the Empress." Jane vowed to hang on like a terrier.

"Ye-es," he said.

"Well, how did that come up?"

"Because she said she contacted him here. Left an envelope for him."

"So she presumed he was staying here," she said. Of course, that didn't mean anything. After all, she'd made arrangements for the desk to take a message for her. And they had.

"I had the feeling," sniffed Mr. Trevellyan, "that she'd hoped to see him again, and seemed disappointed that she could only drop it off."

"So he was presumably charming," she said.

"Well that's the whole thing," said Mr. Trevellyan. He snorted. "She made a point of telling me how attractive this fellow was. I had to act vaguely put out, as if he were a rival. You need a bit of charm to get someone like Lucy to help you. I mean, she doesn't really need the money. You have to butter them up a bit, you know?"

"I see," said Jane, nodding and trying to look as if his powers of persuasion with the female sex were a given.

Encouraged, he expanded on his theme. "That's why you don't go for the young, pretty ones. You go for the middle-aged ones with some fat on them. They like the attention. And besides slipping them a few bucks, you send them a box of chocolates or something."

"Very shrewd," said Jane. "You're telling them they're not really fat." Mr. Trevellyan himself had quite a stomach of his own—the kind Jane usually associated with boozers.

"That's right. Besides, if you send flowers, the other girls in the office want to know who they're from."

"Do you think you could persuade Lucy to tell us this guy's name?"

"I tried," he said. "Just in case you were interested," he added hastily. Again, she sensed just a shade too much expression in this last phrase. Unless it was her imagination, Mr. Trevellyan was an appallingly transparent liar. It had to be a handicap for a private investigator to be saddled with body language and vocal qualities that functioned like a polygraph machine.

She imagined he'd tried to get the guy's name so he could sell him something. Like Jane's name, perhaps.

"Do you think I could talk to Lucy?" she said.

"Oh, no," he said. "She wouldn't want the world to know she was involved in anything irregular."

"And of course, she wouldn't want to think you blabbed her name around," said Jane. "After all, there can't be that many Lucys who call the Third Floor at BC Medical once in a while and ask for addresses and other confidential patient information."

He narrowed his eyes a little, and she thought maybe she'd overdone it with her implied threat. She actually felt a little sorry for him, but she forced herself to move right on to the close.

"Could you call Lucy and ask for the guy's name?" she said.

"It might be a bit awkward," he replied.

"Oh?" said Jane.

"Mmm," he said pensively. "She's feeling a bit skittish after BC Medical questioned her. I've just managed to calm her down. I wouldn't want her all upset."

"Maybe we can see what we can find out at the hotel," she said. "We don't have his name, but we have Lucy's. Or you do. Maybe we can ask if the envelope she dropped off got to the right party. Something like that."

"Umm, we could do that, I suppose," said Mr. Trevellyan in a tone that indicated they weren't going to do any such thing.

Jane decided to take his statement at face value. "Good," she said, pushing back her chair. "How about you just tell them that Lucy dropped off an envelope and you want to see if it went to the right party, and you forgot his name or something."

"Bit thin," said Mr. Trevellyan.

"Maybe you can thicken it up," said Jane, with a nice smile.

"I suppose so," he said gloomily.

"How's this?" said Jane. "Tell him Lucy So-and-so of your office dropped off some papers that were supposed to go to Mr. Smith, but that she mislabeled them, and you're not sure who they really went to. And you have to get them back and you want the name of the party who took charge of the envelope."

"Well, I suppose..."

"Of course, I'd be glad to do it myself. But you don't want to give me Lucy's name."

"Mmm," he said.

"Of course I could try and get her full name from BC Medical," she added disingenuously. She doubted this would work, but she didn't doubt that he'd be put out if his source were compromised by an off-the-wall phone call from her.

"That would never work," he snapped. He ground out his cigarette and looked at her with an analytical eye. She figured he was trying to decide if she was threatening him on purpose or out of stupidity. She smiled.

"Well, I'll give it a try," he said. "No guarantees. I doubt Lucy left her name along with the envelope." He knocked back his drink, with the gesture of a man about to embark on the kind of task he wants to get over as soon as possible. "I'll be right back," he said.

As soon as he left, Jane settled the bill, gave him a head start, then went down to the lobby to see how he was doing.

He was dutifully hanging over the counter and looking appealingly desperate. She sidled up to him and gave the clerk a nervous smile. Trevellyan was obviously irritated that she was standing next to him, and shifted his weight a little from foot to foot.

"Without the guest's name," said the desk clerk, an appealingly well-scrubbed-looking young woman in a peach-colored blazer that matched the decor, "I'm afraid there's not much we can do."

"Oh, it's all my fault," said Jane. "I'm the one who gave her the wrong envelope."

The clerk looked puzzled, but Jane plunged on, wishing she'd stuck to Trevellyan from the beginning. She wasn't quite sure what he'd said. "Did you explain it?" she said to him.

"Just briefly," he said, mercifully catching on. "I told her we delivered the envelope for Mr. Clark to this American by mistake."

"You see," said Jane, "I put the Clark papers in the wrong envelope, and Lucy was going to put the American's name on it, but she was the only one who knew his name, and now she's gone on vacation, and Mr. Clark will be furious."

The clerk didn't seem sufficiently moved by the urgency of the situation, so Jane took a deep breath and added, "It took us forever to get his ex-wife to sign off and now we have the buyer, but without the papers with her signature..."

"There's a substantial real estate transaction going here," said Mr. Trevellyan. "Hong Kong money. Cash."

"My God, I feel terrible," said Jane.

"You should," snapped Mr. Trevellyan with a vehemence that startled Jane.

"She brought it in yesterday?" said the clerk, frowning disapprovingly at Trevellyan for yelling at Jane.

"Yes," said Jane. "He's Lucy's client. All we know is he was an American, staying here. She said he was quite attractive."

The girl was sounding more interested in Jane's problem. "We get a lot of Americans here, naturally," she said. "Let me just go ask if someone else remembers handing an envelope to an American guest."

After a second, she came back. "Could it have been Mr. Johnson? Caroline remembers handing an envelope to Mr. Johnson. He was here from San Francisco."

She clacked away at her computer. "There was a message for him yesterday that there was something for him at the desk." She looked apologetic. "We have a lot of guests. I can't run through them all, I'm afraid."

"We'll give him a try," said Trevellyan, taking hold of Jane's elbow and trying to pry her away from the counter. "We'll just give him a ring on the house phone."

"Oh, but he's checked out," said the clerk. "I remember

him now. I checked him out myself. This morning." She
paused for a minute. Jane figured she was deciding
whether he had been attractive. A little half smile told
Jane she'd decided he was.

"Did he say where he was going?" said Jane.

"I don't think so. Oh, wait, the concierge had arranged
a booking for him. I remember, because she was gone for
a second and he wondered if she'd taken care of it or
not."

"Thank you very much," said Jane.

Trevellyan was looking very uncomfortable. Jane got
the distinct impression he hadn't wanted her to find out
about Mr. Johnson. "May not be the right fellow," he said
gruffly. Which made Jane suspect they had the right man
and he knew it.

She stepped away from the counter and turned away,
so the clerk couldn't see her facial expressions. She wanted
to be firm with him, and so she had to abandon the
persona of the remorseful and browbeaten clerical. "I'll
take care of it from here on," she said.

"All right," he said. He seemed ever so slightly put out,
as if he'd lost face. Perhaps it was because she'd horned in
on his attempt to get information about the other person
who was looking for Brenda. He managed a pleasant
good-bye and said he'd be glad to help her anytime she
needed it. "And give my regards to Mr. Mason," he said,
as if he and Calvin were old chums, which Jane knew
wasn't the case, but which she assumed was his way of
trying to make himself seem more legit. She was delighted
to see him go, and found it incredibly easy to find out
from the concierge where Mr. Johnson was headed.

Mr. Johnson, whoever he was, was going to Tofino.
One of the places where Trevellyan had uncovered a
Brenda MacPherson. Jane had planned to do some phon-
ing from Victoria. Call those Brendas with some story,

still vaguely forming in her mind, and check out the most obvious possibilities first.

But Mr. Johnson had the jump on her. Presumably, he'd done some legwork and decided to start with Tofino. Or maybe he wanted to find Brenda without warning her. Jane was intensely curious about who he was and why he wanted to locate Brenda. Maybe, if she made it to Tofino in time, she could find out.

She went out to her car and reached for her map of the island. Tofino, a small town on the west coast of the island above Pacific Rim National Park, looked very far away, and as if it were at the end of a long and winding road. She estimated the distance at over three hundred kilometers. She checked her watch. She'd have to start right away if she wanted to get there before dark.

She drove along the harbor to the tourist information kiosk, which she'd spotted earlier. It was housed in what looked like a restored art deco gas station. Art "Deco" Nazimova, she felt, would have approved.

Inside, she picked up a handful of brochures on Tofino, glanced quickly at them, and got a quick impression of long sandy beaches, crashing waves, rain forests and whales. She also asked a young man with red hair, who looked like a college student, about the drive to Tofino.

There was only one road to the west coast of the island, with the exception of some rough logging roads. He told her it was paved, with just two lanes with the occasional passing lane. There was virtually nothing on it after Port Alberni except fabulous scenery, so she'd better gas up there. And he warned her that as it was tourist season, "You should probably book a room as soon as possible."

She made a phone call, got the last room available at what sounded like a nice enough place on the water, and headed north on the highway that ran up the east coast of the island, then turned inland to Port Alberni.

It was around seven o'clock, and still light by the time she got there. She drove through a McDonald's and ate as she drove, filled the tank and had them test the tire pressure and check the oil, wished she had a more powerful car than Uncle Harold's old Chevy, and headed west.

Within a few miles she found herself traveling through postcard country, each curve bringing forth a new vista that could have come off of one of the innumerable brochures she'd picked up at the tourist information center.

Vast lakes, looming mountainsides full of fir and cedar bluish in the evening light, and, at the side of the road, sculptural compositions of rock and gravel, interspersed with wildflowers—the bright yellow of Scotch broom, blowsy wild rose and blue lupine, the occasional early daisies and Queen Anne's lace among grasses with reddish clouds of seeds hovering over the stalks.

Traffic wasn't too heavy, but she found herself frustrated to find herself stuck every once in a while behind slow-moving campers and trucks. Because the road twisted and turned, it was hard to find the opportunity to get around them. Negotiating past these slower vehicles became kind of a game to help her pass the time.

As night fell, around nine o'clock, when the signs told her she was about a half hour out of Tofino, she saw the full moon, appearing and disappearing behind mountainsides now silhouetted black against the sky, and, when she passed a huge lake, making a shiny path across the water.

Besides the occasional boat-launching or camping signs, and the red taillights in front of her as she negotiated the broad arcs, climbed hills and descended on the other side in corkscrew turns, there was no sign of human habitation. Logging, though, had left its mark. Vast tracts on the hills were completely clear-cut and bare; other areas were full of heavy stumps, recently burned over, dotted with magenta fireweed and young alders.

She put herself on a kind of automatic pilot, as if the car were being drawn through these mountains, and watched the moon set, almost as if it were a sun, over the mountains until it was finally just a sparkling dot like a star, then vanishing altogether.

She stopped thinking about Brenda, about Jennifer, about Kevin, presumably lying on his bunk in Monroe while she swooped like an owl through this landscape. She had a single focus now, to get this ribbon of road past her, to get to Tofino, and once there, to think of her next move.

But until then, she relaxed, lulled along by the feeling of heading to the end of the road, the end of the world.

When the road did end, with the open Pacific presumably somewhere in front of her in the dark, she turned north again, through the park on a straight road into the town itself, which seemed to consist of a main street with a few spurs off to the side. It gave the impression of something fairly recently thrown up for the tourists. The buildings were low, squarish and simple, some set in grassy, unweeded patches, the whole managing to impart a sense of impermanency. After all, it was nature they were selling here—the buildings were just afterthoughts.

It was easy to find her motel, one of the largest buildings in town, stained a gray-blue and facing a dock shooting out into a bay.

She carried her suitcase up some stairs to the lobby. A young woman, with the kind of polite, gentle, patient Canadian inflection Jane was becoming accustomed to, was explaining whale watching to some elderly German tourists, who, with German thoroughness, wanted to know exactly what to expect about the expedition they were taking the next day.

The wife translated simultaneously for her husband, and Jane, still a little buzzy from her drive, listened in two languages.

The guides took you out in Zodiacs among the reefs and islands nearby. The guide service didn't guarantee you'd see whales, but the word was whale watching had been good the last few days. A few of the grays stuck around all season. In any case, there were other things to observe—sea lions and seals and puffins and eagles if you didn't see whales.

They should walk over to the office across the street and up a ways to confirm their reservation. Somebody might be there now. If they wanted to visit the hot springs, they should bring towels and something to eat, which they could get at the Co-op supermarket next door. Yes, the hot springs were lovely, at the end of a short trail through rain forests. You could sit in rocky pools and stand under a hot waterfall.

The couple debated the merits of the hot springs expedition. They seemed to have a German confidence in the therapeutic qualities of mineral waters.

Finally, they completed their interrogation, and Jane checked in, vaguely wistful she couldn't get out on the water and look for whales. Standing under a thermal waterfall in a rocky grotto in a rain forest sounded even better.

Her room was neat and pleasant, a definite step up from the Ye Olde Tourist Trappe where she'd spent last night. And there was a real bathtub and shampoo and conditioner.

It was too late to look for Brenda right now. Her plan was to just show up. Phoning people just put them on their guard.

She'd go down to dinner, but first she lay down on the bed and flipped on the TV. There were about a million channels—she'd noticed a big satellite dish outside the motel—and she picked up some news from Seattle. After only two days in Canada, where everyone seemed so well scrubbed and wholesome, the American female newscasters looked a little cheap—overcoiffured and over-made-up.

She let her mind wander a little. She had to come up with some story for Brenda, some way to get her confidence before she tried to get her to talk about what Jennifer might have seen. Saying she was a friend of Jennifer's might not be that terrific an idea. After all, they'd parted on less than amicable terms. Besides, from what she'd heard, Jennifer hadn't really had any friends.

Suddenly, she felt a frisson. They were talking about Jennifer Gilbert on the Seattle news. Jane heard her name and turned her attention back to the broadcast.

"In a new development in the University District slaying of office manager Jennifer Gilbert, police have released an Identikit drawing of a man wanted for questioning in the case." A black-and-white drawing popped up on the screen. Jane was sure it was the man Arthur had seen visiting Jennifer a few days before she died. He had a suggestion of a cleft chin, a neat haircut of dark, thick hair, good brows. Of course, like all those police artist pictures, he looked crude and scary. The picture was just there for a frustrating second. Jane thought he looked familiar, but she couldn't place him. Maybe he was Sean's father, the dentist. She imagined Arthur had provided the description, and probably found the process thrilling in a morbid way.

"Police emphasize that the man is just wanted for questioning and is not a suspect at this time," said the announcer. Her solemn face transformed instantly, like some victim of multiple personality. Now she was perky and cheerful. "In a lighter vein, our roving reporter Chuck Lundquist found a man who collects gum wrappers—that's right, gum wrappers. And he's been doing it for a long time." She clicked off the set just as an image of an old codger in a baseball cap standing proudly next to a huge silver ball came onto the screen.

She wanted to see that composite sketch again. Maybe Calvin Mason could get a copy and fax it to her here. But later, when she went down to dinner, she realized why the face looked familiar. It was the man she'd checked out at breakfast this morning in the Empress Hotel. The one who looked so nice and clean and freshly shaven and prosperous and respectable. She knew she was right—as right as anyone could be about one of those composite sketches.

Because the man was here, in the dining room at her hotel. He was wearing a yellow lamb's-wool sweater and khaki trousers, and he was eating a large piece of salmon and reading *Time* magazine as if he didn't have a care in the world.

Chapter 16

She took a deep breath. Should she call the police? She rejected the idea after about ten seconds' thought. It was absurd. Sure, he resembled the composite, but so what? So did a million other guys. And he wasn't even in Seattle. All she knew about him was that he'd been at the Empress Hotel in Victoria this morning.

At first, she'd planned to arrange herself at her table so she could observe him in profile, and so he couldn't see her without turning around. Now she decided she'd let him see her.

"Could I have that table there?" she asked the hostess, pointing to the one next to him.

"Sure."

Jane made a slightly noisy deal of scraping her chair and thanking the woman, and, sure enough, he looked up from his magazine. To her surprise, he gave her a big smile. She found that rather chilling.

But she smiled back.

"Didn't I see you in Victoria this morning?" he said, putting down the magazine with the air of someone who expects to have a long conversation.

"I think so," said Jane, lowering her eyelids in a shamelessly coy gesture—the sort of cheap trick she used to incorporate into her act when she sang in clubs in Europe.

"You aren't following me, are you?" he said easily.

"I was going to ask you the same thing," she said with a sideways smile.

The waitress handed her a menu.

"The prawns are pretty good," he said. Something about the inflection on the word "pretty" convinced her he was an American.

If she were actually trying to pick him up or something for personal, rather than business, reasons, she'd be more restrained. Jane felt that most men, no matter what they said about wishing women would call, were secretly appalled if they actually did, and still basically liked to think the whole thing was their idea. But she forced herself to be a little more forthright. "What are you doing in Tofino?" she said.

She had a silly flash of the man saying, "I'm here to stalk a woman named Brenda. Last week I killed her ex-roommate in Seattle. Perhaps you saw the composite picture of me on TV." Here she was, acting like Mata Hari with this perfectly nice tourist.

"Just looking around," he said vaguely.

"I'd have thought you were here on business. Weren't you wearing a gray suit this morning?" Let him know she'd checked him out enough to notice what he wore.

He smiled. "It's a formal town. What about you? Here on business?"

"I'm going whale watching," she said. "I'm crazy about killer whales."

"That's too bad," he said with a little gleam. "Because they mostly have gray whales around here. The orcas are more on the east coast of the island. In the Strait of Georgia."

Now she felt like an idiot. "I thought I'd do the hot springs too," she said, struggling to maintain her dignity.

He laughed. "I only know about the whales because I just read it in a brochure," he said, apparently aware and amused she was slightly embarrassed. "Apparently, we just missed their big migration." The waitress came back to take her order, and brought him a cup of coffee. She ordered the prawns and a glass of wine.

"Would you mind if I drank my coffee at your table," he said with a tasteful touch of reticence, as if he were presuming but couldn't resist asking.

"Of course not," she said, as if she were somehow remiss in not having invited him sooner.

He moved over to her table with his coffee cup in his hand, stepping over a chair that was wedged between the tables. He did it with grace, but the informal gesture convinced her he was American. Only Americans used space like that. Almost anybody else, she felt, would have slid out the other side and gone around the table.

"You're American, aren't you?" she said.

"That's right," he said. "From San Francisco. Where are you from?"

"Up from Seattle."

She didn't notice any flicker when she said Seattle. If he'd strangled someone there recently, it might have meant something to him. Unless, of course, he was one of those charming and remorseless sociopaths. He didn't seem to be. He seemed to be just a nice guy with a smooth manner.

"Nice town," he said. "How can you tell I'm American?"

"The accent," she said.

"You mean the one I don't have?"

"That's right. More open vowels mostly. Less precision, flatter inflection."

"You must have a pretty good ear," he said with a disarming smile.

"And the way you stepped over that chair," she added. "It seemed sort of direct and American."

"Do you think Canadians are that different?" He frowned a little as if he were concerned he might have missed something.

"They're a little more circumspect," she said. "Wary of offending."

"You're right. And formal. They say 'Pardon?' instead of 'What?'"

He leaned back in his chair and put one arm around the back of it. "So are you all set up for your whale watching?"

Jane frowned. "I'll set it up tomorrow," she said.

He leaned over confidentially. "Word is there's just one lousy whale in the whole place, and they drag all the tourists over in a Zodiac at great expense to see the same one over and over again."

"Oh, come on," said Jane, smiling. "They have a whale museum and everything."

"They have whales all right. But only in the spring when they're passing through. Except for this one. I swear to God." He held up his right hand. "They have her on retainer. It's a female who doesn't want to go down to Baja and have babies."

Jane laughed, and he looked pleased that she did. They were silent for a moment, then she gazed at him more appraisingly.

The waitress appeared, breaking their locked gaze with a plate of prawns.

Jane decided she liked him. Jane believed that most men who looked as good as this one didn't work very hard to be charming, but he seemed to be that rare exception. He seemed rather sweetly pleased he'd made her laugh, which pleased her in turn.

She took another sip of wine, and wondered if he were an exception to her rule it meant he was dangerous.

But she didn't think he was dangerous. He probably had absolutely nothing to do with Brenda or Jennifer at all. She had been imagining things.

She had a brief fantasy wherein this nice man, thrilled to meet a mysterious adventuress like Jane, helped her track down Brenda, to be companionable and because he admired her. The whole thing would be more fun with a little romance interjected into it. Maybe Uncle Harold wouldn't have approved, but Uncle Harold was dead, and she was out of town anyway. She looked down to see if he had a wedding ring. He didn't.

"I really recommend the hot springs," he said earnestly. "And I'd hate to see you get ripped off by the local whale shell game."

She sipped her wine. "Are you one of those people who arrives in a new town and knows all the angles in the first ten minutes?" she said gravely.

"Yes," he said, looking pleased with himself. "I am."

"Well it is a real whale," she said. "So it isn't really a rip-off. It's not as if they dragged you by some large piece of flotsam or jetsam and told you it was a whale."

"No, but it's sort of a tame whale. For all I know they feed her donuts to keep her here. That takes all the excitement out of it. Like Marine World or something." He leaned forward conspiratorially. "We can probably work a deal for the hot springs and slip them an extra ten to rendezvous with the whale on the way out there."

"And ten's only eight-fifty American," she said.

"I hate to see a fellow American get suckered by slick foreigners," he said with a melancholy shake of the head.

He was interrupted by the arrival of the hostess. "Mr. Johnson, there's a lady to see you."

"Yes," he said in suddenly businesslike tones. "I was expecting her." Jane looked over his shoulder and saw a young woman with short red hair and freckles coming toward them. She was wearing jeans and a cotton sweater, and looked slightly nervous.

Her companion rose. "I've got a kind of a business meeting right now," he said. "But maybe later we could have a drink or something."

"I'm tucking in early," Jane said, but with a slow smile that meant she wasn't brushing him off. She couldn't bring herself to seem too eager. She realized that she'd now removed him from the category of a suspicious character to investigate and recast him as a man she was actually interested in. Which meant taking one tangolike step back in order to be able to go two forward later. "Maybe I'll see you around."

"Sure," he said—looking not discouraged but amused at her ambivalence. Jane congratulated herself on how the rhythm of the thing was developing.

Then the red-haired woman came up to the table and threw it all off. She looked curiously at Jane, and said to him, "I'm Brenda MacPherson."

Chapter 17

Earlier that day, back in Seattle, Calvin Mason had taken a slight dislike to Dr. Carlisle immediately. First of all, he was late, but he didn't apologize, striding into the waiting area where Calvin had spent half an hour reading *People* magazine and trying to flirt with the humorless receptionist. Secondly, the dentist was very good looking and had a breezy air of confidence.

"Mr. Duffy here wanted a word with you before his appointment," said the receptionist, using the phony name he'd given her. Calvin had tried to cultivate this woman, because she probably knew all of her boss's personal business, but she wasn't buying any of Calvin's friendly overtures. In fact, she glanced over at him with contempt. "He says he's very concerned about pain. I've scheduled a little consultation time."

It isn't my fault she's so cold, thought Calvin. She'd respond to the real me, but she's under the false impression I'm a wimp.

"Hey," he said to her now, "it's the only thing that scares me, really. Needles, heights, enclosed spaces—no problem. I even beat up a mugger once. But this dentist thing—"

She interrupted. "Just follow the doctor back to his office," she said.

134

Sitting in Carlisle's office, watching him busy himself with a few papers on his desk, Calvin began earnestly. "You see, I've always been simply terrified of dentists. I think it started when I was just a little kid. Old Dr. Philips was a sadist, a real sadist."

This was a lie. Dr. Philips had been a nice old guy who always gave him a lollipop after a session.

"Maybe it was because he reminded me of Uncle Wendell," added Calvin, who always injected some truth into a lie. Now Uncle Wendell *had* been a real sadist. Calvin remembered being lured to his side with the promise of being allowed to examine his old-fashioned pocket watch, then having Uncle Wendell seize him and pin his arm behind his back until he squealed "Uncle," a pun that Uncle Wendell found witty.

Dr. Carlisle seemed very uninterested in the source of Calvin's dental phobia. "We can give you some Valium," he said. "Or nitrous. It's great stuff, actually."

"Yeah?" said Calvin.

Dr. Carlisle gave him a knowing look, rather reminiscent of a sixties college doper. Calvin wondered if the dentist took the edge off with a hit now and again.

Calvin put a hand to his jaw. "I've been putting it off so long."

"Open your mouth," said Dr. Carlisle bossily.

Calvin cringed and feigned reluctance, then opened his mouth and leaned back.

"You've got a lot of fillings in there. You must have had plenty of work done over the years. A nice porcelain crown too. What kind of anesthesia did they use then?" He was starting to look puzzled.

"They knocked me out completely," said Calvin. He closed his mouth and allowed his eye to gaze over at the family picture behind the doctor.

"Nice-looking kids," said Calvin. He supposed the boy was Sean. He was getting absolutely nowhere.

Carlisle didn't seem to want to talk about his family. "We'll put you in a chair, have the girls take a look in there. You're not afraid of a little flossing, are you?"

"It's dentists in general that scare me," whimpered Calvin.

"Well relax," said Dr. Carlisle, flashing a smile. "I have the girls do ninety percent of the work. I just come in and take a quick look when they're through. They're not dentists."

"I see," said Calvin. Not a bad gig. He probably got his assistants for practically nothing, then managed to have half a dozen chairs making money for him at once while they did all the work.

Calvin supposed that his admiration for this lucrative business plan, not unlike that of a successful street pimp, had crossed his features, because Carlisle frowned, and said rather defensively, "Of course I do all the drilling and filling."

Calvin went back into his phobic persona and managed a realistic shudder. "I just can't go through with it," he said, rising hastily. "That word—"

"You mean 'drilling'?" said Carlisle. "We have high-speed drills these days. And I'm telling you, that nitrous..." He leaned forward. "When you're on nitrous and you get one of these girls' nice soft tits up against the side of your face, when they're leaning over adjusting the clamps on that rubber dam—you're in heaven."

The pimp analogy had been very apt. Calvin momentarily considered a quick flossing from one of the girls in Carlisle's stable. Even without the nitrous, it sounded worthwhile. This guy was a good salesman. Calvin summoned up some sales resistance.

"I can floss my own teeth," he said, still thinking in sexual terms. "Why should I pay for it?"

The dentist shrugged and consulted his watch. "Go home, think it over, make an appointment if you think you can take it," he said. "I'm not going to argue with you." He shook his finger. "But I'm telling you, dental neglect is just going to make it worse."

Calvin crept out of the office underneath the withering gaze of the receptionist. Carlisle really was kind of a jerk, he decided. The slight dislike had turned to something deeper. Calvin thought indignantly that he hadn't been sympathetic enough. What if he'd been an actual phobic patient?

It was with some satisfaction that he pulled out of the parking space with Dr. Carlisle's name painted on it. He hadn't been able to find one when he arrived this morning, and Calvin figured the customer should be king and deserved the parking space.

He hadn't come up with much, other than a good long look at the picture of Sean, which he tried to memorize. He figured a drive by the house wouldn't hurt. Maybe he'd find some reason to go knock on the door, get a feel for the situation.

If Sean was your basic adolescent lowlife, living at home and not going to work or school, he'd still be asleep at this hour, maybe just waking up and watching old "Gilligan's Island" reruns or something.

Calvin parked in front of the house, but he made sure his car was obscured by some shrubbery and couldn't be seen from the house. No point letting them know anything more about him than they had to.

The prosperous, old-fashioned neighborhood was quiet. There was no sound except a power lawn mower a few houses away where some gardeners were at work. Calvin had noticed their truck as he'd driven by and seen a big strapping guy, looking vaguely Polynesian, working with a delicate little edger, clipping the border of a lawn, while a tiny dark woman tried to control the massive power mower.

Calvin walked up the front path, forming a brace of stories. The one he chose would depend on who answered the door and what he thought they would buy. If Sean was the loser Calvin thought he was—after all, any friend of Kevin's had to be a loser—and Mom answered, Calvin was ready. He thought she'd like to hear someone had a job for her son. Maybe even that someone believed in him and his sincerity. Calvin tossed some dialogue around in his head. "Yes, ma'am, the young man seemed eager to work, and we sure could use a smart young kid like that. He told me he was ready to make some changes in his life, get some college money together." She'd probably hand him right over—or at least give him a phone number where the kid could be reached. It was a variation on the shabby and transparent "I'm looking for him because I owe him some money."

But Calvin never got a chance to use this story or any other. He heard feet running, barely had time to half turn and get the impression of a big, heavy man before he felt an explosion on the back of his head and fell forward onto the concrete path.

Chapter 18

After Brenda MacPherson had announced herself to Jane's companion, he rose immediately, took Brenda's arm and glided off with her with just a perfunctory nod to Jane. She was glad he'd moved fast. She was pretty sure he hadn't seen her shaking.

She managed to eat a few more prawns, knocked back the rest of her wine, signed for the meal and went up to her room.

Was he out strangling Brenda somewhere? The hostess had called him Mr. Johnson. Who the hell was Mr. Johnson, anyway? She cracked open the mini-bar and poured herself a brandy, adding a splash of soda. Was that girl in danger, while Jane was dithering around flirting?

She stood by the window, arms crossed tightly against her body. No, she decided. Brenda wasn't in danger because he'd met her right there in the dining room in front of her and the hostess and a roomful of people. If Brenda turned up strangled—Jane saw a vivid Ophelia-like picture, her pale body gently lapping up on the beach of smooth stones across the street from the hotel—everyone would know where to look. He couldn't have been that dumb. Or that nervy.

But maybe he could have. After all, he'd asked Art

Deco for directions, hadn't he? On that occasion he might well have gone up and strangled Jennifer. The police must have thought so.

Maybe Jane was imagining the resemblance to that police artist's sketch, but he *had* sought out a Brenda Mac-Pherson, and it was clear they hadn't met before. And someone else was looking for Brenda, she'd learned that in Victoria.

What was puzzling was that he had the wrong Brenda. Art Deco said she was brunette and small. This one was tall and gingery-looking. Her red hair was real—it matched her freckles. And she wasn't a dancer. Jane saw that by the way she walked—a kind of meaty, slouchy, earth-bound walk.

Jane took off her shoes and lay down flat on the bed, her arms and legs stretched out. She was wired from the long drive, and now she was slightly sedated from the wine and the brandy. She was too tired to take the bath she'd planned.

Everything had become more complicated. Now, besides finding Brenda, she had to find out who Mr. Johnson was and what he wanted with Brenda. She should have arranged to meet him for that drink he'd talked about. Now she'd have to make sure their paths crossed again. Had he said how long he was staying in Tofino?

Maybe she should call Calvin Mason. Maybe he knew more about the investigation. She rejected the idea. She was so tired, and besides, he might scold her for leaving town.

She fell asleep lying there with all her clothes on, with the lights on. Later, around four in the morning, she woke up, feeling seedy. As soon as she remembered where she was, she undressed, set the alarm for seven, turned off the light, and fell asleep again.

By morning, she felt reasonably energetic again, but the mirror told her she was pushing it. Her eyes looked puffy. Damn. She couldn't coast on youth anymore.

She showered and dressed in a big T-shirt and jeans and went down to the desk. She was sure she had the wrong Brenda, but she had to see her anyway—she wanted to find out what she could about Mr. Johnson, and a story designed to elicit that information from Brenda was forming in her mind.

At the desk, she asked for directions to the address she had for Brenda MacPherson. The clerk took out a map that looked as if it had been hand-drawn and run off on a Xerox machine. Jane leaned over it, pushing her hair out of her eyes and behind one ear as the woman drew an arrow down the main street, then a curving line off to one side, then an X where the house was. "You shouldn't have any trouble," she said.

Jane thanked her, and then straightened up and stepped back, bumping into someone. She turned.

"Good morning," said Mr. Johnson, looking all newly shaved and smelling like the same hotel soap she'd used. His eyes drifted to the map and she swept it off the counter, with a movement she was afraid wasn't casual enough. His eyes followed her hands as she folded it in half.

"I looked for you in the bar after I came back, but I guess you'd turned in," he said.

Jane was slightly miffed that he'd expected her to be hunkered down at the bar, waiting for him to return. She also knew he'd seen the map. Had he spotted the X and did it mean anything to him? Had he driven Brenda MacPherson home last night? Was Brenda safe?

He smiled a little shyly, and Jane found herself deciding he wouldn't hurt anyone.

"I thought I'd check out those hot springs," he said. "We talked about them last night. Want to come?"

"Sure," said Jane, smiling. She began to feel easier now, more in control.

"Can you leave in about an hour and a half?" he said.

"All right. I have an errand to run this morning."

He raised his eyebrows inquiringly and looked at the map in her hand. "An old friend of my Uncle Harold's," she said with a level gaze. "I promised I'd look him up." Lying was getting easier and easier.

"Looks like he lives near that Brenda MacPherson I met with last night," he said. Jane felt herself tingle a little. Was she blushing? God, she hoped not.

"Just what business are you in, Mr. Johnson?" she said calmly.

"Insurance," he said. "And how did you know my name? I was just about to introduce myself."

"The woman who brought that Brenda MacPherson into the dining room called you that, didn't she?" said Jane.

"Did she? Well it is Johnson. Steven Johnson."

"Jane da Silva," she said, extending a hand. He shook it and gave her an appraising, amused look beneath slightly lowered lids. It could have meant he saw through her and knew she was lying and what she was really thinking—which was, after all, what flirtation was all about anyway, seeing through the subterfuge that was coyness, and declaring yourself not fooled in your own coy way.

"I hope the young lady bought a policy," said Jane with a little sideways smile.

"Another lousy lead," said Johnson, with an ironic smile of his own. "Meet you here at nine-thirty, okay?"

"Okay," said Jane, wondering what she was in for.

"I'll have the hotel pack us a nice lunch," he added rather cozily, his sinister edge fading. "And I'll get them to throw in the resident professional whale on the way over."

The clerk, a motherly looking older woman, beamed discreetly at them. She thinks we're sweet, thought Jane, and that our little outing is the beginning of a romance.

The clerk had been right about one thing. It was no trouble finding Brenda's house—a small cabin on the road out of town, with a hardscrabble look to the yard— big firs providing a dark canopy over a weedy lawn, and a big orangey-looking stump of crumbling cedar sprouting a huckleberry bush. It looked as if the place had been hacked quickly out of the wilderness, without any particular love for nature, or for civilization.

There was an odd collection of objects around the place: next to a little outbuilding was a stack of bundled foliage—leathery dark green leaves. There were some red mesh sacks lying around too, the kind onions came in, and some tools hanging from hooks by the door.

Brenda was home. She answered the door wearing jeans and a sweatshirt.

"Hi," said Jane rather breathlessly. "You're Brenda MacPherson, aren't you?"

"That's right." Brenda looked surprised, but not suspicious. She raised her eyebrows as if she wanted to be helpful but needed more information. An uncitified reaction to a stranger at her doorstep.

"This sounds kind of silly," said Jane, "but I've lost track of Mr. Johnson, and I knew he was going to be looking you up, so I thought I'd come by here."

"The American gentleman?" said Brenda in her genteel Canadian way.

"Yes," said Jane, looking over Brenda's shoulder at the interior. There was a big waterbed with a patchwork quilt made out of velvet, some furniture that looked as if it were made of two-by-fours, and a strip of kitchen on the wall facing the door.

"I don't know where he went," she said. "I was the wrong Brenda MacPherson."

"I don't know what to do," said Jane. "He was supposed to leave a message at the hotel."

"Oh." Brenda was still confused. Jane's strategy was to leave her that way so she'd start volunteering information.

Instead, Brenda just stood there looking pleasant but puzzled. She was sweet, Jane decided, and reasonably intelligent-looking, but the wheels in her brain seemed to revolve without much speed.

"Did he come to sell you some insurance?"

"Insurance? No."

A man wearing a plaid shirt and jeans came into the room, went over to the kitchen and plugged in an electric tea kettle. Americans never seemed to have these appliances. Strange, thought Jane, that we should have missed out on a gadget. The man was skinny and ruddy-cheeked, around twenty-five or so. He nodded at her politely.

"I'm sorry to disturb you," she said to the man. May as well get him involved too, and prolong the encounter in hopes of gleaning something. "I'm Jane da Silva, and I'm looking for someone called Johnson."

"Come in," said Brenda.

"Thank you," said Jane, pleased at how friendly they were. "I'm sorry to bother you, but I didn't know what else to do." She stepped inside. There was a wood stove, and an old what-not with some bone china teacups. There were a lot of navigational charts pinned up on the walls. White for water, yellow for land—mostly islands.

"This is my husband, Doug," said Brenda. She turned to him. "She's looking for Mr. Johnson."

Doug looked wary. "Oh yeah?"

"She wanted to know if he was selling some insurance." She paused. "Says she's a friend of his."

The man looked at her suspiciously. Jane decided she didn't want them to think she was his friend.

"No, it's not that," she said hastily.

"You were having dinner with him, weren't you?" said Brenda tentatively. "In the hotel?" She went over to her husband's side.

"We wondered what he was up to," he said indignantly. He turned to his wife and stroked her shoulder. "You didn't say anything about insurance." He had a protective manner about him Jane found touching. She wondered whether anyone would ever worry about her again like that. Probably not. She'd been on her own so long, she didn't look like she needed help. Once, when she'd been young and soft like Brenda, she'd had a husband who worried about her like that.

"He hit my car in the hotel parking lot," Jane said. "Just a little fender-bender, and we were supposed to exchange information—insurance companies and all that. But we didn't get around to it. He said he was in the insurance business. I remembered your name from the hotel."

"Insurance business? He told us he was a lawyer," said Doug. "Some kind of a scammer, I guess." He turned to his wife. "I told you he was. I should have gone with you."

"Gosh, he seemed like a legit guy," said Jane. "But maybe he's just run off. I guess I'm covered anyway, but I'd sure like to find him." She turned to Brenda, and then noticed some big plastic tubs on the kitchen counter.

"*Percebes!*" she said. The tubs were full of barnacles she'd seen them eat in Spain. Strange creatures with long, leathery stalks coming out of a triangular mosaiced shell that looked like a dinosaur toe.

"Goose neck barnacles," said Doug. "What did you call them?"

"*Percebes.* I never knew the name in English. This is where they come from? Do you eat them?" She figured she was looking at a thousand dollars' worth of the things.

He picked one out of the tub. There was a bit of seaweed clinging to it. "We gather them on the reefs around here and sell 'em to a guy who ships them to Spain and Portugal," he said. "I guess they had their own, but they fished 'em out, eh? I understand they fetch a pretty high price over there."

"They sure do," she said. "I hadn't seen one in years. They're orange underneath that skin, right?" she said.

"That's right."

"You do that full-time?" said Jane, fascinated, and momentarily forgetting her errand.

"Lot of people around here go after barneys," said Doug. "I was a regular fisherman, but it's getting so you can't make a living. Brenda and I dig Manila clams too, but they're getting scarce. The Vietnamese poach them, eh."

"And we do salal as well," said Brenda.

"You mean the plants? From the wild?"

"That's right. We cut them in the woods and bundle them up. Florists use them. They keep so long, see."

"Want some barneys?" said Doug. "I'll steam you up some."

Jane had never been a big fan of *percebes,* but she didn't think she should refuse.

"Are you sure?" she said.

"I got plenty," he said. He rummaged around in the tub. "The market likes 'em nice and thick," he added, gathering up a handful and clattering around in a drawer full of pots and pans, stopping when the kettle whistled. "Anyone but me want coffee?" he said.

Brenda shook her head.

"No thank you," said Jane. "So Mr. Johnson told you he was a lawyer?" she said to Brenda. "Did he leave you a card or anything?"

"Push those things off the chesterfield, and sit down," said Brenda hospitably. Jane imagined a chesterfield was a sofa, and moved aside some folded towels in pastels.

Brenda sat down in a chair opposite and blushed. "No. He said I was the wrong one. He was looking for a Brenda MacPherson who'd inherited some money in the States. He asked me who my mum and dad were and if I'd ever lived in Seattle, and a few more questions, then said I was the wrong one. I guess I should have known it was too good to be true." She shrugged, as if it had been somehow presumptuous of her to think she could be the right one.

Doug chimed in. "I was out helping a friend with his boat, so I didn't go with her. He said she might have inherited five thousand dollars. American."

"If he was some kind of a scammer, he would have said it was more," said Jane with a frown.

"I'd have taken the five thousand," said Brenda with a rueful smile. She had a crooked incisor, which gave her a sort of sweet, lopsided look. "He was very nice about it all. Seemed sorry he couldn't give it to me."

"Asked her what we did for a living and wanted to know if we made a decent living with the barneys and the clams and the salal," said Doug contemptuously. "Pretty rude, don't you think? It's none of his bloody business."

Jane glanced around the room. There was an expensive stereo in the corner. They certainly weren't starving. "Where did he say he was from?" said Jane, reminding herself she was supposed to be trying to track him down because he'd hit her car.

"Seattle," said Brenda.

"And you've never lived there?"

"We're from the Prairies," said Brenda. Jane marveled that a couple of kids from Canada's dry, treeless plains would have ended up foraging for the flora and fauna of this lush, overgrown place.

"The whole thing's pretty weird," said Jane.

"It sure is," said Doug. "He told you he was in insurance, eh?" He came over and handed her a plate of barnacles. She tried to smile. They looked like hors d'oeuvres from another planet. "Should be woman's work, but she doesn't cook them right," he said with a grin at Brenda, who didn't seem bothered by his antediluvian attitude.

"I hope you like them," she said to Jane. "I don't. Doug," she chided her husband, "not everyone likes barneys."

He ignored her. "Let me fix them up for you."

"Get her a serviette," said Brenda. "They squirt all over." He went back to the counter and got Jane a paper napkin, then sat next to her on the sofa and started peeling the leathery skin, exposing the bright orange meat. He handed her one and helped himself to one. "I love these things," he said.

Jane bit into it. They tasted like lobster, but not so sweet. "Terrific," said Jane, who could take it or leave it.

"What kind of a vehicle was he driving?" Doug asked Jane.

She panicked for a second, but then she said, "I didn't actually see him hit me. He told me inside the hotel that he had." It just occurred to Jane that they might see her car was undamaged.

"It wasn't a camper?"

"I don't know," said Jane, gamely tackling another barnacle. This one spurted forth orange juice. She wiped at herself.

"The guy in the camper wasn't the same guy," said Brenda to her husband. She turned to Jane. "Some guy in a camper was parked outside our house a few days ago. He stared at me for a while and pulled away after he saw I had the dog with me. It gave me the creeps."

"What did he look like?" said Jane.

"Like a tourist. An older guy. Bald. I don't know."

"That doesn't sound like Mr. Johnson," said Jane, sighing. "Well, I'll see what I can do back at the hotel. If you hear from him again, would you mind doing me a favor?" She took out one of Calvin Mason's cards. "This is my work number. Call collect and leave a message. I'll write my name on here."

Doug took the card. "You're from Seattle too, eh?" he said.

"Yes," said Jane. Maybe it was stupid to have identified herself. But how else could they have got in touch?

She rose, hoping they didn't decide that Seattle was too much of a coincidence, or that if they did, that she'd be gone by then. "Thanks for the barnacles. I really appreciate it. I didn't know they had them around here."

"There's plenty of 'em if you know where to look," said Doug. "But a lot of people are after them. The Natives collect them too—to sell, not to eat. You have to know where the virgin rocks are and get there when the tide's just right."

She went out to the car, thanking them profusely for the barnacles. Doug stood behind Brenda. Neither of them seemed to be looking at her car for any damage, thank God.

Instead of answers, she had more questions. Was the bald man in the camper some sort of scout for Mr. Johnson? Or was he looking for Brenda too? Or was he, and this was most likely, just a lost tourist? And what was Steven Johnson up to?

The next thing on the agenda was to find out what she could from Steven Johnson. She briefly turned over in her mind the idea that Brenda could have misunderstood; that the five thousand dollars was some sort of a life insurance payoff. Maybe he was a lawyer who worked for an insurance company.

But why come all the way up here from San Francisco, or Seattle or wherever he was really from, to give someone five thousand dollars? Surely that was something that could be done over the phone, or with a little ad that said Brenda MacPherson, formerly of Seattle, should contact him and learn "something to her advantage." Jane smiled, realizing she'd picked up this last phrase from old novels, and there was probably some modern equivalent.

To find out, she had to get close to him.

Which she did, sooner than she expected. An hour and a half later, she and Mr. Johnson were both removing their clothes.

Chapter 19

After being unceremoniously decked in the Carlisles' front yard, Calvin Mason lay there for a second, feeling woozy. He half expected a pair of feet to start kicking him now that he was down, but it didn't happen. He pushed himself up from the pathway, or at least he tried to. His arms wobbled.

He decided rolling over on his back made more sense, but it would make him feel vulnerable to more attack. Instead, he crawled off the concrete, through a narrow bed filled with geraniums, and onto a damp square of lawn.

Out of boot range, he allowed himself to sit up. "What the hell was that about," he said, looking up at a scowling man. His assailant's hands were still in fists, a touch Calvin didn't like. Even more alarming, the guy wasn't holding a brick or a sash weight. He must have pounded the back of his head with one of those closed fists.

"You son of a bitch," said the man. "Tell me where the kid is."

"What kid?" said Calvin. At least he was talking. This was a good development. Calvin felt more comfortable in a verbally adversarial relationship than a physical one. At the same time, it occurred to him if the guy came at him

151

again he'd grab him around an ankle and pull him down so they were both on the ground.

"You know. Sean," said the man.

"Oh," said Calvin, getting slowly to his feet. "Sean. I'd like to find him myself." He smiled. Maybe he and this gorilla could work together. Whoever he was, he was highly motivated.

"Get that damn grin off your face," said the man, his face turning red and blotchy. "We're gonna drag your ass and his through the courts, but I'm going to kick the shit out of both of you first."

Calvin shook his head. He was still woozy. "If you want to go to court, you'll need a lawyer," he said, reaching into his pocket. He handed over a business card.

"Don't give me that," said the man, peering down at the card. "You're a dentist. A rich dentist."

"You think I'm a dentist?" said Calvin. "Did you follow me?" It slowly dawned on Calvin. This big thug had seen him pull out of the parking space marked Carlisle. If Calvin hadn't parked in Carlisle's spot, this jerk wouldn't be thinking about working him over. Guys like Carlisle always managed to wriggle away from trouble and make sure someone else got nailed in their place.

"I just stole the dentist's parking space," said Calvin. "I'm a lawyer, honest." Slowly his faculties began to return to him, and he started to get red in the face himself. What was he doing handing business cards to some jerk who'd sneaked up and bashed him in the head? Some weird instinct had taken over while his mind was inoperable. "If anyone's getting dragged through the courts, it's you," he shouted. "You can't go around assaulting people. I'll call the cops and sign a complaint, then I'll sue you in civil court. Jesus, a head wound like this, I'll have neurologists on the stand saying I'm practically a vegetable and it's all your fault. What assets do you have, and is that your car over there? Whatever you own, I can get it in a lawsuit, you know." Calvin gestured to an elderly Datsun.

A look of fear came over the man's face and he turned and ran. Calvin took off after him up the sidewalk. Feeling was coming slowly back into his body, and it now seemed that his mind was reconnected.

Unfortunately, the guy was pretty fast for a big guy. Calvin was gaining on him, though. For a while, it looked like he could catch up with him, which of course meant he'd have to tackle him, but Calvin decided he'd worry about that later.

But it never came up. Calvin dashed in front of the hilly lawn where the gardeners were working. The little woman was dragged into Calvin's path by gravity and the huge mower she was operating. He tried to run around her but he knocked her over, got tangled up in a big canvas catcher, managed to twist it half off the mower with his foot, and emerged covered with damp grass clippings into the cloud of blue smoke coming out of the snarling, overturned machine. By the time he got the small woman up on her feet and wrenched her equipment back up on its tires, the guy had managed to get into a car—not the Datsun Calvin had spotted, but something that looked blue—and raced down the street.

"Damn," said Calvin, picking off grass clippings from his jacket.

Chapter 20

"Damn," she thought as she removed her underwear, hoping it wouldn't leave unattractive red impressions of straps and elastic on her skin. She folded her clothes neatly, as if she were at the doctor's office, and set them in a pile on a rock, then wrapped herself in the towel.

The hot springs, which she had somehow imagined as a bubbling and miniature version of Old Faithful, surrounded by picturesque ferns, were instead a series of steaming natural hot tubs in which people soaked. She had forgotten about the conversation she had overheard between the German tourists and the desk clerk about bringing towels.

She and Steven Johnson had set out on this excursion as soon as she arrived back at the hotel. He had the amiable, take-charge manner of a good traveler, which she appreciated, and he seemed refreshingly interested in the surroundings, rather than in her, which had made it all seem less like some awkward high school date. Until now, of course.

They had come up in a rubber Zodiac manned by a laconic hippie guide, battering over the water with a lot of thumps and wind and salt in their faces. They cruised past rocky reefs that emerged and vanished with the tides, full of barnacles and kelp and gulls—past vast deserted beaches, full of pale logs, bleached by the salt.

The bits of land seemed alien and incidental in the expanse of water—a gray-blue-green northern sea, where the water looked thicker and more dense than the shiny waters of the tropics.

When they arrived on the dock, the guide told them he'd catch up with them later at the hot springs in an hour or so, and they set off on the path that led to the hot springs.

Jane forgot her mission entirely. Worming the truth out of Johnson seemed like something better done in a smoky bar over some stiff drinks, with maybe a languorous hand drifting over to his at some point.

The sense of being at the edge of the world, the vast sky and water, drove sneaky thoughts out of her mind entirely. She felt too pure and fresh, and too happy with him for having brought her here.

They walked as they had come over on the Zodiac, in companionable silence, with Jane murmuring "gorgeous" once in a while, just to be polite. Anything more would have been obtrusive.

Jane had thought of northern rain forests as dark, forbidding, sinister places, where life was too rampant— plants sucking the life out of one another, competing for every inch, as if drunk and disorderly on the constant water from above.

This trail looked instead young and crisp and green, landscaped with neat, overlapping ground cover. Brilliant green moss bristling with reddish spores enveloped rock and wood like soft, muffling fabric. Tall, straight tree trunks branched above into a canopy that cast dappled light on the springy trail, cushioned with rust-colored needles.

Each bend in the trail provided a distinct, harmonious vista. The cool damp air smelled of cedar—sweet and slightly spicy.

Every once in a while a creek would appear. Water rushed white and silver over smooth oval stones, making an urgent, musical, lovely sound—a continuous sound that seemed to be ignoring the noise of their feet on the wooden bridge above.

Finally, the trail took a turn through a dark patch of old-growth forest, emerging onto a rocky beach.

To the left was a huge rock wall, like something painted on canvas for an old production of a Wagner opera. To the right were more rocky outcroppings, and in front of them was the water.

Jane walked without thinking to the water's edge, where waves washed frothily on kelp-covered rocks, fingers of tumbling water rushing into the spaces between stone before being sucked back into the sea, leaving the glistening seaweed bare again, except for the tide pools. These bowls of rock were lined with wine-colored spiny urchins, and clinging purple and orange sea stars, their fluid arms embracing the shape of the pool, huddled together like puppies beneath the clear water.

Johnson came up beside her, slipping one arm out of the pack he'd brought with their lunch, and looked out over the water. They stood there in the breeze for a moment, then looked at each other and smiled.

He pointed to the huge rock wall, a sort of ziggurat, terraced here and there. "Shall we climb up there?" he said.

She started to say "sure." It seemed natural to want to reach the highest point, and look out to yet another spectacular vista. But then she remembered why she was here, who Johnson might be. It would be easy for him to push her off and say it was an accident. She couldn't take the chance.

"I don't think so," she said, trying to look as if she were happy enough with her surroundings. Then she worried he'd think she was a sissy. "I hate heights," she lied.

They heard voices and turned toward the sound. From between two tall rocks, a man and a woman emerged. They were both dripping wet, stark naked, quite pink and definitely out of shape. What they weren't, was self-conscious. They smiled as they strolled past, and went up the beach to a cluster of small tents. They both had long hair, and the man had a beard. They looked rather like time travelers from some bucolic sixties be-in.

"Aha! The hot springs," said Johnson. "Did you bring a suit?"

"No," she said.

"Well you're in luck," he said, looking vaguely amused. "Neither did I. But the desk clerk did press some towels on me as we left the hotel. Want to go in?"

"Maybe," she said, walking over to the rocks. She looked into the crevasse from which the two nature lovers had made their appearance. Rising up from the water's edge, between two rock walls, was a staggered series of pools. A cascade of water fell in a cloud of steam into the first one, and each one overflowed into the one below. The last pool was filled from above by the stream of water, and from below by waves from the sea.

"It looks fabulous," said Jane, trying not to look self-conscious about tearing off her clothes with a handsome stranger. But personal modesty seemed trivial in this Eden-like setting.

He handed her a towel. "We can take turns if you want." He had rather a sweet, apologetic expression, as if he were trying to make her feel comfortable, which naturally brought out the same reaction in her.

"It's all right," she said breezily. "I'm a graduate of a half dozen European topless beaches, and plenty of coed hot tub immersions." She realized it would have been easier if he hadn't been so attractive. That took it all out of the realm of simple communion with nature.

"Well, there are a bunch of campers up there, so if I go berserk or anything, you can scream," he said gesturing behind them to the cluster of tents, and managing to make her feel self-conscious again.

"And so can you," she said, smiling and taking the towel. "I'll leave my clothes somewhere where I know they'll stay dry," she said, climbing away and finding a grassy little spot behind a rock. She drew the line at tearing off her clothes in front of him.

Wrapped in the towel, picking carefully with bare feet over the rocky terrain, she regretted having sloughed off the last few weeks lately on her workouts. She was coasting on past effort. A certain amount of exercise was required to keep her stomach reasonably flat and her butt reasonably unflat. Coming from California, he was probably used to aerobicized hard bodies with breast implants and tucked stomachs. Anyway, she told herself smugly, at least her breasts were real and her legs were long, and recent intense scrutiny at the backs of her upper thighs had revealed no sign of the dreaded cellulite. All in all, she was in pretty good shape for her age, which was the result, she realized with humility, of incredibly good luck more than anything else. She supposed she could fall apart at any moment, but it hadn't happened yet.

Her companion, she knew, probably hadn't inventoried his own physical charms as she had. It was ironic that in any naked encounter, women were usually more concerned about their own bodies than about their partner's, and were more than willing to put up with an out-of-shape lover if he was sufficiently appreciative of her body. In fact, the act of love could take on aspects of a mutual worship of the woman's body.

She told herself to stop thinking about sex, just because she had her clothes off, and went to the edge of the first pool, the one being fed by the steaming waterfall, where

Johnson was now submerged up to his chest, his arms stretched out on the rock ledge, his eyes closed in a blissed-out attitude, his head back and his hair wet and curling. He opened his eyes just a crack as she unfurled the towel and stepped into the water. Then closed them again in a gentlemanly fashion.

The water was very hot.

"Start under the waterfall," he said sleepily. "It's fantastic. I had this little kink in my neck from sleeping funny on the hotel mattress and I blasted it with that water."

She stood under the waterfall. It was actually just a little too hot, but she soon got used to it. She realized her neck and shoulders had been tense. All that driving hadn't helped. She sighed happily, and felt the force of the water push the heat into her muscles.

"A hundred and ten degrees, they say," he murmured.

After about a minute, she sat down opposite him. The heat, and the way the steaming cascade agitated the water, made the whole thing into a natural Jacuzzi.

"Great stress reliever," he said. "You are stressed, aren't you? You're nobody if you're not stressed, these days."

"Lack of stress can be stressful too," she said.

"Aha! Another adrenaline junkie. I knew it."

"Maybe I am. I always think I'm calm, but I like being around energetic people and new situations." It occurred to Jane this sounded like a line from a skimpy résumé.

"A thrill-seeker," he said. His eyes were still closed.

"Maybe a vicarious thrill-seeker," she said. She wasn't sure she wanted to be some over-the-top nutcase, but there had been times when she suspected she was. "Does that mean you won't try and sell me a policy? Because I look like a secret hang glider or something? What about you? Do you like the idea of leaping off cliffs, attached to life by only a fraying bungee cord?"

"No," he said, "but I used to be a police officer."

She tensed up. A police officer? Good cop gone bad? Somehow, she couldn't see him strangling anyone, but having been a cop put him in an entirely different category. He had looked like a businessman. "Was it thrilling?"

"It had its moments. But mostly you spend time trying to get a bunch of stupid drunks to shut up and calm down. What do you do for a living, if you don't mind my asking?"

She thought for a second. She couldn't tell him the truth. After all, she was here to find out what he was up to. And in any case, the Foundation for Righting Wrongs was supposed to be kept secret. The board members said Uncle Harold didn't believe in doing good in a flashy way. Jane suspected this was also because the board didn't want anyone from the government telling it how to spend Uncle Harold's money, and asking for tedious reports. Besides, her work for the foundation had so far been a failure. A few charitable advances could hardly be construed as a living.

But Jane knew also that a weak part of her wanted Johnson to admire her and think she was a competent, interesting person. She racked her brain for some plausible lie that would hold up under further scrutiny, and came up with absolutely nothing. Great, she thought to herself, not only am I an unemployed flake, I can't even make anything up.

"Did you forget?" he said gently.

"Actually, at the moment I don't do a damned thing," she said. "I suppose I'm having some kind of midlife crisis." It occurred to her this was close to the truth.

"Premature midlife crisis, I'm sure," he said gallantly.

"Like those skin care ads for premature aging," said Jane, laughing. "I hate that. Aging is aging. How can it be premature?"

"I've been accused of suffering from midlife crisis," he said. "Actually, I thought I was still having adolescent adjustment problems." Jane imagined some outraged woman, nattering at him that he couldn't commit.

"I suppose they can sort of fuse together," said Jane. "If you work it right you can be maladjusted forever. Maneuver your way right into senility that way." She moved her arms back and forth below the surface of the water, and caught him glancing for a millisecond at her breasts. She didn't mind, because they were floating and looked their best.

"Tell me about being a cop," she said. "Did you ever kill anyone?" She may as well get right into it.

"I hate to disappoint you," he said, "but I never did. Never fired my weapon off the range."

"I'm not disappointed," she said. But she was because she wasn't getting anything out of him to explain what he was doing looking for Brenda MacPherson.

"What exactly brings you up here?" she asked.

"The waters," he said lazily, stirring them a little with his hand as if to demonstrate. "I came for the waters."

"And Brenda," she said. "Wasn't that her name?"

"That's right." His eyes opened. They were a darkish blue. "Tell me how it went with your old family friend."

"Just fine," she said. "Of course," she added, "he is getting on in years. But really a fascinating old guy," She leaned back against the warm rock, closed her eyes and continued, knowing it all sounded inane but, driven on by nerves, finding herself unable to stop as she got comfortably into the lie in any case. "Speaks seven languages. And he's an authority on Persian miniatures."

"And just think," he said. "He lives right next door to Brenda MacPherson."

She heard sarcasm in his voice, and opened her eyes. He was smiling.

"In fact, our friend Brenda told me all about him. He's teaching her Urdu. Or is it Croatian."

"I don't think Croatian is in his repertoire," she said coldly. "Maybe you're mixing it up with Serbian." Damn, damn, damn, she thought.

"Why don't you tell me what you're up to," he said. "We seem to be looking for the same person."

"What makes you say that?" she said. But she was pretty sure she knew. That weasely Englishman. Or Cornishman, if he preferred.

"I thought you did this for a living," he said. "But the Persian miniatures gave you away."

"Did what for a living?" she said.

"Persian miniatures stand out too much. You've got to keep it all bland—the stories, I mean."

Jane tried to look as if she were alarmed because she was talking to a crazy person, rather than being alarmed because she had been unmasked. "What are you talking about?" she said, shrinking back against the side of the pool and worrying that she was overdoing it. It occurred to her that if she really thought he was nuts she would have acted calm and unruffled and soothing while plotting her escape. This was too Lillian Gish.

"You got a list of Brenda MacPhersons from a private investigator in Victoria," he said impatiently. "You did say your name was Jane da Silva?"

Damn Calvin Mason for steering her to that lowlife.

"Next time I'll find someone in the Yellow Pages," she said. "Is that why you asked me here? To grill me? You could have done that back at the hotel."

"Thought it would be better to get all your clothes off first," he said lightly. "Classic interrogation technique. They never approved of it when I was in uniform."

"Well," she said, "you're out of uniform too." For emphasis, she let her gaze fall down from his face and linger on his naked chest. There was a heart-shaped patch of golden brown hair there, no stragglers, but neat borders, like something in a well-kept garden. "Presumably with your defenses down, you'll tell me what you're doing looking for Brenda MacPherson."

"I take your use of the present tense to mean you didn't find the right one, either," he said. "Actually, I don't really care why you're looking for her, I was just curious. And I didn't really know at first you were Jane da Silva. I just thought you looked like a nice person and we were both traveling alone." He smiled and held up his hands, palms out, as if to indicate he was unarmed. The tips of his fingers were wrinkled. "It's getting hot. The pools get cooler the closer you get to the ocean."

He got out of the pool, steam rising from his shoulders, his body shiny wet. He had nice long muscles and classic proportions. He looked like a Greek god and he knew it, of course. Women had probably been telling him for years. He had the look of someone who felt completely at ease in his body.

Jane was furious. He had taken the upper hand, let her know he knew who she was, acted as if he didn't care, and had revealed nothing much she didn't already know. He didn't answer her questions, just went on with his own script.

What was most galling was that he'd made her feel stupid about her fictional friend and his Persian miniatures—really unfair, she thought, because she could just see the old gentleman, surrounded by glowing examples of his collection, pointing out the details of some of his finer specimens with a long bony finger. And now, Johnson, if that was his name, having told her she was an idiot, was standing there naked, looking casual and not even bothering to gloat, which was worse. If he'd been gloating she'd have something to work with.

And to think she'd thought he was kind of sweet. All an act to lure her here, supremely confident, no doubt that she'd run right after him.

"Coming?" he said pleasantly, offering her his hand. Now he was taking charge, deciding what temperature water they'd sit in.

Jane had no choice but to go along. She ignored his hand, rose dripping and steaming, and followed him, stepping over a low rock wall and sliding silently into the next pool.

It was just a few degrees cooler, enough to be completely refreshing. While Jane didn't really believe there were any known scientific health benefits to soaking in mineral-laced hot water, she knew plenty of people who swore by it, and had once spent some time in Aix-les-Bains, convinced she felt fabulous because of the waters. Right now, even though she was frustrated and angry, she still felt an incredible sense of well-being. She settled in with a little murmur, then submerged her head, tilting it back on the way up so her hair would lie wetly away from her forehead. The air was cool on her damp face, and she heard the sound of gulls above and the surf below.

"Are you an investigator for that insurance company?" she said, wondering why she hadn't thought of it before. It fit. He was an ex-cop. "Is that why you're looking for Brenda?"

"Why don't you tell me why you're looking for her first," he said.

"It's a personal thing," she said. "Something to do with her roommate. Jennifer Gilbert."

He nodded but didn't react to the name of the dead woman. "So you're not a friend of Brenda's?"

Jane shrugged.

"She skip out on her half of the rent or something?" he persisted. Jane liked it better when he was guessing than when she was.

"That's moot now," said Jane. She didn't add, though, now that Jennifer's been strangled.

She watched him carefully. He didn't flinch.

He shrugged. "Be as mysterious as you want. I'm just suggesting we find her together. It won't take long." He was implying that it wouldn't take him long, and Jane could tag along. As if to emphasize the simplicity of the task, he added, "To be perfectly honest, I made a bigger deal of this than there was, because I wanted to come up here and look around." He smiled a boyish lopsided grin. He was acting sweet again. "I like to get away from the city, you know? It's wonderful here."

"Why did you want us to find her together?" asked Jane.

He sighed with exasperation. "Because you're pretty, and smart, and I thought you'd be an interesting companion. All right?"

She laughed. "But now I seem like too much trouble, right?"

"Only because you won't tell me what you're doing," he said. "Do I seem that untrustworthy?"

"No," she said. "Actually, you don't."

"So what's the big deal?"

The big deal was, she didn't want anyone horning in on her hopeless case. And she thought she should think he was untrustworthy. Why didn't that composite picture on TV scare her? It should have.

"Although," he added, "I suppose a little mystery is okay too."

"I've taken all my clothes off already," she said. "There's no mystery there. I have to keep something in abeyance."

"Ah," he said, tilting his head. "Women always have something in abeyance."

"You mean we're inherently mysterious?"

"To us, you are."

"But you don't think we do it on purpose, do you? That we're basically dishonest?"

"Of course you do it on purpose."

"We're just too subtle for you," said Jane. "And you get confused. But sometimes we do it on purpose. To drive you mad."

"This is a historic moment in my life," he said solemnly. "One of you admitted it."

"I try and be honest," said Jane. "When I can. And to show you how brutally honest I am, I'll tell why I try to be honest. Because men find it disarming, and therefore intriguing. So I have a basically dishonest reason for being honest."

He narrowed his eyes. "You're right. You are subtle. And disarming, and intriguing. I haven't decided how honest you are, though. And I still don't know what you're up to."

She smiled. She had decided what to do. And now that she had a plan, and felt in control once more, she felt happy, and magnanimous in an almost flirtatious way.

Later, after they had worked themselves down to the last pool, and experienced the cold tide rushing in at intervals, stirring up the hot water with a cold blast, and filling the rocky pool with another foot of water with every beat of the wave; after they had wrapped themselves in thick hotel towels and sat on flat rocks on the beach and eaten smoked salmon sandwiches on rye bread and grapes and twist-cap bottles of white wine; after they had put on their clothes and hiked back through the incredible rain forest and sped back in the bouncing Zodiac, Jane felt a little regret at her plan. But she forced herself to carry it out.

Chapter 21

Calvin Mason, still picking bits of grass from his clothing, walked slowly back to the Carlisles' house. He had a pretty good idea where his assailant might be headed. If he was right, it would prove the big thug wasn't the smartest guy in the world. But then, would a smart guy start bashing in someone's head in broad daylight?

Calvin decided to test his theory and drive back to Dr. Carlisle's office. The guy had seemed determined to have it out with the dentist, and it had finally penetrated his thick skull that Calvin was not Carlisle. Now that he'd learned he'd made a mistake, he might go back there and find the real dentist and try to work over the right man.

Being nearby while a confrontation took place might reveal why the guy was looking for "the kid," presumably the elusive Sean. There was also the added benefit of perhaps being able to see the rich, suave, confident Dr. Carlisle on the receiving end of some inelegant but effective battery.

As he was getting into his car, Calvin saw a thirtyish woman with lots of curly light brown hair all tied up in an ethnic-looking scarf. She got out of an old station wagon parked in front of his car, then went around to the rear of the vehicle, flipped open the back and proceeded to yank an unwieldy vacuum cleaner out of the car. There was a bumper sticker on the car referring to a female deity, and another suggesting that world peace began at home.

This looked promising. She set down the vacuum cleaner and pulled out a plastic bucket full of rags and cleaning preparations.

Here in Seattle, cleaning ladies tended to be working on degrees from hazily accredited naturopathic institutes or running yoga schools by night, or making jewelry in their spare time. Calvin knew and liked the type—hearty earth-muffins, cheerful, brave and uncompromising in their pursuit of spiritual riches and worldly failure.

He decided to tell her the truth. Once in a while, it made sense. Usually it didn't, because the truth was often so flaky, but this was a woman, he sensed, who was unfazed by flaky.

"Excuse me," he said. "Do you work for the Carlisles?"

"Yes," she said, slamming down the station wagon door and examining his face. He imagined it looked bad where it had met the sidewalk. Her gaze flitted down to his shoulders, and he brushed off a little more grass.

"I'm sorry to bother you," he said. "But I thought I should tell you something." No use telling the entire truth. An overlay of altruism wouldn't hurt. "I was walking up the path to their house, and this guy attacked me. He seemed to think I was Dr. Carlisle." Calvin rubbed the back of his head and winced theatrically.

"Attacked you?" Her eyes grew wide. They were light blue, surrounded by long pale lashes, and she had a translucent quality to her skin. Calvin figured she was a vegetarian.

"Hit me on the back of the head." He shrugged. "I guess I'm okay. I was just thinking the Carlisles should be warned."

"A head wound can be dangerous," she said.

"I am feeling a little dizzy," he said, putting one hand on her car and leaning heavily into it with a sigh.

"You'd better come inside and rest." She peered into his eyes. "Your pupils are the same size, but you could have gotten a concussion," she said. "You want to call the police?"

"I don't know," he said. "I guess I just wanted to be sure the Carlisles knew this character was after him. Who would want to hurt them?"

"I don't know," she said. "I never see them. I have a key."

"But you must have an idea about them from cleaning their house," he said, following her up the walk. She was fiddling with a huge bunch of keys.

"Oh, yeah," she said. "It's amazing what you can tell about people when you clean up after them."

He helped her drag the vacuum cleaner up the steps and followed her inside. "This character seemed to be looking for their son," said Calvin.

"Sean?"

"I think that's it. You see, I was just walking around the house putting together an estimate for new gutters. I'm a contractor. This guy comes up and hits me, knocks me down and calls me Dr. Carlisle, then he demands to know where Sean is. I finally straightened him out and he took off."

He looked around the hall. There was an antique hat rack and some botanical prints. "Where's the phone?" he said.

She led him into the kitchen, and walked over to the sink, frowning at a lot of dirty dishes there.

"I'll make you a cup of Red Zinger tea," she said. "A mild stimulant will do you good." She busied herself with a tea kettle while Calvin pretended to be looking through the phone book.

"What's the deal, did this Sean disappear or something. Is he in trouble?"

The woman shrugged. "He's been gone for weeks," she said. "I haven't cleaned out his roach-filled ashtrays or picked up his old beer cans for quite a while." She drifted back to the sink. "Three cereal bowls. If he's here he didn't have breakfast. Actually, he used to be here while I cleaned. Asleep in his room mostly. I get out of here by eleven every week. A real jerk. I'd be vacuuming and he'd come down and yell because the noise woke him up." She shook her head.

After a suitable interval flapping phone book pages, Calvin called his own number and talked into his machine. "Well have the doctor call me right away," he said. "This is Clyde Balfour, from Balfour Gutter. I came by to do the estimate and some guy hit me on the head. Right on the path." He paused and pretended to be listening, hoping the woman wouldn't hear the beep of his machine.

"You could sue them," said the cleaning lady helpfully, handing Calvin a steaming cup. "They probably have lots of insurance."

"Yeah, well he has my number," said Calvin into the phone. "And tell him I'm too shook up to do that estimate. I'll do it later in the week. Oh, and tell him the downspouts look pretty bad."

Calvin hung up, and gazed over at the refrigerator. There was a collection of snapshots held on by magnets. Calvin recognized the dentist and his son. A pretty blond lady and a slightly chubby teenage girl apparently completed the household.

There was also a French impressionist calendar hanging over the phone. Beneath some Monet water lilies was a grid of dates and appointments. "Softball game—7:30"; "Eve and John's—cocktails—7:00"; "Aerobics"; "Nails." But there was one entry that caught Calvin's eye and caused a little leap of adrenaline. "Sean. UAL #52. 3PM." It had to be a flight number. And the date was for next Saturday.

Chapter 22

The hardest part was smiling prettily when she said she'd take a nap and see if she felt like dinner later. "Call me around six," she said.

Under ordinary circumstances, a nap on cool, starched hotel sheets after the hike and hot springs, then drinks and a good dinner bristling with romantic tension, would have constituted a perfect day. She could well imagine facing him across a table while that delicious, teetering feeling crept up on her. Somewhere in the evening, a look, a remark, an admission, a glimpse at his vulnerability, would push her over the edge—and she'd fall into a state of deep affection, admiration and lust.

But by six, Jane was long gone, driving the winding road back to the other side of the island, watching the late northern dusk cast long rosy light over the darkening stands of fir.

As soon as she'd checked out of the hotel, she'd made a stop at the offices of the Royal Canadian Mounted Police, conveniently situated across the street from Tofino's Whale Museum on the left-hand side of the street that took her out of town.

Maybe she was finally growing up. During her lifetime, she'd trashed dozens of plans, changed dozens of itineraries because of an attractive man. And why had she found so many men attractive? Probably, she thought with irritation, because if they found her attractive, she figured they must be discerning, terrific people.

Not that she regretted any of them. They'd all been nice enough. Some of them had become friends once the excitement had worn off. But it always had. Which was all right too. It left her free to fall in love again. But it seemed to Jane now that if she'd spent less time falling in and out of love, she would have accomplished something else more permanent along the way. God knows she'd never had much sense of purpose. Not since her husband, Bernardo, had died, anyway.

Inside there was a long counter, with a handful of employees working in a large office area beyond. She waited and cast an eye over the bulletin board. There was a picture of a missing child, and a typed TOURIST ALERT, which seemed to be messages for travelers.

Joseph Cross of Winnipeg, call your sister Marie. Dietrich Himmelman of Stuttgart; Yves and Marie-Claire Gauthier of Nice; Claire Hanson, Yonkers. All enjoined to call home. Jane imagined some drama behind every message.

A pleasant-looking uniformed officer came up to the counter.

"I was watching one of the Seattle stations last night," she said, "and they had a composite picture of a man wanted for questioning in a murder down there. I think he's staying here in Tofino." She tried to sound reluctant, rather than eager. A good citizen, squeamishly doing her duty.

"I see," he answered in the noncommittal tone of policeman everywhere.

"The resemblance was striking," said Jane, "but later, when I talked to him and learned he'd just been in Seattle, I thought I'd better tell someone."

The officer took the name of the hotel and Mr. Johnson's name.

"I hope I'm wrong," said Jane. "He seemed very nice. But when I teased him about his resemblance to the picture, he got very tense."

The officer nodded thoughtfully.

"He grabbed my wrist, rather hard," said Jane. She thought she'd better jazz it up a little with a Hitchcockian touch. "His face got kind of scary, and I guess he saw I was nervous, and then it changed back into pleasantness, but I was frightened and I thought I'd better tell you." Now she'd probably overdone it.

"We might go round and have a chat with him," said the officer. "Thank you for the information. Could I have your name?"

"No," said Jane. "I'd really rather not. As I say, I was frightened, and I'd rather just leave town quietly, to be honest."

The policeman gazed at her thoughtfully for a moment. He had big round brown eyes. "We'll look into it," he said. "But if you are frightened, wouldn't it be better to leave your name with us?"

"I just want to go home," said Jane. "The whole thing has been very upsetting. The man in the composite, he may have killed a woman. Strangled her." Suddenly it occurred to her that her Mr. Johnson, the man with whom she had moments ago fantasized falling in love, might have done just that. Was there some denial mechanism working here, some force that made it impossible to believe a nice, personable man could have strangled someone? Why wasn't she frightened?

Paradoxically, it began to frighten her that she wasn't frightened.

"I hope you don't think I'm being hysterical," she said.

"I just thought it was my duty to tell someone in authority."

He clearly seemed to approve of her instincts in the matter. "You did the right thing," he said.

She felt a schoolgirlish pleasure in his saying that, but then reminded herself she wasn't being a good citizen at all, she just wanted to slow Steven Johnson down.

"Well, thank you." She made a rather clumsy retreat, got into her car, put it in gear, and felt a huge sense of relief as she left town.

The next Brenda on her list lived on Denman, a small island halfway up the east side of Vancouver Island. She hoped she'd have a good start, hoped the RCMP would come by the hotel, hoped Johnson would get all tangled up telling them his story, whatever it was. If she made the first ferry in the morning to Denman, she'd beat him. She vaguely remembered reading somewhere that the Mounties had much broader powers than American law enforcement agencies. Maybe they'd keep him.

Of course, she felt guilty. She'd led him on, and she knew he thought they were having dinner together. Instead, he'd find she'd turned him in. He'd probably think she was a duplicitous bitch. For a moment she thought about what it could have been like to have dinner with him, go along with his plan, travel with him, let him lead her to the real Brenda. Along the way, she'd find out why he was looking for her.

Hours later, after night had fallen, she arrived in Qualicum Beach on the Strait of Georgia, less than a hundred kilometers south of the ferry to Denman Island. She stayed in a nice, quiet motel room, fell into bed hungry but too tired to eat, and reflected in the small moment of wakefulness that, despite her guilty feelings, Johnson would understand her turning him in like that. He seemed to like the idea she was a rival. And it served him right for being so smug. She couldn't believe she'd actually been tempted to have dinner with him. She also decided that there was indeed something medicinal in those hot springs. Despite hours in the car, her whole body felt terrific. She fell asleep feeling relaxed and floaty.

By morning she was starving. She ate a big breakfast, then drove to the Denman Island ferry, which took fifteen minutes to make its crossing. It was a small vessel, with an open deck. Across Buckley Bay lay Denman, long and low and covered with fir, except for a large grassy oblong where a farm stood.

The passengers had a festive air about them. They were wearing shorts and T-shirts, driving campers or vehicles with kayaks strapped to the top. A lot of the passengers, presumably the ones who actually lived on Denman, were chatting with one another, keeping an eye on their children.

At the end of the short run, she drove up a hill, then turned left at a tiny wooden church half obscured by big shady maples. On her right was the general store, white with green trim, which looked as if it had been built in the twenties. It was a big square building with a false front, a gas pump in front, a deep shady porch. A couple of people were sitting on the porch—one of them a leather-jacketed young man with peroxided hair. Jane wondered if he wasn't hot in his leather jacket. He was talking to a middle-aged woman with an explosion of corkscrew curls bunched in here and there covered with a gauzy scarf, a tie-dyed tank top and khaki shorts. Perhaps they were mother and son.

A sign announced that the store was also the post office and government liquor store. She pulled up and went in, stopping first to check the collection of posters on the bulletin board. The Polka Dogs, live from Toronto, were playing at the Community Hall. Someone had some prawns for sale. The Ratepayers' Association was meeting. Fish-net was available for fencing.

The old wooden screen door made a comfortable, summery bang. Inside, there were shelves of groceries, and, up on higher shelves, items like gumboots and film. Off to one side, past the *Toronto Globe and Mail*, the *Times-Colonist* and the *Vancouver Sun*, was the restaurant with a collection of oilcloth-covered tables. Glass doors led to a terrace and a small counter with some old-fashioned chrome stools. A young blonde girl was making a milk-shake, and there was a lot of socializing going on at the tables and on the terrace.

Clearly, this was the hub of the island. She supposed if she sat here long enough, Brenda MacPherson would be bound to come by eventually. But how would she know her?

She bought herself an apple, and, over by the screen door, discovered a box with the local newspaper. The honor system was in force. She put a red two-dollar bill into the box next to it and took it out into the sun.

The front page had a story about a crow who had been adopted by a local boy after it fell out of a nest. On the back page was an ad for the Kaleidoscope Market. She smiled happily. They had espresso.

It was just a stroll down the quiet street, across from a worn and friendly looking baseball diamond in a grassy field.

She bought herself a cappuccino, and asked the man behind the counter if he knew a Brenda MacPherson. "Sounds familiar," he said. "Have you checked the phone book?" He showed her a yellow construction paper book-let stapled together. She was right there. Brenda Mac-Pherson. There was a phone number.

She took her coffee out to the phone booth in front of the first store, walking along the middle of the sunny street. Now that the ferry traffic had abated, the street was empty, except for a couple of dogs.

A sleepy-sounding male answered the phone. "Penny-whistle Herb Farm." He sounded the h in herb.

Jane asked for Brenda, and was told she'd been gone all week, to visit her sister in Bella Coola. Jane loved the name Bella Coola. "When do you expect her back?" she asked.

"Tomorrow. Around noon."

The man's lazy voice made her wonder if he hadn't been smoking some of his crops. She thanked him. "Hey, it's all right," he said, in a peculiar overlay of Californese over Canadian.

She needed a place to spend the night. She polished off the espresso, absentmindedly petted a yellow lab and went back to the general store. It also had the BC TouristInfo logo on its crowded face.

By that afternoon, she was installed in a bed and breakfast on the far side of the island, facing the next island, Hornby, a big green wedge of an island across a narrow blue channel.

There weren't any hotels here, and a bed and breakfast sounded grim to her. She imagined waking up on a creaking hide-a-bed in some cheap little stucco house, listening to someone yell at the kids through paper-thin walls.

Instead, she found herself driving down a long, forested driveway to a meadow where an old farmhouse surrounded by outbuildings sat, looking as if it had been there for a hundred years. Three of the outbuildings were trim little cottages, surrounded by a rose garden. The whole thing looked like a magazine layout in some country living kind of magazine.

The place was run by Mrs. Bannon, a brisk Englishwoman in her sixties with steel gray shingled hair, a cotton twin-set, pearls and linen tweed skirt ensemble like some-thing the Queen Mother would wear for a casual weekend at Balmoral. Two meek-looking Bedlington terriers followed her around. Jane doubted they had Englishwomen like this in England anymore. One had to come to the outposts of Empire to find them.

Mrs. Bannon charged a fortune, but Jane felt like a houseguest—a houseguest with a hostess who didn't expect anything. She spent part of the afternoon getting a tour of the garden while Mrs. Bannon dead-headed the roses. "Of course the deer eat absolutely everything, so we have to keep all the garden behind a fence," she explained, wielding her pruning shears decisively. "Here's a lovely old rose. Not showy at all, but a lovely scent, rather like cinnamon, actually." Jane bent to smell it. The garden was interlaced by meandering flagstone paths with thyme growing in the cracks. Besides the roses, there were wide borders, with clumps of lavender and old-fashioned perennials like sweet William, Canterbury bells and teetering delphiniums. The garden was encircled by a lattice-topped fence heavy with clematis. "We hang Irish Spring soap in the orchard. They absolutely hate it."

She spent another couple of hours in a hammock, reading one of the books she'd found in her cottage— Stephen Leacock, the Canadian humorist, whom she'd read as a child, and still found funny in a nice gentle but sprightly Edwardian way.

But the roses and the bees in the honeysuckle and the general air of life slowed down and under control failed to distract her completely.

She finally set down the book, lay back in the weak sun and thought about why she was searching for Brenda— such a slender thread, really, to the events at the Coxes' pharmacy. Just that Brenda and Jennifer, who might well have seen something, busted up that same day. So it was a day Brenda might remember. And the fact that Brenda's picture was taken from Jennifer's apartment. But even if Brenda remembered what had happened to her room-mate, even if she knew, would any of that be admissible in court? Wouldn't it all be hearsay?

And where was Sean? Would his father have hired someone to silence a witness—would he have done it himself? Had Jane tipped him off? But how would he have known who was in the pharmacy that day to see his son kill Mrs. Cox? Mr. Nguyen wouldn't tell her. Would he tell Sean's father? Would the elusive Mr. Cox have told him? Not likely. He'd made it clear he believed Kevin was guilty.

And he wasn't the only one. The boy's own mother, his attorney and, through a druggy haze, even Kevin himself believed he'd done it.

So why was she chasing Brenda MacPhersons all over the map?

And why was Steven Johnson doing the same?

Maybe Kevin did kill Mrs. Cox. There was still some-thing else going on here. Or Jennifer wouldn't be dead. And she and Steven Johnson wouldn't be chasing Brenda. Maybe her hopeless case wasn't a matter of saving a wrongly accused boy—well, young man, actually—from prison. Maybe she would find another hopeless case in the midst of her search. That irritating committee of old geezers, however, might not like that. They'd given her a hard time before because she had found out she'd been pursuing the wrong trail, and then, when she'd presented the right solution, they'd rejected it. She wouldn't let that happen again. If this case panned out, she wanted it all to herself. She wasn't going to share it with anyone—not even the police.

Chapter 23

It rained in the night. In the morning, the air smelled fresh and damp, and the ground was wet.

Jane walked down a long, muddy drive to the Pennywhistle Herb Farm, picking her way through ruts filled with water. On either side of her was a wall of fir trees. Their trunks were wrapped in sheets of moss, and the moss glistened with a million raindrops clinging to a million woolly green strands.

She'd parked her car on the main road, but when she got to the end of the drive, she saw another visitor who'd driven up there in his four-wheel-drive camper. She didn't have to see the American plates to guess the man was American.

For one thing, he spoke a decibel louder than a Canadian. He seemed to be lecturing a short young woman in a heavy Cowichan Indian sweater—geometric patterns in gray and brown on white—jeans and rubber boots. Her hair was dark and she was short. Maybe she was the right Brenda.

"If these things worked," he said, gesturing toward rows of dreary-looking plants set in rows in a muddy garden, "don't you think doctors would prescribe them?"

Jane thought he had a point, but she also saw an immediate opening. If this woman was Brenda, Jane

181

would make an instant ally of her. "But the doctors and the big pharmaceutical companies don't really want people to take care of their own health," she said. "They'd be out of business."

The woman looked at Jane and smiled, managing to cast a piteous sidelong glance at the man in the baseball cap.

The man shook his head sadly, and walked off down a row of some gray-looking leaves. "What's this for?" he demanded over his shoulder, pointing at a row of peaky-looking plants.

"It's terrific for arthritis and other inflammatory diseases," said the woman rather defiantly. "Many people find it a very helpful herb." She pronounced the h in herb.

"Mind if I look around some more?" he said, disappearing behind a rather pathetic little greenhouse that seemed to be made of rickety two-by-fours and flapping plastic sheeting.

"I know these things do a lot of good," said Jane solemnly. "Because women have traditionally been herbalists, their knowledge has been denigrated by the men who've controlled science."

"Absolutely," said the woman, nodding with an air of wisdom, and the satisfaction felt by someone who finds her views reinforced.

"Is there anything for hay fever? I have a nephew who has terrible hay fever."

"Let's check on that," said the woman, leading Jane to the door of a dark little shed. Inside was a shelf with a few books and a clutter of earthenware pots. From the roof hung a row of crystals, looking like giant earrings.

The woman began flipping through a large, well-worn paperback book. The cover showed a vaguely art nouveau portrait of a woman's face with stylized flowing orange hair and wide gray eyes, surrounded by a border of green leaves.

Jane thought that Brenda, if she was Brenda, having to look it all up in a book detracted from the wise woman of the woods mystique, and, although she agreed with the man in the baseball cap about the value of most of these herbs, she found herself disappointed nonetheless.

"Goldenrod," she said.

"Poor little guy," said Jane. "It makes him so irritable." She wasn't sure hay fever made children irritable. Maybe it made them listless.

"A few drops of lavender oil in the bath soothes irritable children," said the herb lady. It occurred to Jane that if this was true, the remedy would be more widely known, but she just nodded. "Of course a lot of irritability is allergies to all the horrible things in the environment," continued the woman, rummaging in a drawer and coming up with a small plastic bag of dried leaves. "Brew it up into a tea," she said, with the cozy air of a benevolent sorceress. "Do you want some lavender oil too?"

Jane took the bag of goldenrod and a vial of lavender oil and paid her ten dollars, which the woman folded up and put into the front pocket of her jeans. The whole thing had the feel of a drug transaction.

"You do crystals too?" said Jane, looking around the shed.

"Yes, I've been doing it for quite a while now. The body heat activates their powers. There are special ones for special needs. The way I see it, the herbs cure the body, the crystals blast a message right into your soul. It's more a spiritual thing." She fished into her sweater and pulled out a leathery thong with a purplish-looking hunk of rock. "For prosperity," she said.

"How's it working?" said Jane, reflecting that at ten dollars (Canadian) per plastic bag, the woman was going to have to do a pretty hefty volume, and her location on a remote island made that pretty unlikely.

The woman's face clouded over a little. "Pretty well. I had a life reading, though, that said my karma this time is involved with money. I was very rich during a lifetime in China. I was a princess and I didn't have compassion for the poor."

Of course you were a princess, thought Jane. When it came to past lives, everyone had been a princess. No one had ever been an accounts-payable clerk or anything like that. Still, there was something sweet about this woman. She had the slightly beatific face of those who choose to believe what they want to believe, because it's more interesting and fanciful, and then hang in there with abiding faith. She had a cute little turned-up nose, and her big cushion of puffy hair had the shrubby pattern of growth of some of the mounds of herbs around the place.

"Actually," said Jane, "I came on another errand entirely. I'm looking for a Brenda MacPherson."

"I'm Brenda." The woman looked surprised, but, thought Jane, congratulating herself on ingratiating herself quickly with her, she didn't look wary.

"Did you ever live in the States?" said Jane.

She wrinkled up her nose. "I lived in Los Angeles for a while." Jane found this easy to believe. "To study polar foot massage. But I didn't like it. A lot of negative energy down there, even though many people are spiritually aware."

"I was looking for a Brenda MacPherson who used to live in Seattle." Jane felt she should embellish. "A friend of a friend," was as far as she got.

"That's really weird," said Brenda. "Someone called me this morning looking for another Brenda MacPherson too."

"From Tofino?" said Jane.

"He didn't say where he was calling from. But he sounded like an American."

"His name wasn't Johnson, was it?" said Jane.

"Yes," said Brenda.

"Her ex-husband. I was trying to find her to warn her. He's been let out of jail and he's looking for her."

"Oh my God," said Brenda. She put her hand to her cheek. "I told him I knew about someone with my same name. She's a stripper in Nanaimo. Some friends of mine were over there and saw her picture outside the place and they were joking with me about it, like I was over there stripping, you know. Not really my style. Anyway, her stage name was Stephanie Chantal, but my friend was with someone who knew her when she went to U Vic, and her name was Brenda MacPherson. Do you think it was his wife?"

"Could be. Do you remember the name of the place?" said Jane.

Just then the man in the baseball cap came up to them. "I noticed some foxglove over there. It's poisonous, you know. You aren't recommending that, are you?"

"No, I'm not," said the herbalist impatiently. "But it has the same thing they use for heart medicine."

"Digitalis is poisonous if the dosage isn't right. And how can you get the dosage right if you're just gathering this stuff out in the yard?" He shook his head.

"Is there something I can help you with?" said Brenda coldly, with the reluctant air of a habitually nice person who had finally been pushed to the limit of her tolerance.

"No," he said, looking a little irritated she wasn't going to argue with him anymore. Jane smiled at him. In spite of his rudeness, he'd made it easy for her to ingratiate herself with this particular Brenda. "Actually," he continued, "I've been camping over at Fillongie Park, and my wife sent me into town for a few things for dinner. I thought I might pick up some garlic here. They don't have a lot at the store, do they?"

"I've got some," she said. "Just a sec, okay?" She held up her hand and turned back to Jane.

"The name of the place?" prompted Jane.

"The Regency in Nanaimo. There was this big sign with the girls' names, and it was right there. Stephanie Chantal."

Jane reached into her purse for a scrap of paper and a pen. "Here's my name and a phone number in Seattle where you can leave a message. If Mr. Johnson calls back, or if you hear anything else about this other Brenda MacPherson, give me a call. But don't talk to him if you can help it. He's violent." Just in case he called back, Jane wanted to make sure he wouldn't get any cooperation.

The woman looked down at the paper. "Jane da Silva. Okay, I will. Gosh, I hope you find her before that other guy does."

Jane thanked her, and Brenda the herbalist turned her attention to the man in the baseball cap. "It prevents colds, you know," she said. "Garlic. And it prevents intestinal disturbances. And mucus."

He rolled his eyes in disgust. "We just want it for spaghetti sauce. If we have any other problems, we'll try the doctor." He gave them both a grim little smile, because he'd managed the last word.

"A real charmer," said Jane as he ambled off.

"Some people are so closed-minded," said Brenda. Jane thought that when it came to being narrow-minded, the herbalist and the man in the baseball cap were probably neck and neck.

Chapter 24

Jane had imagined the Regency would be some dingy bar with painted plywood siding and a few desperate characters lurking outside.

Actually, it was part of a rather pretty-looking old brick hotel, near the harbor in downtown Nanaimo, a town about forty-five minutes' drive south of the Denman Island ferry.

She went inside rather nervously. A motherly looking older woman in a hand-knit sweater, who reminded her of a French concierge, was working the door. From behind her, through a smoked glass door, Jane heard some perky canned rock music. Apparently the place was open all day long.

"I'm looking for the manager," said Jane. The woman ran her eye down Jane's body, and raised an eyebrow. "It's not about a job," Jane said. "I think I'm fifteen years too late for that."

"We've got some girls your age in pretty good shape," said the woman kindly. "A lot depends on their personality."

Jane rather doubted that when it came to marketing female flesh to a bunch of testosterone poisoning victims, a winning personality could substitute for twenty-year-old breasts.

"I'll take your word for it," she said. "Actually, I'm

187

looking for someone who danced here." Jane was hoping she could find Brenda without having to take a seat in the front row among a lot of drooling jerks. "She's my best friend's little sister," said Jane. "Stephanie Chantal." She smiled nicely. She didn't want the woman to think she was here to save Brenda from a career in vice.

"She doesn't work here anymore," said the woman. "They rotate them a lot, you know."

"I imagine the fellows like new talent on a fairly regular basis," said Jane.

"That's right. It's too bad really, but the chaps just don't get as excited after they get used to the girls' bodies, even though they seem to get personally fond of them."

"That fits with what I've noticed about life," said Jane, who didn't believe human behavior changed all that much. She had a quick vision of wandering cavemen, driven into the next valley by some imperative of nature to spread their genetic material as broadly as possible. "Do you know where she went?"

"We never give out that information," said the woman. "But maybe you can ask Bob." The woman gave her directions down a short corridor to a door marked PRIVATE.

Jane thought about knocking, then decided to just go in.

Bob, whom Jane had imagined as a greasy pimp with a lot of gold jewelry, turned out to be a wormy-looking little guy with thin hair sitting behind a desk with his plump hands folded in front of him.

In front of his desk sat Steven Johnson, with a big, stupid grin. He was listening to Bob, who was saying, "Why don't you stick around for the lunch show? We've got a new black one, you can bounce a quarter off her stomach."

Jane closed the door behind her, and the two men turned toward her.

"Sorry to disturb you," she said, avoiding eye contact with Johnson.

"You here to sign up for amateur night?" said Bob. He didn't look as skeptical as the little old lady at the door, but perhaps he encouraged any woman who wanted to dance naked in front of him, whether he thought they had commercial potential or not.

"No," said Jane. "I don't think you could bounce a quarter off any part of me."

"Don't sell yourself short," said Mr. Johnson. "I don't know if she can dance, Bob, but Jane here is a very attractive woman. I've been privileged to have a good look at just what she has to offer."

Jane gave him a contemptuous look and turned back to Bob. "I'll wait until you're through here. I just had a question about one of your dancers."

"Go ahead," said Johnson, rising. "I'm all through here." He passed Jane on his way out the door, giving her a little sneer, waved at Bob and said, "Thanks a lot," and gave him a conspiratorial wink.

Jane had been so irritated at finding Johnson there, and then at being insulted by him, she hadn't focused properly on Bob. She tried to make up for it now by giving him a big smile.

"Sit down," he said, addressing her chest. Jane would have thought that working with naked women all day would have dampened his interest in checking out women's bodies, but maybe it was just a professional habit.

"I'm looking for a dancer. Stephanie Chantal. I was supposed to meet her here last week, but I heard she left already. Can you tell me where she went?"

"We never give out that information," said Bob. "Have you called the booking agency?"

"But didn't you just tell Mr. Johnson?" said Jane.

"Of course not," said Bob. Jane felt sure he was lying.

"But he thanked you. I heard him." Now she'd called him a liar. A bad move that didn't allow him to save face and eventually come around to wanting to help Jane.

"Sorry," said Bob coldly. "I can't help you."

Jane buried her face in her hands. "God, I hope you didn't tell him. What did he tell you? He's crazy, you know. He beat her up and now he's stalking her. I want to find her and take her to her sister's house in California so she'll be safe."

She looked up at him again, thrilled that she'd produced a few tears, or at least a glassy-eyed look. She sniffed to add to the effect.

"You're saying he's got some personal thing with her?"

"Yes. She left him and now he's stalking her. The man's an animal."

Bob cleared his throat and looked guiltily away. "I'm not sure I believe you. Mr. Johnson is with an insurance company."

"He's such a good liar. I don't blame you for telling him. He can be very convincing. I understand that you did what you thought was right."

"He told me he had a payment for her for a claim. She was in a car accident and he had a check for her."

"Couldn't he have mailed it?"

"I asked him that," said Bob. "He said she had to sign something first." He looked worried now. "And there was some kind of time limit on it. She'd skipped out without taking care of it."

Jane felt like saying sarcastically, "An insurance company is knocking itself out trying to pay a claim?" but felt there was nothing to gain by informing Bob that he was an idiot.

Instead she said, "Just tell me where she is, so I can warn her."

"I don't know what to believe," said Bob. "This is pretty weird."

"Why would I lie?" said Jane. "Why would I try and tell you all this about Stephanie and that guy if he were a legit insurance guy?"

"He told me you'd be here and that you'd lie," said Bob.

"Of course he did," said Jane. "Don't you see how manipulative he is? But what motivation would I have?"

"He said you were her sister—some religious nutcase trying to stop Stephanie from working in stripper bars. You were some kind of a fanatic who wanted to drag her back home. He said you'd disrupted some of her performances."

"He was lying."

"Freedom of artistic expression is very important to me," said Bob sanctimoniously. "This is a clean industry, and everyone has a right to enjoy erotic entertainment. Up here in Canada we do it a lot classier than you do in the States with a bunch of hookers and drug addicts. Frankly, if you're trying to screw up a good thing, and maybe lose Stephanie a job, I don't want to help you."

"So you're saying you think I'm trying to save a lost soul from life as a stripper?" Jane tried to sound as if she didn't think Bob was pretty dense.

"Look, all I know is this Johnson guy comes in here, seems like a nice guy, and he tells me he's looking for Stephanie on account of this insurance deal. And he tells me that some crazy woman is going to come in here trying to find her and lying and whatever to get me to tell where she is. So then you come in with this story, just like he says you will."

Jane didn't want to waste any more time. Johnson already had a head start. She leaned across the desk and said in a low, steely voice, "I want to help Brenda and save her from this son of a bitch. I don't care if Brenda's stripping or if she's got an act with a German shepherd and a Tijuana mule, or if she had to go down on you and all your friends to get this job."

"I guess you're okay," said Bob, after a slight pause. "She headed up to Port Hardy. You might find her dancing at the Tomahawk Club."

Chapter 25

The rain had cleared up a little, thank God, but the worn wooden bleachers at Ross Field where Calvin Mason sat with Carol, watching her son, Raymond, play, held water like a sponge, and they were still wet.

At the bottom of the fifth (Little League games only went for six innings, but they seemed interminable to Calvin), Raymond's team, Bill's Auto Detailing, was getting badly waxed, trailing Ballard Kitchen 'n' Bath by a humiliating nineteen to three.

Carol's boy was at bat. Unappealing as the kid was—kind of jug-eared and knock-kneed, furtive-eyed and a mumbler—Calvin had developed a perverse desire to see him do well. He found himself strangely touched by the sight of Raymond awkwardly suited up and out there on the field looking slightly terrified when he wasn't looking overconfident.

The Kitchen 'n' Bath coach said to his pitcher casually, "Smoke 'em in there, buddy. You got this guy."

Calvin felt Carol tense up on the bench next to him. Raymond, as he always did when concentrating, stuck his tongue out of the side of his mouth just a little.

Raymond's coach looked irritably at the dugout where Raymond's teammates were horsing around, ignoring the game and trying to lag spare baseballs into batting helmets and generally bouncing off the fencing. "Pay attention to the game," he said. "Let's hear some chatter from you guys." He turned his attention to Raymond.

"Swing at the good ones, Raymond," he said. Raymond, who read a lot of books about boys saving the game with one powerful out-of-the-park hit, had a tendency to go for anything with everything he had. There were two outs and runners on first and third.

"Choke up on the bat, Raymond," yelled Calvin.

Behind them, a mother, who'd been talking throughout the whole game, continued her monologue. She shut up, Calvin noticed, only when her kid was at bat.

She specialized in horrible things that had happened to people she knew. The first couple of innings she'd covered various obstetrical and gynecological horrors of which she had personal knowledge. The woman was a walking textbook of medical malpractice.

Now she was talking about bad things related to ear piercing. She had covered off-kilter jobs and various kinds of horrible infections caused by not changing earrings often enough or using cheap earrings.

"And my cousin's daughter," she was saying now, "she wore these huge big earrings all the time and they stretched out her holes so bad she had to have stitches."

The pitcher sailed one right over the plate. Raymond just stood there.

Calvin winced, but the umpire called it a ball.

How these adult umpires could tell what was what standing behind little kids who were four feet high was a mystery to Calvin, but he was sure the pitch had been good. "Good eye, Raymond," said Calvin encouragingly, nevertheless.

"Anyway," the woman behind him was saying, "the holes were, like, huge. The doctor said they could rip right open anytime."

Raymond wound up for another hit, swung a nice, level, hard swing and the ball arced up in the air and into the outfield.

Raymond took off for first, encouraged by shouts from the bleachers. The other team and its parents urged someone named Max to get underneath the ball and catch it. A minute ago, Max had been drawing intricate patterns in the dust with the toe of his cleats, completely oblivious to the game, but the shouts from the bleachers galvanized him into action, and, squinting up into the cloudy sky, he waited patiently for the ball to fall into his glove. Which it did, much to Max's own astonishment and the cheers of his parents and teammates.

As Bill's Auto Detailing gathered up their gloves and ran out to the field, Calvin leaned over to Carol and went for the payoff.

"Know anything about that murder over in the University District," he said softly. "That office manager?"

"Best lead they've got is some guy who was seen in the building that day. The manager saw him. Apparently, she let the killer in, he strangled her, dragged her body into the bedroom, went through the desk, and left through the back door, out onto a terrace. Hard to know if anything's missing, because she lived alone."

He was squeamish enough to drag the body out of sight before he went through her stuff, thought Calvin. An amateur touch, maybe?

"Have they had the funeral?" said Calvin. He thought vaguely about dropping by. You could learn a lot at funerals. He didn't want to run into any homicide detectives, though. The last thing he wanted was for anyone to know he was involved in any way with this case. He thought again about Jane da Silva. He'd been an idiot to let her get involved. He never should have told her about that juror.

"No funeral," said Carol. "She belonged to that Christian Science Church in the U District."

"Brick. With Greek columns," said Calvin.

"But they don't have funerals. Death's an illusion anyway, or something." Carol shrugged. "They just cremated her."

Behind him, the chatty woman was on again about her cousin's kid's ears. "She had stitches in both ears, but her insurance didn't cover it. They said it was cosmetic. You'd think if they were about to get sliced clean through it would be covered. I mean, it could get all infected and stuff."

Two wires connected in Calvin's head and produced a spark. He needed to find out more about Jennifer. Maybe he could call someone at that church.

Chapter 26

As she walked back out down the hall of the Regency and out to her car, it occurred to Jane that while she had been indignant as hell that Bob hadn't believed her, she had lied through her teeth the moment she walked in his office. Her only true statement had been the finale; she really didn't care what Brenda did for a living.

She felt in her purse for her keys as she walked. She was excited now. This could well be the Brenda she was looking for. A dancer. Even that sleazy Cornishman had said she might turn up in a stripper bar.

Should she try to get in touch by phone? Would that be her way of getting a leg up on Johnson? After all, he'd phoned Brenda the herbalist when he'd been slowed down.

Johnson had a head start of just a few minutes, really. And he was probably smugly assured that Bob hadn't told her anything. Port Hardy, she knew, was the northern tip of the island. It would take hours to get there. She had a good chance of catching up.

Should she be warning Brenda?

But what if that meant she missed Brenda herself, if Brenda made herself scarce or refused to see her? Jane ran a few sample conversations through her mind. "Something's happened to Jennifer." It would only scare her. The best thing to do would be to find her, get her confidence, then try and find out what she knew about the day Jennifer had picked up her prescription at the Cox Pharmacy.

Maybe she didn't know anything at all. In which case, Jane had been spinning her wheels. But whatever happened, Jane had to find out what Johnson was after.

Johnson, no doubt, was on the road now, heading north. She wished she knew what he was driving. She could keep an eye out for him.

But Johnson wasn't on the road. He was leaning against her car, his arms crossed over his chest.

He came straight to the point. "You didn't have to turn me in to the police back there in Tofino," he said. "If you had a problem, you should have talked to me about it." He had a slightly aggrieved tone, as if he were going to say, "I thought we were friends."

"I'm sorry," she said. "But it seemed like a good idea at the time. You didn't have to tell Bob there that I was some kind of an antistripper crusader."

"It seemed like a good idea at the time," he said.

"I suppose that line about having had 'a good look at what she has to offer' was a good idea too," she said. She reminded herself just how sleazy that was. And what a betrayal, somehow, of the springs and the rain forest and the swirl of the hot water mixing with the icy waves.

"Okay," he said. "That was tacky. But I was pretty steamed. I thought we were going to have dinner together, and you sneaked away. I felt like a fool, you acting all one with nature and like you were having a peak spiritual experience when you were just grilling me and then deciding to set me up. This may come as a shock to you, but I enjoyed being with you and I wanted to spend more time with you."

"Well, you got out of the clutches of the police, anyway," she said, realizing how unattractively sulky she sounded.

"That's right. They were going to put me on a chain gang in the Yukon, but I convinced them I didn't have anything to hide. Maybe I can convince you too. If you give me a chance. Which is more than you have so far."

"So you weren't the guy at the Moorish Court Apartments?"

He sighed. "I went there. I questioned Jennifer Gilbert. She was alive when I left. I didn't know she'd been killed until the Mounties paid me a call. I spoke with the Seattle police, and I'll be meeting with them as soon as I finish up here," he said rather formally. He looked puzzled. "What I don't understand is what you have to do with all of this."

"We've been over all of this."

"The Seattle police didn't seem to know what you have to do with this either," he said.

"You told them about me."

"Of course I did," he snapped. "This is a homicide investigation. Jesus Christ."

"I know," she said thickly, feeling dumb and rather sick. Why hadn't she talked to the Seattle police? Calvin Mason had tried to get her to. Instead she'd disappeared.

And why? The answer was rather shameful. So she could solve a hopeless case, like some kind of sorority girl pledge initiation stunt. And get those nasty old trustees to give her lots of money to buy pretty things. And so she could prove to herself that she wasn't just a hopeless case herself, an empty stylish shell, hoping to find some sort of substance within, some area of competence, the ability to right a wrong, set things right, give some sort of shape to a messy, petty, shabby little world.

"Look," he said earnestly, impatiently, entreatingly, his head to one side. "You can come with me. He told me where Brenda is. We can talk in the car. I'll tell you what I'm doing, and you can tell me what you're doing."

Maybe she should. She imagined his nice brown hands on the wheel while she sat with her head tipped back in the seat, eyes closed, her tired voice explaining everything. Maybe he could help her make some sense of it all. Maybe he could tell her what to do.

Right now, she wanted someone to tell her what to do.

"You seem to be mixed up in something that's over your head," he said in a soft voice.

That softness almost pulled her in, but it gave her an icy little chill of wariness at the same time.

"I don't know," she said. Could she really be contemplating getting in the same car with him and driving off into the wilderness?

"You haven't got much choice," he said. He stepped away from her car and stood next to her. "This is your car, isn't it?"

"Yes," she said.

"In case you hadn't noticed," he said, "someone slashed all four tires. A pretty thorough job." He looked genuinely puzzled. "You have any idea who might have done that?"

"You bet I do," she said. Her face tightened with anger. "I should call the cops. Again."

"I guess that means you're on your own," he said. "But if I were you, I'd worry about whoever did that to your tires."

An hour later, she'd bought three new tires and had them and the spare mounted, and she headed for the TouristInfo office. She figured she may as well get herself a reservation (a "booking" in Canadian) at some place in Port Hardy. All she needed after what she'd been through was to spend the night in the bus station or something.

The clerk there made a few phone calls for her, and

while she waited she amused herself by checking out the
TOURIST ALERT memo on the bulletin board. The man from
Winnipeg was still being enjoined to call his sister. And
Dietrich Himmelman of Stuttgart and the Gauthiers from
Nice and the lady from Yonkers were there too, just as
they'd been in Tofino. She skimmed further down the
list, and was startled to find her own name. Jane da Silva
of Seattle. Call Calvin.

Excusing herself from the counter for a minute, she
rushed out to a pay phone. What could he have to tell
her? She prayed he'd be home.

His machine was on. "I can't come to the phone right
now," he said, "but leave a message at the tone and I'll get
back to you." To Jane's delight, however, there was more.
He'd left a personalized message for her on his machine.
It was good to hear his voice, even on tape. "If this is
Jane, where the heck have you been? Thought you'd like
to know I've got a rendezvous with the little father
planned. And, your friend Arthur's late tenant was a
Christian Scientist. A *devout* one. Think about it. Call
when you can."

She went back to the counter, pleased that she had a
reservation and eager to hit the road. Good for Calvin
Mason. His message was clear, even though he'd avoided
using names. He'd found that weasel Sean. And Arthur's
late tenant was clearly Jennifer.

After thinking about it for a while, she had to agree
Calvin had stumbled on to something of potential
significance.

Later, after she had headed north, through acres of
forest in various stages of development, she thought
again about Steven Johnson.

It occurred to her that if he'd wanted to disable her
car, he could have been much slicker about it. He could
have pulled the distributor cap or drained the tank.

There was something fierce about the sight of those tires with their jagged cuts. Maybe he had been trying to scare her.

She thought about that on the long drive north. The road hugged the coast for a while, past totem poles, signs for salmon resorts, fast-food restaurants and the occasional strip mall, then at Campbell River turned off past a huge paper mill into a real freeway cut straight through heavily timbered mountains.

Here she felt she had left civilization behind, and in fact there was very little between here and Port Hardy at the northern tip of Vancouver Island, except three hours behind the wheel and about a billion trees.

The scenery was in various stages of growth. There were areas of thick, dense forest interspersed with burnt-over clear cuts. In between were sections of varying heights, neatly labeled by the timber company. HARVESTED 1926, HARVESTED 1949, HARVESTED 1968.

The signs and the stands of uniform fir trees were a reminder to anyone from a city far away who had formed a vague impression of greedy, land-raping timber companies slashing and burning, that trees were a renewable resource. They just took a long time to grow back.

But when they grew back, they looked like a neat, dull crop rather than an artful landscape of mixed species illuminated by slanting shafts of light dancing with red cedar dust.

The clear cuts had a bleak, creepy appeal of their own. In between the charred stumps with their gnarling roots grew a feverish assortment of scrubby undergrowth—the kind of growth familiar to anyone who had ever weeded a garden bed in the wet Pacific Northwest, where any bare ground doesn't stay bare too long.

Unfortunately, while Jane didn't know what Johnson was driving, he knew what she was driving. She had considered renting a car in Nanaimo, but then she decided she'd waste valuable time filling in a lot of paperwork.

She was close to Brenda now, she knew it, and she felt more and more that Brenda knew something that would help her. She corrected herself. Something that would help Kevin, anyway. It was funny how little she thought about Kevin. He wasn't really important—just a means to an end. Who knew what he was up to now? Watching TV or sitting around in his cell or weaving baskets or making license plates. Jane imagined that prison life must be like combat as she had heard it described: long periods of boredom punctuated by moments of terror.

Which, she reflected, as raindrops slammed onto her windshield, caught some of the spirit of her own enterprise. The road seemed interminable, and now that the rain seemed to be coming down in sheets, feeding all those thirsty trees, there was a real monotony to the drive. It was a monotony made worse by a squeak from the wipers.

A passing truck with a load of peeled logs threw a tidal wave over the window and she couldn't see a thing for a second. She fiddled with the wiper control and set it for the maximum number of sweeps. The squeaks speeded up too.

Finally, although she knew she was in a race to get north, she seized on a rare roadside sign that indicated a restaurant as an excuse to stop. It was the first evidence of human habitation she'd seen for miles.

Her nerves were getting frayed and she hoped the rain would settle down a little while she had a cup of coffee and maybe a sandwich.

She turned off the road and went down a short spur toward a lone white building with some gas pumps in front. She kept her head down, the rain beating on the back of her head, as she picked her way through the dirt and gravel turning to mud of the parking lot. She nearly collided with a group of men coming out; from her crouched stance, she got a brief impression of plaid shirts, jeans and work boots.

Inside, she shook herself like a wet dog. The air was warm and full of the sweetish smell of Canadian cigarettes. Some innocuous, vaguely countrified Muzak played. The place was full of loggers, hunched over their coffee and talking with animation. The walls were lined with rough-hewn planks, and there were blown-up photographs of old turn-of-the-century tinted photos of life in the woods. Lumberjacks with handlebar moustaches standing with quiet pride next to gigantic stumps; steam locomotives pulling cars full of logs through the woods, groups of unsmiling men shouldering axes and carrying giant saws. Back then they got through acres of virgin timber with hand tools, thought Jane, but their great-grandsons, drinking coffee around her, looked plenty tough still.

She had a cup of coffee and a grilled cheese sandwich and wondered just what she would say when she met Brenda MacPherson. Maybe it would make sense to just tell the truth. A novel approach. Jane was ashamed at the sneaky pleasure she took in making up convincing lies when she was running around doing Uncle Harold's work. Maybe she should tell Brenda that Jennifer had been killed. Brenda would see how important it was that she help if she could.

Brenda the stripper seemed an unlikely roommate for the prim young woman Arthur the landlord had described, but surely she would feel some sense of responsibility to her old friend. And Brenda needed to know too that Johnson was looking for her.

Jane put down her coffee. What the hell was she sitting

here for? The sooner she got to Brenda, the less chance Johnson would have to come up with some smarmy lies of his own. She threw some bills on the table and went back outside.

Hunched over under the rain, her eyes scrunched into slits, she didn't notice as she slid behind the wheel. It was only after she started the engine and tried to back out the car that she realized there was something terribly wrong.

She got back out and into the rain. The new tires were practically sitting on their rims. And it wasn't that they hadn't been properly mounted or anything. The tires had the same angry, jagged cuts in the rubber that had appeared before, outside the Regency in Nanaimo.

Chapter 27

It was at this point that Jane felt like bursting into tears. She looked through the blinding rain to see if Steven Johnson were here. Across the parking lot, barely visible through the rain, was a car with a male occupant. He appeared to be reading a road map. She wasn't sure. It could have been Johnson.

All that time in Nanaimo she'd spent buying tires, sitting in the shop having them mounted—it was all for nothing. She felt like going over to that car, peering in to see if he was hiding behind that road map, and then pounding on the car window and shrieking at him.

How could she have thought he was attractive? Right now, she hated herself. She was a weak and foolish woman, susceptible to any kind of flattery. If she hadn't been so determined to find herself a hopeless case, she'd probably have slept with him. And would he have cut her up like he cut up her tires?

In Nanaimo, okay, it might have been some vandal. But to have the vandalism repeated here, when no one knew who she was on this damn island besides Johnson—it was too much.

She shuddered at the thought that they'd sat naked together in that warm water. What was the matter with her? She was barely sane, flirting with danger like this.

As she often did when things seemed unbearable, she thought of Bernardo, her husband, who had wrecked his car and killed himself, making her a widow when she was twenty-seven years old. If he were here, as he should have been, he could protect her. Instead she was a rather pitiful creature, trying to do hard things without the steel to follow through on them.

At times like this, she was angry with him. He had been a Formula One driver, so it wasn't so strange his having died the way he did. He lived with the threat of death. She went into her life with him knowing that, as much as a girl of twenty-three knows anything. But if he had loved her as much as he had loved winning and going as fast as he could, would she be in this parking lot now, at the mercy of some sociopathic thug?

I will not, she said to herself, fall apart. I will not give that son of a bitch Johnson the satisfaction. She gave the tires one last look—why, she didn't know. Perhaps she was crazy enough to think she could wish them whole again.

They weren't whole. She straightened up and sighed.

A man approached her. Her whole body tensed, expecting for just a second that it was Johnson, but it was an older, burlier man in a baseball cap.

"Boy, what happened to you," he said, looking down at the tires.

"I'm not sure. They were okay when I pulled in here," she said. She knew she'd seen him before, then she realized he was the irritable tourist she'd met at the herb farm.

"Weren't you buying some garlic a while back?" she said. "On Denman Island."

"That's right, at that hippie herb farm." He snorted. He looked back down at the tires. "Do you belong to Triple A? You're going to have to get a tow. Way out here in the middle of nowhere. It could be a real hassle." He said it without sympathy; more as a matter of interest. And with the same sense of superiority he'd shown at the herb farm. You stupid woman, he seemed to be saying. Why did you have to get your tires slashed out here.

She waved a hand dismissively at the car. "I don't have time for a tow," she said. "I've got to get somewhere. I'll worry about the car later."

"I'm going north," he said. "To Port Hardy. There isn't much between here and there as far as I know. I could send a tow truck down for you if you want."

"Do you think you could give me a lift?" she said.

He frowned. His disposition hadn't improved much since he'd been challenging the Denman Island herbalist. "I suppose," he said.

She glanced over at the car whose occupant was still hunkered down behind a map. Nobody needed to look at a road map that long.

"I'll pay for the gas," she said, rather desperately.

"It's okay," he said, sighing morosely.

She grabbed her bag from the trunk and followed him over to his camper, a big hulking white vehicle. He opened the door for her and she climbed up. Inside it was warm and a little steamy. There was a bundle of maps and tourist pamphlets and a wicker fishing basket on the seat. She pushed them aside to make room for herself. The rain beat heavily on the roof of the vehicle. He came around to the other side.

Please, she said silently, pull out of here and get going. She tried not to look anxious. He took off his baseball cap and ran a chubby, veined hand over his bald head. It seemed to take him forever to get the car in gear and get out of the parking lot.

She watched the other car in the side mirror. Its lights went on, then it disappeared from view. She couldn't turn around and look out the back window, but she feared they were being followed.

After they had been on the road for a few miles, she relaxed. At least nothing could happen to her here in the car. She tried to force herself not to look in the side-view mirror. She didn't want this guy to think she was being followed.

"That's terrible, someone ripping your tires like that," he said. "You don't expect that up here. In the city, maybe. With all those crazy kids running around. But up here in the woods?" He shook his head.

"I know," she said. "It gave me the creeps."

"You should have called the police," he said.

"I just wanted to get away," she answered. "I really appreciate your giving me a lift." She glanced back in the mirror, read, OBJECTS IN MIRROR ARE CLOSER THAN THEY APPEAR. There wasn't any sign of that car she thought might be Johnson's. She relaxed a little more.

"You up here fishing?" she said, glancing over at the wicker basket.

"That's right. Camping a little. It's not bad up here." He was still frowning, which made Jane think that he was one of those habitually irritable men who seem to think they're supposed to disapprove of everything, even when they're having a good time.

She leaned back and combed out her wet hair with her fingers. He was going at a nice seventy miles an hour, thank God. They should be in Port Hardy in an hour and a half or so.

"What brings you up here?" he said

"Oh, business," she said vaguely.

"What kind of business?" he said. The windshield wipers clacked furiously.

Another sign from the timber company, advertising the

fact that the trees they were passing had been planted in 1948, flashed by. FORESTS FOREVER it said.

"The timber business," she said. Then, in case he asked her anything about it, she added. "Pretty boring really. I'm in the accounting department."

"I was an accountant for years," he said gruffly. "I didn't think it was boring."

"Oh, you're retired," she said. She'd rather talk about him than about accounting procedures, of which she knew absolutely nothing, and be exposed as a fraud. "Are you enjoying your retirement?"

"Do a lot of fishing," he said laconically.

Jane had a theory that no one was really boring. Even bores had a half hour or so of material in them. This gentleman, however, seemed to be the exception. Which was probably just fine. She really didn't need much more excitement. A little hiatus was a good idea.

"If you don't mind," she said, "I could use a little nap. I've been working hard and traveling a lot."

"Mmm," he murmured.

"Audits," she added by way of explanation, and put her head against the window. She doubted she could sleep, but she wanted to think rather than make conversation.

But a second later, with her eyes closed, she found the motion of the car had actually made her sleepy. It was kind of a relief not to be driving herself. Maybe she should call the restaurant from Port Hardy. Tell them she'd be back later for the car. She could find the name of the town from the map. There was only one restaurant in town.

Right before she drifted off, another thought teased her from her subconscious. Something about garlic and the herb farm on Denman Island.

Chapter 28

She didn't know how long she'd been asleep. When she
woke up, she was looking at more trees. The road looked
a little narrower, though. It was two lanes, with a bright
shiny new yellow line painted down the middle. What was
it that she'd thought about just before she went to sleep?
Garlic.

Bernardo had loved garlic. He thought it was good for
colds and chomped away at cloves of it. She smiled. She
wasn't angry with him anymore. Who knows what would
have happened if he'd lived? Lately, she'd begun to think
they might not have been together by now anyway. Hardly
anyone else they had known back then was still together.
People change. But of course Bernardo couldn't. He
would always be the same wonderful, charming person
he'd been on the day he crashed. When that oddly
consoling thought had first leapt into her mind, she'd felt
guilty. Now she was getting used to it. She no longer
looked wistfully at old couples who'd been together for
years.

Old couples together. Garlic. That was it.

"How was that garlic?" she said. "That you bought at
that herb farm?"

"Garlic is garlic," he said.

"Did your wife like it?" she said. "You said she'd sent you out for it as I recall." Why was he alone?

He looked over at her. "It was okay."

"Where is your wife?" she said now, puzzled.

He didn't say anything for a long time. In that silence, Jane felt a prickle cover her whole body, as if every pore had tightened.

"She's not feeling well," he said after a while. "She's taking a nap in the back."

"I'm sorry to hear that," said Jane.

The long pause before his explanation convinced Jane he was lying. And he'd said it defensively, as if he didn't care whether she thought he was lying or not.

Suddenly he turned the wheel sharply to the left, off the road and onto gravel. Some kind of a forestry sign flickered by.

"Where are we going?' ' she said sharply. "Is this the road to Port Hardy?"

"Shortcut," he said. "Logging road. They have a lot of speed traps up here."

The landscape had changed dramatically. Skimpy alders, a few feet high, lined the road, growing like weeds out of the gravel, cordoned off by a tuft of dusty horsetails.

They went past the rusted-out hulk of a clothes dryer and some unidentifiable strips of metal, a burnt-out quarry, flooded over with brown water.

This was logged-over territory, without even the delicacy of a fringe of forest to protect the motorist from the sight of ravaged land. Ahead loomed two peaks of naked rock. The rock was peppered with stumps, but the earth had washed away.

"Where are we going?" she said sharply again, knowing that a firm tone would make no difference, that she was completely at this man's mercy. Was he an opportunistic deviant who, once she had climbed into his car, decided she was his, to do with as he pleased, then perhaps junk her like a rusted-out old clothes dryer?

They raced past a river littered with gnarled stumps, curly roots waving in the air, wedged into a gravel bank; past rocks covered in yellowish moss and blackened by slash burning.

She couldn't leap out of the truck. There was nowhere to hide. But he did look out-of-shape. She might be able to outrun him if she plunged into the hideous landscape.

"Wow," she said disingenuously, "I thought the road to Port Hardy was pretty clear and straight. Are you sure we want to take these old logging roads?"

She sounded stupid. What was he supposed to say? "I guess you're right. I'll turn around and take the route you think is best." That wouldn't jibe with any male behavior she'd ever observed.

He grunted in reply.

"Got a map or anything?" she said. "I can't imagine where we are."

Suddenly he startled her by sounding frightened. "Shut up!" he said. His voice almost squeaked.

"What?" She didn't know whether the fear in his voice should give her hope or scare her even more.

With horror, she watched him, one hand on the wheel, the other scrabbling in the fishing tackle basket next to him. He came up with a knife.

"I'll use this," he said. "I swear to God I'll use this."

Just then he swerved to avoid a lumbering silky black bear, nosing around the side of the road, followed by its cub. The bear moved around inside its skin as if it were a size too big, the pelt sliding around the giant shoulders. "Damn," he said.

"I don't understand," said Jane, for whom the bear held little interest. "Please. What is it you want?"

He didn't answer. He was driving very fast now. But in

his right hand he held the knife. It was stainless steel with a serrated blade. The kind of thing you would use to gut a fish.

When the car stopped, then she should make her move. Run for it. Climb a tree. Isn't that what you were supposed to do if a bear was after you? He didn't look like he could climb a tree after her. He'd give up and go away. And then she'd hide like an animal, creep out later, maybe hail some passing vehicle—a logging truck driven by some safe, kind person. There couldn't be a lot of sociopaths out here. In small, sparsely populated places like this, they'd be spotted right away. Not like this madman, with his nervous, mean face.

Climb a tree, that's what she'd have to do. She hadn't actually climbed a tree since she was a kid, but she thought she could do it. She imagined pulling herself up, arm over arm. He'd be pulling at her ankles. Yanking her to the ground. Gutting her like a fish perhaps.

The road grew worse. Rocks blonked against the undercarriage of the vehicle. She glanced over at the ignition. Her only chance was to get him out of the camper and get away in it. But how in God's name could she do that? Could she pull the keys out of the ignition, stop the vehicle?

At least then she'd be closer to the main road. Who knew how far these logging roads went into the woods. They'd been logging in British Columbia since the nineteenth century, as far as she knew.

She felt a horrible pang of despair and pity for herself; she could die out here, in this scabby, ruined landscape. Her body would lie for weeks, maybe forever if he chucked it into a ravine. Then the animals would scatter her bones. No one would ever know what had become of her.

Tears of fear and rage began to form in her eyes. There had to be a way. She'd always believed she could talk her way out of anything. But she was afraid to talk to this man. He had seemed so frightened. Now, barreling along, he seemed purposeful, focused on the road.

If she was silent, maybe he would forget about her entirely. She tried that for a moment, but the sheer terror that inaction created in her was too much to bear. Better to try something. Anything.

Perhaps if she managed to invoke pity in him. Surely somewhere there must be some core of goodness, of pity. She sniffed. "Please don't hurt me," she whimpered. And she added, "I have children."

"Shut up," he said. This did seem to upset him. In fact, it seemed to enrage him. "Shut up about your kids."

"I'm sorry," she said, hating herself for apologizing. But she took some solace in the fact that his reluctance to hear about her fictional children seemed to be based on some flicker of guilt.

She kept scanning the surrounding landscape, searching for some way out. Looking for an escape in case through some miracle the car stopped and she could leap out. Here and there the forest started up again, making the road dark and cool-looking, providing inky openings into the dense undergrowth, openings that looked like safe caves. Irrationally, she projected herself mentally into those caves as they flew by.

If guilt wasn't enough to stop him from whatever it was he planned to do, maybe fear would do it.

"There was a guy in that parking lot where we started out," she said. "He saw me leave with you."

He frowned. "I didn't see anyone," he said. Something about the trace of doubt in his voice, as well as the tinge of guilt she'd heard before, convinced her this guy hadn't done a lot of this in the past. After all, she had practically begged him to give her a lift. If he planned to rape or kill her, maybe it was a crime of opportunity.

And if she did get raped or killed or both, it would be the fault of Johnson, slashing her tires like that.

"What are you going to do with me?" she said.

"I don't know," he said. "Don't worry about it," he added ludicrously.

"I'm sorry I asked you for a ride," she said. "Just drop me off here, leave me here, I won't tell anyone. I'd be so grateful that I wouldn't tell anyone. You didn't mean to hurt me. I don't believe you're really a bad person."

Like hell, he wasn't a bad person, she thought to herself. While she was pleading, trying not to whine or let fear come into her voice, trying to sound calm and reasonable, she was imagining cutting him up with his own knife, slitting his throat, leaving him here to die in the woods, his blood seeping out of him into some of the yellowish moss that draped the burnt-out rocks.

They passed another fork in the road. There were three battered, metal, bullet-riddled signs stacked on a tilted pole—DEVIL'S BATH. KATHLEEN LAKE. ETERNAL FOUNTAIN. She memorized them in case she managed to escape somehow and had to hike back out. He stayed on what seemed like the main route, toward Devil's Bath.

"Of course I'm not a bad person," he said rather indignantly.

She felt a little leap of hope.

"That's why you'll let me go."

What he said next startled her. It cast doubt on her theory of the lone creep with a screw loose, bent on rape or the thrill of killing a woman, suddenly snapping, taking advantage of opportunity, perhaps even telling himself it was all justified because she'd asked for a ride.

"You're name is Jane da Silva, isn't it?" he said. "That's what you told that herb woman. You gave her a card and you wrote your name on it. And she said Jane da Silva. I heard her clearly."

"Why do you care what my name is?" she said. Could it have something to do with looking for Brenda? After all, he was there with the herb lady, and her name was Brenda MacPherson. "Look, I don't know your name, and I don't know who you are. If you just leave me out here it will take me hours to get back. You can get far away, and we can forget this ever happened."

Of course, we are on an island, she thought to herself with some tiny satisfaction. If she did get out of here, she could call the cops and maybe they could watch all the ferries leaving the island. Maybe they'd catch him and put him away for years so he wouldn't terrorize anyone else again, ever.

To her amazement, he pulled the camper sharply off the road up a slight rise into what looked like a turnaround for logging equipment. There were big tire tracks in the mud and gravel. Maybe he was backing out. Maybe he would leave her there. Jane said a prayer—saw Christmas card angels from her childhood swooping down, lifting her aloft, flying away with her.

On three sides of the area was what looked like a drop-off into forest—on the fourth side, the side nearest the passenger door, there was a steep wall of rock about twenty feet high. Salal and huckleberry and moss grew there in patches.

She'd go over the top of the rock, rather than down over the ridge into the forest. Not only was he a heavy guy, but he looked to be in his sixties. Downhill was tempting, because on the rock he could see her and she could see him and her impulse was to get out of his line of sight, but the rock would be harder for him to get up, and she could stomp on his hands if he climbed up after her.

Downhill, he'd catch up with her just by letting the sheer weight of him propel him down on top of her.

Before the vehicle had even come to a full stop, she tore open the door, threw herself out and flung herself at the rock. It was easier going than she'd thought. From the turnaround it had looked more vertical. She was six feet or so up before he had time to get his bulk around the car and come after her.

She grabbed some salal for a handhold and felt its shallow roots pulling out of the little crevice where it grew. She switched to a huckleberry bush and barely cleared the top of his head. She could hear him huffing and puffing beneath her. Damn. He had looked so out-of-shape and old and sedentary, but men, even old crocks, were always stronger than you thought they were.

Maybe the son of a bitch would have a heart attack scrambling up that rock. She'd like that, watching him wheezing and gasping, red in the face, dying on his back in the muddy tire ruts in that bleak little spot.

Did she dare kick him? His head was right beneath her. Could he grab her ankle and yank her down? She kept scrambling—sideways this time where there were footholds—and then up again. By the time she got to the top of the ridge she had a couple of seconds on him.

Her heart was beating in her chest like a huge bird flapping its wings against her ribs. She could almost hear the blood racing through her body. She reached down and picked up a big rock. But if it was small enough to lift and throw, would it be big enough to hurt him? She dropped it and found another one, a bigger one, and bending over because she couldn't get it above her waist and move at the same time, she went over to where she expected his head to appear.

He was faster than she thought. She had imagined dropping it on that bald head from a foot above. Instead his head and torso had already cleared the ridge.

Before he had a chance to let go of his handhold and

pull himself up, she dropped the rock on his left hand. He let out a yelp of pain and slid back a little.

She turned and scuttled away like a crab. All she'd managed to do was slow him down. And she saw that his other hand still held the knife.

She was upright now—she could run. But she only ran a few feet before she realized she was looking at the tops of trees. She was standing on a high cliff and below her was a lake unlike any other lake she had ever seen.

It was far beneath her, maybe a hundred and fifty feet down from the top of the cliff to the surface of the water, a perfectly circular lake with sheer rock walls most of the way around.

From where she stood, she could look across at the cliff across from her, a rocky moonscape, a litter of peeled logs and boulders. Horrified, she stared down beneath her feet, into the eerily still water below. A jumble of logs and a gnarled old stump floated there in the center, all higgledy-piggledy, like a child's game of pick-up-sticks. They were still, and covered with moss trailing off into the water like a slimy green veil. Smaller trees grew on the backs of the logs, as if they hadn't moved in years. The surface of the water, a grayish blue, was flat and dead.

Two thirds of the way around, the tall sides of this strange lake looked as sheer as the naked rock wall across from her, but where she stood there was vegetation— cedars and Douglas firs and ferns. It all seemed to be growing out of the rock wall itself, like a hanging garden, and she knew that if something grew there, there had to be some horizontal planes somewhere on the rock wall to accommodate soil and provide a space for the seeds that these trees had once been to lodge and grow.

He was right behind her now, the knife in one hand, the other hand covered with blood.

She had no choice. She had to go over the edge. A few feet away there was bare rock, and she could dive into the water from up here. But even if she could have dived into the water, like a cliff diver in Acapulco, she could break her back if she landed wrong. And she had no idea how deep the water was.

She would have to go over the side with the trees and branches. She'd get scraped and scratched and bruised, and maybe she'd fall anyway and kill herself, but the only other alternative was staying here and struggling with a man armed with a knife on top of a cliff.

Chapter 29

At first, her descent was basically a fall, broken a half dozen times by tree limbs and roots. Finally, the fear of falling overtook her fear of the man, and she grabbed for a rough, dark fir limb.

She didn't know if he was coming down after her. She was making so much noise herself, gasping noisily in fear until she told herself she shouldn't hyperventilate, and tried to breathe more shallowly.

She propelled herself downward, feeling desperately with her feet for footholds—any niche in the rock or well-placed sturdy limb, gauging whether it would hold her weight before daring to let go with her hands and working her way down further.

The sounds of her body against snapping branches and thrashing leaves seemed incredibly loud in the stillness above the strange lake. Scratchy twigs whipped against her face, and she was gasping for breath, again, partly from exertion, mostly from fear. When she heard herself moan, she told herself to snap out of it, and again she tried to regulate her breathing. She thought it would help her to think more systematically.

What was she going to do when she got to the water? She was counting on the fact that he'd be reluctant to scramble down after her.

She wasn't sure where he was; she didn't hear him thrashing after her. That realization gave her a second's relief, a brief surge of achievement.

But then she wondered what would happen once she reached the bottom. There was nothing there but that still water and that pile of logs in its center. Would he come down and get her eventually? She couldn't scramble up the other side. It was sheer rock. And if she did, he could come around and get her.

She was about ten feet above the water when she heard him. From the yell above her it sounded as if he were still up on the cliff. "Where the hell do you think you're going?" he said.

"Just go," she shouted. "You can drive off now, and we can forget all about this." She had yelled it as loud as she could. There was a shimmer of an echo in the rock basin.

She clung to a tree trunk, waiting for his answer.

"If you make me come down there after you, it'll be worse," he said in a peevish voice.

"I'm not coming up," she shouted angrily. What the hell did he think, she was going to claw her way back up so he could slit her throat?

She waited for an answer. When it came it was voiceless, just the thrashing of foliage. And then he swore. It was clear he didn't want to come down after her. It was all she had, so she had to use it. She gazed over at the pile of logs and the inverted old stump. Then she tried to figure just how much he could see and what his angle of vision would be from the cliff as he worked his way down.

She climbed down the final ten feet or so to the water, and stood there for a second on a slippery log, the water soaking into her shoes.

It was cold, just as she feared.

"No, no," she screamed as theatrically as possible. "Go away." Her voice bounced off the stone walls.

And then she flung herself into the water sideways, aiming her body so she made as big a splash as possible.

The water was absolutely bone-chilling and well over her head. She submerged her whole body, on the theory that the cold wasn't so bad if all of you was wet, surfaced and tilted her head back to get her hair out of her eyes. Treading water, she listened. There was the sound of branches snapping, but he wasn't coming down nearly as fast as she had.

She slapped the still surface with her hands, making thrashing sounds, and wondering how long it took someone to drown, or at least to pass out while they were drowning. Not too long, she supposed.

"Help. Help," she screamed. "I can't swim."

With a lot more splashing, and turning and tossing of her head, just in case he could see her properly, she made her way a few yards to the pile of logs in the center, trying to make real swimming look like panicky splashing.

She remembered hearing about people going down for the third time, so she made a few desperate appearances above the water line, sputtering and choking, before slipping underneath and gliding underwater a few more feet until she came up to the collection of logs in the middle of the lake.

What she did now had to look good.

She submerged as long as she could. She couldn't see much underwater. The logs floated above her, making it even darker underneath; one of them, wedged between some others, knifed down at a forty-five-degree angle and disappeared into the dark below. The gnarled roots of an old stump dangled in front of her, immobile. She took care not to get her clothes snagged on any of the dead tree limbs. She imagined she could get stuck underwater that way and actually drown.

Finally, exhaling slowly, she allowed her body to rise and float, facedown, until her head bumped against a log.

She was as still as the logs themselves. Her goal was the huge old stump. She wanted to look as if her drowned body was wedged in there somehow, between the curling roots.

Moving slowly, trying to look as if she were drifting, she arranged herself in a V shape between two arms of the stump, her head half submerged in the water, but turned away from the cliff so it would look as if her mouth and nose were underwater.

The way she was positioned, one ear, one eye and her nose were above the water line. She hoped fervently that first of all he'd think she had drowned, and secondly that he would save himself the climb down to make sure.

If he was smart, he'd get back up there and clear out, hoping like hell that if she was found they'd call it a suicide or an accident. Of course, they'd wonder how she'd got into the area in the first place. There wouldn't be a vehicle for her.

Maybe he'd go for help, pretending he'd tried to save her. For now, she had to lie still, and will him away.

She strained to hear signs of movement from the cliff. To her horror, she heard lots of agitated thrashing of foliage. She maintained her painful stillness. The cold was much worse when she wasn't moving. Staying perfectly still was excruciatingly difficult. If there had been any movement in the water, she could have cut herself some slack, but the water was as still as death.

She told herself it was all right, he might only come as far as the water's edge, just to see if she was dead. If she could convince him she was, then he'd go away.

But another thought occurred to her. There had been tire tracks on the logging roads. Somebody must come by here now and then. What if he decided to make sure the body was submerged—weigh it down with stones?

One thing was sure: he probably wouldn't try and get her body back up the cliff.

She listened to more thrashing foliage, then felt her heart sink as she heard the noise of someone entering the water, followed by the sounds of a sure, steady swimming stroke.

Chapter 30

She braced herself. When he got over to where she was, she'd fight like hell and scream bloody murder. With the echo off those stone walls, maybe some lumberjack would hear her. Or maybe this guy would get scared. But she'd play possum until the bitter end.

Maybe he'd just poke her a little to see if she was alive. She lay as still as possible. Some trailing moss had wrapped itself clammily around her shoulders. She heard those strokes coming toward her and willed herself to float like a dead thing.

She couldn't bring herself to wait, though. She felt a presence right next to her in the water, and instinct took over. She turned over on her back, pulled herself up on a log and kicked him in the chest. He grabbed her ankle and she shook it off, then propped herself up on her elbows. Nothing could have been more astonishing.

"What the hell are you doing here?" she demanded.

Treading water, and looking equally astonished at her recovery from drowning as she was at his appearance, was Steven Johnson.

"I'm rescuing you, goddamnit," he said. "I heard you scream you couldn't swim."

"But there was a guy, an older guy..." Jane felt slightly

dizzy. It was like in a dream, where one person turned into another in midnarrative.

"He's still up there for all I know," said Johnson.

Just then, they heard an engine start up and a vehicle leaving the area.

"Correction," said Johnson. "He's on his way out of here."

"Were you in his camper all the time?" said Jane.

"No, you idiot. I was following his camper. I saw him tear up your tires at that coffee shop, and I followed."

"I thought that was you in the parking lot," she said. Now that she was mostly out of the water, she was cold. Her teeth started to chatter. "But I didn't know you were behind us."

"That's the whole point," he said. "Not to be observed. And once he got on these logging roads I followed his treads in the mud. Jesus, what do I have to do to get you to believe me? Are you coming out of the water now, so we can go follow the guy out of here? Or do you want him to get away while our lips turn blue?

"You can swim, I take it. You were trying to fake it, right? Not a bad idea, but you wasted a lot of my time. I could have been finding out who the hell that guy is."

Jane pushed herself off from the jumble of logs and swam to shore. What else could she do? He swam next to her.

Johnson pulled himself onto the tiny strip of shore first, then gave her a hand and yanked her up out of the water.

Without much enthusiasm, Jane surveyed the cliff in front of them. Up would be worse than down. He went first, and she was glad he didn't turn around and watch her progress. She felt clumsy and numb. As they clambered, dripping and puffing up the side of the cliff, Jane asked him, "Why did you let me go off with him if you saw him slash my tires?"

"Because you wouldn't believe me," he said simply. "You thought I did it to your tires in Nanaimo, and you'd think I did it there too." He shook his head in exasperation. "Every time I mix it up with you I get arrested or yelled at. This time I just decided to keep an eye on you. I'm glad I did. What the hell happened? Did he throw you over the side here?"

"No," she said, "that was my idea. He threatened me with a knife."

"Anybody you know?"

"Not exactly. Ow." He'd let a branch snap back into her face.

"Sorry." He didn't sound particularly remorseful.

"Care to tell me why you were following me?" she said, testing a branch with her soggy tennis shoe. She'd learned that Douglas fir was more stable than cedar, and less slippery when wet.

"I don't like it when I can't figure out what's going on," he said. "I especially get upset about it when I find out someone I have a routine interview with in Seattle winds up murdered."

"Jennifer Gilbert?"

"That's right. And I want to know who you are and what you're doing and who our friend was too. Is he mixed up in this, or is he just some loose cannon you took a ride with?"

"I think," said Jane, "that's he's mixed up in this."

"If you want a ride out of here," he said to her sternly, "you're going to have to tell me everything. Otherwise, you walk. And I saw a couple of bears going in. The place is lousy with them."

"I saw one too," she said. "A black bear. They're not very dangerous. We have them in Washington." She didn't add that they could get nasty when they had cubs.

He'd reached the top, and he was leaning over to pull her up after him. She felt like managing on her own, but she was too tired. She gave him her hand.

Standing there on top of the rock wall that flanked the turnaround, she glanced nervously down. The camper was gone. Instead, there was a white Ford. It had rental plates.

She looked at Steven Johnson. She supposed it was rather ungracious of her not to thank him. Presumably he'd scared off her assailant, and he'd tried to save her from drowning.

"Thank you," she said stiffly.

"You're welcome," he said with unsmiling dignity, as if he were starting their relationship over on a more civil basis.

She didn't smile either. She wanted to sit down, catch her breath, let all the adrenaline and fear that had been pumping through her subside, maybe even collapse on his shoulder, which would probably irritate him. She didn't let herself. She was wary of him, and paradoxically, she also wanted his respect. She wanted him to think she was competent and able to keep going. She wanted to think that about herself too.

"We need to talk," she said. "Brenda, the real one, is in danger." If his impulse had been to save her, presumably he'd feel the same way about Brenda.

"We can talk in the car," he said, scrambling down the other side of the rock wall. "I'm very curious about this guy with the knife. Who the hell is he?" She followed him, skidding down the rock. Her wet canvas shoes squeaked. "And I'm also curious about you," he added.

"We can turn the heater on in the car," he said. "Maybe dry out a little." When they got to the car, though, her heart sank.

"That son of a bitch," said Johnson, pounding the car's roof with his fist. All four tires were sliced up. He'd done it again.

"That's what he wanted to do with me," she said.

He got behind the wheel. "We'll go as far as we can on the rims," he said.

She slid in next to him. "Have you got the keys?" she said with alarm.

"No," he said sarcastically. "I left them down on that log where I found you. We'll have to go back." She believed him for a half second, but he pried the keys out of his wet trouser pocket and held them up in front of her face.

She started to laugh. Her laugh sounded a little giddy. Something about being inside a nice, shiny car made her feel as if she were already closer to civilization.

He put the key in the ignition. It made a small click.

She stopped laughing and he went out and popped the hood. She went out and stood next to him. Where the distributor cap was supposed to be, there was a collection of cut rubber hoses.

"I guess we do walk," he said. "I trust you're right about the bears."

"Whoever he is, he's getting more efficient," said Jane. "Tires *and* the distributor."

"Overkill. The guy's an amateur," said Johnson. He rummaged around in the car and came up with a canvas suitcase and a briefcase trimmed with leather. "Who knows when we'll get back here," he said. As an afterthought, he added the car rental folder from the glove box.

"How far do you think it is?" she said.

"Maybe eight, ten miles," he said. "We might get lucky and run into some logging vehicle. Can you make it? You can stay here if you want. Lock yourself in the car."

"You're thinking I'll slow you down," she said. "I promise I won't."

"I'm thinking you've been through a lot and you might not be in great shape. Emotionally, that is." His stupid remark to the creep in the Regency about what kind of physical shape she was in came back to her. After what she'd been through it didn't seem so important.

"I'm fine," she said. "I'm very angry and I want to get to Brenda before he does. I tend to fall apart after a crisis, not during it."

"Okay," he said.

They started out on the still path. She felt the gravel through the thin rubber soles of her shoes, and tried to walk in the tire tracks where the ground was smoother.

"Why are you looking for Brenda?" she said.

"An insurance scam. Health insurance," he said.

"So you work for an insurance company?"

"That's right. Why are you looking for her?"

"Because I thought she might know something about a murder. Jennifer might have been a witness. Brenda was her roommate. They had a big fight on the day in question. I thought she might know what Jennifer saw. Now I think Jennifer didn't see anything. But maybe Brenda did."

"Go on."

"Jennifer was a Christian Scientist. Sometimes they go to doctors anyway. But I just learned Jennifer was pretty strict. So what was she doing in a pharmacy, picking up a prescription?"

"If Jennifer was a Christian Scientist," he said, "she'd either be miraculously healed or she'd be dead. Because according to her health claims, she was a diabetic. Had to inject insulin every day."

"Do you think she let Brenda use her name and Social Security number for the insurance she had at work?" said Jane. "That's what I think."

"That's what I suspected," he said, as they trudged along. "And Jennifer confirmed it when I visited her in Seattle. She broke down in about fifteen minutes. She felt guilty as hell. But she didn't tell me anything about a murder in a pharmacy."

She turned to him. "I can't believe the insurance company would send you after poor Brenda just because they switched names. How much money are we talking about, anyway?"

"The insurance companies don't want anyone to know just how much fraud like this there is," he said. "They take it pretty seriously. People have been convicted for mail fraud, wire fraud, and conspiracy for pulling this same stunt." He sounded just a tiny bit defensive. She was glad he did.

"Seems kind of harsh, doesn't it?" said Jane.

"Someone else has to pay every time someone lies like that," said Johnson. "Look, everyone knows our health care system is a disaster. But when people lie and chisel it doesn't fix the system and it screws up everything else. Believe me."

"You're right. It all turned into something much worse. It all makes sense now," said Jane. "Brenda was impersonating Jennifer for the insurance. She was a student, sort of vaguely employed now and then. It must have been a shock for a Canadian to come to the States and find out there's no national health insurance. Jennifer had insurance, but she never used it."

"Sometimes policies cover Christian Science practitioners," he said. "So what happened in the pharmacy? Is that how you got involved? And who the hell is that guy in the camper? I got his plate number. It may not be too hard to find out who he is."

"I'll tell you who he is," said Jane. "At first I thought he was a hired thug for a dentist named Carlisle who wanted to keep his kid out of trouble. Now I believe his name is George Cox and he's a pharmacist who killed his wife."

Chapter 31

"He was looking for Brenda too," said Jane. "That first Brenda MacPherson in Tofino, the forager. She saw someone like that sitting outside her house. A bald guy in a camper. And then I ran into him at the other Brenda MacPherson's herb farm."

She turned to him, stopped in the stillness. "He didn't approve of her herbal medicine. He wouldn't. Being a pharmacist."

They started walking again. She told him about Kevin, about how he'd gone into the pharmacy, how Mrs. Cox had fired a shot at him. How juror number ten convicted him reluctantly for firing back and killing her, but noticed that magazine on the floor. How the prescription label led to Jennifer.

Johnson had been very patient, but now he said, "Jennifer, who was really Brenda, and who got scared because she knew if she was questioned they'd find out she was scamming an insurance company."

"That would explain why she left the scene—and the country."

"But what did she see?" said Johnson.

"I don't know. Maybe the killer doesn't know, but he's scared enough to have gone to Jennifer's and strangled her soon after Kevin's lawyer told him there might be a witness. We even asked him whose prescription label his wife was typing when she died." Jane tried not to think about that angle. They'd led him right to her.

"Maybe he was just trying to find out what Jennifer knew," Jane continued. "She'd just finished telling you about the fraud, there's no reason she wouldn't have been honest with him. He searched the place. And he took Brenda's picture from the wall. He must have known her by sight. After all, she was a customer at the pharmacy."

Johnson was blessedly silent. They both kept walking along purposefully. Something about the rhythm of their feet made it easy to think, made it easy to fit all the pieces into place.

It made a lot of sense. Mrs. Cox scares off Kevin. Mr. Cox comes in from the back room at the sound of the shot. His wife tells him what happened. He picks up the gun Kevin dropped and shoots her at point-blank range.

Jane described the scene as she imagined it. "Maybe it was just too tempting. There he is. Standing in front of her with a gun. All he has to do is say he came in a second later, after Kevin killed her. He sells off the pharmacy. Gets to go fishing whenever he wants."

"Probably collects some hefty life insurance," said Johnson. "But there are some problems with it. He'd have powder burns. The kid wouldn't. There might be prints on the murder weapon. And you say Brenda was sitting in there the whole time, reading a magazine?"

"Who knows what she saw?" said Jane. "The point is, it all fits. It wasn't until I started asking around that he went to see Jennifer in Seattle. And he would know right away it was the wrong Jennifer. He knew Brenda by sight, but he knew her as Jennifer. That's why all he had to do in Tofino is sit outside her house. Why all he had to do at the herb farm place was hear her name and eliminate her."

Jane frowned and tried to remember. "He was standing there while I gave her my story about finding another Brenda MacPherson. She told me about the one who was stripping at the Regency under the name Stephanie Chantal. And he must have got himself over there just after I did. In time to slash my tires. He heard my name at the herb farm. He knew I was working to clear Kevin."

"Mind telling me why you are doing that?" said Johnson.

"I was afraid you'd ask that," she said. "Can't it wait? We have to get to Brenda before he does. He could be in Port Hardy, killing her right now."

"She's not there," said Johnson. "She's due in a little place in Victoria. The Tip Top Club. As soon as I figured out she was Stephanie Chantal, it was easy." He opened his briefcase and pulled out an eight-by-ten glossy photograph. "Her booking agent is in Vancouver. I called him. They bicycle these girls around British Columbia on a circuit. She couldn't get along with one of the other girls in Port Hardy. Took off a few days. We can catch up with her, let her know this Cox character is after her."

"And find out what she saw," said Jane. She took the glossy photograph. Brenda was arched over backward in a modern-dance-looking pose. She had black curly hair, narrow, feline, dark-lashed eyes and good teeth. She was wearing a pair of five-inch spiked heels and a little chain around her waist. She had small, round breasts with dark nipples, which were smartly erect for the photograph, and long smooth haunches and muscular legs. One knee was coyly bent, which had the effect of moving her thigh forward and covering her crotch.

"What can you tell about her from this picture?" said Jane.

He looked over her shoulder. "She's not shy," he said. "And she's probably a pretty good dancer. Because she's more flat-chested than most of the women who do this. Hasn't bothered with implants."

"So you're saying there's a tit-to-talent ration in this business?" said Jane.

He shrugged. "You can judge for yourself when we get to Victoria. We've got a couple more hours on foot here, then we try to rent a car in Port Hardy and head south again. I don't know how long it will take with the RCMP."

"The RCMP," she said. "Why are we going to talk to them?"

"Because you've been assaulted, a murderer is running around loose, and you think he's stalking Brenda. It's very simple."

"I've got to take care of this myself," she said.

"Why? We've got plenty of time. Tell me why. Why you're involved in this and what you're doing."

"It'll cost me a job if I don't take care of this myself," she said.

"What kind of job?" he said. "Someone pays you to run around solving felony crimes outside the law. Give me a break."

"They haven't paid me yet," she said. She sighed. "It sounds screwy, I know. It was all my Uncle Harold's idea."

She told him. She told him about Uncle Harold's will and the board of trustees, and how she'd tried before to find and solve a hopeless case, and how the board had found it wanting. Surrounded by the twisted, alien land-scape, completely silent—even, it seemed now, devoid of birds—plodding together down that muddy gravel road, it seemed natural to tell him.

"It sounds flaky," he said.

"I want to do it," she said, now headily honest, completely unguarded, worn out, "because there doesn't seem to be anything else for me to do. I'm thirty-seven years old, I've had a million stupid jobs, nobody takes me seriously, I've been too broke too long. I want to be a respectable, attractive widow with a mysterious source of income. I want to put in a few weeks a year clearing up somebody's old mess—I'm not bad at it, really I'm not—then I want to relax and lead a pleasant life. Is that too much to ask? I don't mind being alone, I'm used to it. But why should I be broke and alone?"

"There are other ways to earn a living," he said.

"I've faced it," she said. "If I'd wanted to make something of myself, I would have done it long ago. Basically, without Uncle Harold, I'd just be Euro-trash with a maxed-out Visa card."

"So what kinds of jobs did you have?" He had a quirky little smile. He seemed to find her raffish past intriguing. This pleased her, but she found it rather irritating at the same time. It wasn't that cute that she'd never got on track.

She waved her hand dismissively. "When I bolted during my junior year abroad it was because I got myself a job as a governess. With some very rich French people. I liked that a lot actually. I'm still in touch with my little charges.

"Then I married, and just kind of racketed around. After my husband died, I found out his manager had siphoned off most everything. And a lot of it was in Brazilian currency. When it crashed, I went down with it." She shrugged. "I still have a nice old Jaguar in storage in London. And I get a case of Scotch every Christmas. A brand Bernardo endorsed."

"Bernardo?"

"He was a Formula One driver. Very famous in Europe. I got spoiled young. Afterward, I did a lot of things. I was a hand model." She held up her hands. "Very boring. You hold products—Q-Tips or nail polish bottles or crackers, and you have to move things very precisely if you're doing film or video and hold things very still if it's photography. Holding still like I did when I was pretending to be drowned."

She held her hands up over her head. "Right before you shoot, you hold the hands over your head so your veins drain."

"You do have nice hands," he said, inspecting them as she lowered them.

"Thank you. They were a little big for hand modeling, but the fingers are nice and long. I did a lot of other things too, and finally I ended up singing."

"You could do that again," he said.

"No I couldn't. I wasn't that good, to tell you the truth. I sang standards—Gershwin, Cole Porter. I got away with a lot because I was an American singing American stuff in Europe. If I tried it here, I'd probably get rolled over by any young kid in beaded chiffon from the lounge of any airport Holiday Inn."

She thought about this for a minute. "It's not that I didn't have a certain style. I know a lot about phrasing and making the lyric and the music work together. And my voice is sort of low and soothing. But I don't have a lot of range. And I'm getting older."

She looked over at him. "Does it sound like I'm whining?"

"It sounds like you're at a crossroads in your life," he said. "Some people can't hold a straight job. It's not in their nature."

"I know. I used to feel slick 'cause I made it by on my wits and my charm. Now I think I've been an idiot, but that Uncle Harold stepped in to save me. There's a lot of money at stake."

"And that's what keeps you going?"

"I'd lie if I said it didn't." She gave him a sidelong glance. "But there's more to it. It sounds kinds of corny, but I do understand what motivated Uncle Harold, although I think his style was probably a lot different. The fact is, there are a lot of jerks in the world, getting away with a lot. Because most people don't care or don't notice." She laughed. "Uncle Harold had a big engraving of Saint George wrestling with a dragon over the fireplace. I've kept it there."

She turned to him. "Why did you want to be a cop? I take it you did? You weren't lying about that, were you?"

"I think I wanted to be a cop because somebody has to do it," he said. "And I figured it might as well be me. I'm a pretty reasonable guy. At first, I actually liked it when I had my own little beat. There was a problem, I could take care of it. On the street, you make the decisions as they come along. Defuse situations. Calm everybody down. Make everything run smoothly. I started out pretty idealistically. Like all kids. But there was something else there. A kind of take-charge thing. I admit it. A feeling you know what's best. It can get out of hand."

"I usually think I know what's best for other people," said Jane. "Not for myself necessarily."

He laughed. "That's right. If you think about what you're supposed to be doing, you don't have time to sort everyone else out. Anyway, when you're a police officer, the higher up you go, the bigger hassles you have with administrators who think they know what's best—mostly for their own careers—and there's tons of paperwork and the money's not so hot, so I work for myself now. I have a couple of big clients. I work as much as I have to in order to make what I need to enjoy the free time."

They walked along in silence and clammy coldness a little longer. Her clothes weren't the least bit dry as far as she could tell. "Something about this landscape brings out revelation," said Jane. "When we were walking on that perfect little trail at the hot springs we didn't talk at all."

She looked around her. Aesthetically, this place was a

disaster. Burnt over, chopped up, messy, out of balance. The rain forest they'd walked through before looked planned. It had to have been. There had to have been some divine plan behind it. She thought of her Christmas card angel.

"When he was coming at me," she said, "I prayed for a guardian angel to come rescue me. I guess you were it. Plucking me out of the Devil's Bath."

"I'm no angel," he said, "any more than your uncle was Saint George. We're just a couple of people who mess around with bad stuff because we think we're supposed to."

"And we don't know what else to do," she said. "Listen, if the RCMP get involved," she said rather urgently, "they might scare off Brenda. I want a chance to talk to her. Let me call her and warn her. We can call the police in twenty-four hours."

"So you can get your hands on your uncle's money," he said.

"That's right. If I get paid, then I'm not an amateur anymore."

Chapter 32

Calvin Mason never liked it when the phone rang late at night like this. It generally wasn't good news. Good news could always wait. Late-night phone calls usually meant bailing out some sleazeball client, or some emergency with a tenant in the building he managed—a flood or electrical problems.

He let the machine answer.

"Calvin? This is Jane da Silva."

He picked it up and shouted over his own recorded voice. "Hang on, hang on." He turned on the light on the bed stand.

"Where the hell are you?" he said. "Did you get my message?"

"Port Hardy. At the northern tip of Vancouver Island. I'm staying in a hotel at the dock. A big trawler just came in and the elevator smells like fish. They've got a one-man band in the bar. Yes. I got your message and it helped me make sense of it all. I know who did it. I know who killed Mrs. Cox."

"You mean it wasn't Kevin?" he said.

"No, it was—"

"Stop!" he said. Did he want to know this? Maybe not, if she wasn't going to tell the police. If she was going to try to be some one-woman vigilante squad so she could get her hands on Uncle Harold's money.

"Stop? Don't you want to know? It's your client I'm saving here."

"Are we going to tell the cops about this?" he said.

"That's why I'm calling. I want you to get to work doing whatever you have to do to get the State of Washington to extradite him."

"Where is he? Who is he?"

"He's Mr. Cox. The pharmacist," she said. "I think he killed his wife, Betty. And I think he's still on Vancouver Island. Kevin dropped the gun. Cox picked it up, shot his wife and called the police. Tell me again, did he say he saw Kevin do it?"

"No. He said he came out of the back room and the deed was done."

"That's because Kevin had left and he never really saw him. And maybe because he didn't want the police to find Kevin. It would have been better for Cox if it had been some mysterious robber who fled the scene."

"Did Brenda tell you all this? She wasn't even there."

"No. I haven't found her yet. That is, I've found her but I haven't reached her yet. Calvin, Cox tried to kill me. I'm pretty sure he killed Jennifer. And Brenda was there. She was impersonating Jennifer so she could use her health insurance."

Calvin thought for a moment. "There weren't any powder burns on Cox."

"There weren't any on Kevin, either. And he's sitting in Monroe."

"Start at the beginning," he said.

"I can't, I have to get some sleep. I have to get the moss out of my hair. We have to get up early and get down island."

"We?"

"I hooked up with an insurance investigator. He scared off Cox and tried to rescue me from drowning, but I wasn't really drowning—at a lake called the Devil's Bath—the most godforsaken spot—we had to walk out of there on their weird logging road because Cox ripped out the distributor and slashed the tires. It's a long, long story. We got to the main road—thank God we didn't run into any bears—and hitched a ride with a mill hand into Port Hardy and we can't get a rental car till tomorrow morning."

Chumped again. Here he was, getting beat up on some dentist's lawn and putting in time fixing Carol's garbage disposal and she was shacked up with some slick son of a bitch in Port Hardy.

"Who is this guy exactly?"

"His name's Steven Johnson. The main thing is he knew that Brenda had been using Jennifer's insurance. Actually, he's the guy who visited Jennifer before she was killed."

"Terrific!" said Calvin. "He probably strangled her. He's probably working for that slimy dentist. Jane, the guy you're with is a person of interest to the police here. I got that from a reliable source in the department. I have half a mind to call the Mounties and send them over to that fishy hotel. How are you registered? As Mr. and Mrs. Smith?"

"I already turned him over to the Mounties once," she said. "He talked his way out of it. He's an ex-cop. He convinced them he was perfectly legit and he talked to the Seattle police already and he's going to come in and tell them everything he knows when we get back to Seattle."

She sounded completely sold on the guy.

"And besides," she added, "he wanted to go to the Mounties himself. I talked him out of it because I said you'd be telling the whole story to the Seattle police in the morning."

"Be careful," he said. "Really, Jane, this whole thing sounds very screwy."

"I can hardly wait to see you and tell you everything," she said. "I think I did it this time. I think I found a hopeless case. We just have to nail Cox and get a new trial for Kevin. How long will that take? Do you think the board will give me the money before he's acquitted?"

"You sound kind of manic," he said. "I think I'd better get up there. I can get a float plane from Lake Union. Meet you somewhere on the island. Or I can get one from Lake Washington that lands up at some of those salmon resorts."

"No," she said. "I need you down there. See if you can figure a way around those powder burns. After I talk to Brenda, I'll know more. I'll call you after that."

"When are you going to catch up with her?"

"I can't get in touch with her. We tried. But I'll see her tomorrow. All of her. She starts stripping at noon at the Tip Top Club in Victoria."

"Sounds like a great witness," said Calvin. "Call in, will you? Let me know what you're up to."

"I will. Talk to you soon. Bye. You're wonderful," she said.

He didn't like that last "you're wonderful" one bit. It felt like a pat on the head. And he hated himself for being jealous and making that Mr. and Mrs. Smith crack. He really doubted the guy was a strangler. After all, the RCMP had let him go, and they had pretty broad powers up there.

He sighed and looked over at good old Marcia, who slept through anything. Marcia was a beautician, so she changed her hair all the time. At the moment, it was red and curly, and splayed out over the pillow, except for one curl that clung damply to her cheek.

Not without tenderness, he brushed it away, turned out the light and reflected that it was completely illogical and unfair of him to get bent out of shape about Jane da Silva fooling around with a boring insurance guy. But there was never any logic or fairness to these things.

• • •

After she hung up, Jane, wearing a T-shirt of Steven Johnson's, fell back on the bed. Her legs ached from the hike, even after the hot bath she'd had. Calvin Mason, she was sure, imagined her now making riotous love with Steven Johnson, who was safely down the hall in his own room, having kindly lent her some clothes. She had kissed him lightly on the cheek, in a sort of cocktail-party greeting way at her door, and thanked him.

It felt rather glorious to be all alone in a locked room, away from Mr. Cox and his knife or wild animals. Grooming instincts took over. She had rinsed out her own clothes and thrown them over the towel rack, taken a hot bath and washed her hair with a bar of soap, and picked out most of the shreds of moss.

After they'd checked in, they had eaten very tasty burgers and fries—nice and greasy the way she liked them—washed down with Scotches in the hotel pub, and watched the one-man band—a pale young man in shredded jeans and a tank top who sang seventies rock tunes as he played the guitar with his hands and kicked at various mechanisms connected to computers and synthesizers with his scuffed boots to create prerecorded drum rolls and more guitar licks. Some of the trawler crew shot pool behind them and some local Natives sat primly at the tables drinking beer.

She had managed to convince Johnson not to call the cops until after they'd talked to Brenda, mostly by playing on his desire to see the job through and give her a chance to interview Brenda. She also pointed out that they hadn't been able to find her, so the police probably couldn't either. When he finally caved in, she thought it was probably from exhaustion.

Phone calls to the Tip Top Club had elicited the information that Brenda would be staying in rooms above the bar when she arrived for a week's engagement, but she hadn't arrived yet and wasn't due until noon the next day.

Right before she fell asleep, the synthesized bass line from the one-man band reverberating a little through the floorboards, it occurred to her she was just a little irked he hadn't come on to her now that they were back in civilization. She realized it was mostly her own vanity that made her feel that way. Although, it might be rather pleasant to be curled up with him right now, after all they'd been through together.

The next day they got a rental car with cruise control and a terrific sound system. He drove fast and she slept for a while, then woke up, and feeling sort of teenaged-middle-aged crazy now that they were getting so close to Brenda, she sang along to old Motown songs on the radio. He told her she had a good voice and was just as good as anyone in the lounge at any airport Holiday Inn, and added that she looked good in his rolled-up, cinched-in jeans and dark blue shirt, which cheered her up immensely.

They arrived at the Tip Top Club in Victoria, tucked away on a street just a few blocks away from the teacup shops and kilt emporiums aimed at the tourists, but in a block the tourists never penetrated.

A flapping fabric sign outside the building read, AMATEUR NIGHT—SUN. NOON. The bar was in an old hotel, a squat stucco building that looked like it had served commercial travelers in the premotel era. There was a hand-lettered sign that said ROOMS in a smudgy upstairs window, a handsome old carved doorway, its lines obscured by a dozen coats of paint, and a couple of windows with neon beer signs. A reader board stuck out from above the door. It proclaimed, LESLIE 44DD WED.

"Amateur Night at noon is an oxymoron," said Jane as they pulled up in front. She turned to him. "I'm nervous."

"About meeting Brenda?"

"No. About going into a stripper bar. I'll be the only woman there. I know it's dumb. I mean, this is a matter of life and death, but still—all those men."

"Don't be ridiculous," he said. "They won't be watching you. These are red-blooded Canadian men. They'll be watching naked women on the stage, seeing as it isn't hockey season."

Inside there was a beautiful old mahogany bar, cluttered up with more neon beer signs. The bartender had black hair, slicked back into a ponytail.

The rest of the bar had been cheaply remodeled, and consisted of raised tiers of tables and chairs. Like an island in the center of the large room was a stage about table height. There were four brass poles at each corner, a row of blinking lights around the perimeter, and, off to one side, a cheap-looking fiberglass tub and shower. It reminded Jane of something a parsimonious landlord would install.

The place was about half full of men—many of them alone, some with a friend or two. It was your basic T-shirt and tractor cap crowd, with a few military men in uniform. There was an Asian man in the corner, sitting with a long-suffering little woman who appeared to be his wife. A lot of them seemed to be eating lunch—hamburgers and sandwiches.

"It'll be better if you ask for her," he said, leading them

to a table near the back. "I can't imagine they let the customers at the girls."

"We should wait till her set is over," said Jane.

They sat down, and a waitress with sturdy legs, wearing a T-shirt and black drawstring shorts, white socks and tennis shoes, and looking like someone from a college PE class, came over and took their order for two Kokanee beers. They hadn't had lunch yet, so Johnson ordered a French dip sandwich; Jane went for a basket of prawns and chips.

The beer arrived at about the same time a disc jockey's voice announced the arrival of Melanie. Jane, who had vague notions of satin gloves and beaded evening gowns, long red nails and eye shadow, was fascinated to see that Melanie looked well scrubbed and wholesome.

She was blonde, about nineteen or twenty, with minimal makeup and long silky-looking hair, short pale nails. She danced around a little to some vaguely disco-ish music, looking like a teenage baby-sitter.

Within seconds she had peeled off her clothes. She had started out in a little navy blue short knit skirt and a stretchy white blouse with three buttons that showed her nipples through the fabric. It was an outfit a teenager might wear to the mall, except for the five-inch spikes. Underneath, she had on a lacy white thong.

She danced around some more, twirling herself around the poles and landing bouncily on her spikes, shaking her hips, gathering her hair up on her head and letting it spill back down, smiling like a cheerleader. Once in a while, she pinched her pale nipples between thumb and forefinger, with an accompanying stylized rolling of the eye, flung-back head and toss of her silky hair.

All the while, the men sat hunkered over their hamburgers and beer. They were hardly a bunch of frenzied animals. They'd just managed a few whoops when the skirt and blouse had come off and she'd deposited them in a neat little pile on one side of the stage. They showed a little more polite interest when she peeled off the scrap of white lace between her legs and tossed it neatly with her other two items of clothing. Now she was down to her heels, and she pranced around some more, tossing her head like a pony and occasionally running her hands over herself.

Her pubic hair was trimmed to a neat blonde oblong. Jane suspected it was bleached to match.

She turned to Johnson. "She looks so wholesome," she said. He was paying more attention to his French dip than the stage. "Like the girl next door if the girl next door had a great body."

"And tore off her clothes," he added. "They look sleazier in the States," he said. "Even though they have to keep a G-string on. At home they make their money on tips. Here, I understand, they get a salary. It's a little less demeaning, I suppose."

He took a sip of his Kokanee. "I had to do a surveillance once on a guy who hung out at these places all the time. I got pretty sick of it. It got so I got excited when the girls put their clothes back on. And the drinks were terrible."

Jane smiled at him. He was looking at her rather earnestly. "Yes," she said, "and it's very sweet of you to maintain eye contact with me, but seeing as we're here, I really won't be offended if you look. I know it's sleazy, but she is very pretty." Jane had made a mental note to start working out again seriously as soon as she got home. Melanie didn't have an ounce of flab on her anywhere. Everything was smooth, tight and perfectly proportioned. Jane watched the men surveying all the dancer's body parts. They could have been at a horse auction, looking for breeding stock.

He laughed. "You want to hit a couple more places after we find Brenda?"

Melanie had now fetched a blanket, a homey sort of quilt that you might take on a picnic, and she spread it out on the stage, rather like a housewife throwing a tablecloth on the table.

"I've heard about these Canadian stripper bars," he said. "They call that row of guys right at the edge of the stage gynecology row."

"You're kidding," said Jane.

Melanie crawled around on her hands and knees for a while, a maneuver that only someone with perfect breasts could carry off with any panache, keeping her spiked shoes up in the air, rolled over a few times like a puppy dog in front of the fire, and then lay on her back and spread her knees as if she were about to get a pap smear.

A foot in front of her, a customer shoved aside his paper plate with his hamburger and fries remains and lit a cigarette, gazing thoughtfully at her crotch.

"That guy looks like he's watching TV," said Jane, horrified yet fascinated.

"Probably a regular. All numbed out."

Melanie parted her labia and made a few unconvincing masturbatory gestures, before springing perkily up and folding her blanket neatly after the music ended.

The disembodied disc jockey voice suggested that with some applause, Melanie could be convinced to step into the shower. A round of polite clapping brought on a big smile, and she stepped over to the plumbing display and wet herself down with a European-style hand-held shower, rinsed out her hair, shimmied a little in the spray, sat on the edge of the plastic tub, bounced a little, acted playful and childlike in the water, then stepped daintily out and toweled briskly off like someone in a locker room and clambered neatly into her mall outfit once again. She walked out of the bar, carrying her little quilt, and looking once again like a sweet young girl, albeit with a slightly sulky expression. The sight of the fully clothed, not terribly attractive customers stuffing french fries into their faces while they inspected Melanie's reproductive organs made the whole thing grotesque and silly. Melanie, however, did have a great body, and it was well lit. In fact, despite the tackiness of it all, her white young body managed to look pure somehow, even in the noisy, sleazy surroundings.

"Is it my imagination," she said, bemused, "but is there something rather innocent, refined and Canadian about Melanie's act? She managed, somehow, to look like a virgin."

He smiled. "I bet she isn't."

Jane laughed. "Well, then she's probably preorgasmic."

"Maybe. But these guys don't care."

"Do I sound envious? I don't mean that at all. I just think it's interesting that she's too young to have much style. Maybe I'm kidding myself," she said, "but I think my old retro torch act, in which I remained fully clothed and vertical throughout, had sexier moments."

She realized as soon as she said it she sounded vain and defensive, when she was really feeling bemused and analytical—trying to make sense of it all.

"I'm sure you managed to raise the tension level in the room," he said. "With your knowing sly moves, your voice, your fully clothed but very nice body"—he put down his beer and touched the tips of her fingers—"and your pretty hands."

Had he thought she was threatened, envious, fishing for compliments? "Perhaps. But I doubt these guys would have bought it. You're very sweet," she said, running her hand through her hair and trying to sound self-possessed. "Maybe I'm overanalyzing something very simple."

"Melanie's act is simple," he said. "Yours is more complex."

He'd used the present tense. Was every woman on all the time, Jane wondered. Can we help it? Is it our fault, or theirs? Can we ever stop seeing ourselves through men's eyes?

But she didn't get a chance to think about it much longer. The DJ's voice boomed into the room. "And now, gentlemen, from Vancouver, returning to the Tip Top Club—I know you've been waiting for her—the very lovely and exciting Stephanie Chantal."

"Brenda!" she whispered. She had indeed been waiting for her for a long time.

Chapter 33

Dorothy's mother didn't ask too many questions. She'd been as delighted as he thought she'd be. Calvin had simply called her. "Mrs. Fletcher? My name is Calvin Mason. I understand you have some papers you'd like served on Sean Carlisle."

"Yes, yes," she squealed. "Where is he?"

"I have reason to believe he's coming in on a flight from Denver this Saturday."

Damn. Why had he told her that? But he supposed he had to come up with something reasonable, or she wouldn't think he could help her.

"I don't suggest you serve him yourself," he said. "I'm an attorney. I'll make sure it's done properly." He paused. "My associate, Mrs. da Silva, gave me the impression you aren't represented in this matter."

"Not really," she said cautiously.

"Well I'll just serve him, then we can talk about any further work you might need later," he said casually.

The way he figured it, he could worm his way in there pretty easy. After all, he'd found the guy. No one else had been able to do that. A nice fat paternity suit, with a line of credit from Dr. Carlisle, might not be bad at all. Calvin was sick of these low-rent cases he always got mixed up in.

Now that it seemed Sean didn't have anything to do

with Kevin and the murder at the Cox Pharmacy, he may as well try and salvage something. Calvin congratulated himself on his ingenuity.

"Uh, okay," she said. "I've got it all here."

"Fine," he said. "You can drop it in the mail to me, or I can pick it up, if you want."

"I can come by your office," she said.

Calvin usually tried to avoid that since he didn't like people to know he operated out of his living room.

"Do you work downtown?" he said.

"Yes. In the Smith Tower."

"Perfect," he said. "I'll be in court tomorrow." This was a big lie but it made him sound busy and professional. "I can come down at a break in the proceedings and pick it up."

Now he was standing there at the airline gate, looking up at the monitor that said the flight was on time, when he saw Carlisle and his wife and daughter.

He ducked behind an espresso stand. He didn't know why he was being so cagy; they'd find out soon enough, but it was awkward.

He was skulking there, thinking about buying himself a latte, when he saw him. The guy who'd laid him away on Carlisle's lawn.

The man saw him too.

He came over to him.

"Hey buddy," he said. "You aren't the process server, are you? No hard feelings, I hope."

"Who are you?" said Calvin. A nice-looking woman in her forties and a sulky teenager with a baby on her hip came up behind him.

"Mr. Mason," said the woman. "I'm Barb Fletcher. And this is Dorothy and Charlie. And my"—she grimaced a little—"my ex-husband, Norman."

"Please to meet you all," he said warily.

"Mom didn't want us to come, but I wanted to see Sean," said Dorothy.

"And I wanted to see Sean too," said Norman.

"Don't hit him the way you hit me," said Calvin firmly. "It won't help your case."

"Dad!" wailed Dorothy. "You hit him."

"I thought he was that bum Carlisle," said Norm shamefacedly. "He pulled out of his marked parking slot and I followed him to Carlisle's house."

"Norman is a little overzealous," explained Barb in a confidential tone. "He's been out of our lives for years, but when he heard what happened to Dorothy and this Sean being so irresponsible and all, he got himself involved."

"That's sweet," said Calvin, "but you'd better not go assaulting people from now on. There's some free legal advice for you."

Dorothy checked her watch. "Shouldn't we be at the gate?"

"No!" said Calvin. "Let me handle this!"

But she had drifted off with the baby on her hip.

Calvin maneuvered around away from the espresso stand. "Well, maybe you can help ID him," he said.

He recognized Sean as he got off the plane. He was scruffy and unshaven, and he had a big duffel bag on his shoulder. The kid looked like he'd been to war or something.

Before his own parents and sister could greet him, Dorothy had made her way up to him.

Sean stood there, looking at Dorothy with a bemused face, then he reached out a hand. The baby reached out and touched him. Calvin hustled over there. "Sean Carlisle?" he said, slapping the papers at him.

A second later, the dentist and his wife were standing there.

"Sean," said his mother, embracing him with tears in her eyes.

"This is Dorothy, Mom," he said.

The dentist scuttled up looking horrified. Sean's sister had a nasty little smirk on her face.

Sean's mother looked down at the baby on Dorothy's hip and burst into tears. "He's beautiful," she said.

Behind him, Dorothy's parents were whispering. "Just stay out of it," said Barb. "Let them work it out."

"Where have you been, Sean?" said Dorothy shyly.

"Wilderness survival camp. My parents made me. It's supposed to straighten you out. We killed weasels and stuff and ate 'em. It was awesome."

He looked back down at Charlie. "I thought about this little guy when I was out there in the woods," he said. "I thought about him a lot. I'm really glad you're here."

Calvin felt his whole case slipping away.

Chapter 34

Brenda didn't look like the girl next door. She was smaller than Jane had thought from her photograph—but perfectly proportioned. But then, her old landlord Art Deco had said that she was too short to get a lot of dancing jobs.

She came strutting in wearing a turquoise blue beaded cocktail dress with long sleeves and pearl drop earrings—hardly the girl next door. More like the young trophy wife overdressed for a charitable event and unwittingly alienating all the first wives.

The dress was held together by one button on her hip. She undid it in a flash, slithered out of it and flung it dramatically down on the ground, raising up her arms in a vaguely Martha Graham gesture. She was now wearing a matching turquoise one-piece garment cut in a big scoop to and up the sides of both hips in back, and slashed in front to five inches or so below her navel. And, of course, she kept her five-inch spikes on.

Which made it all more spectacular when she executed a back flip. Brenda was no slouch when it came to athletic ability. The guys applauded appreciatively. Jane also reflected that Brenda was no dummy when it came to choosing a costume. Having seen her publicity shot, it was clear her legs were her strong suit—she had a dancer's body, all right—and her outfit showed off her best assets.

Unlike Melanie, she didn't smile. She had a purposeful, serious look on her face. Her choreography—undulating arms, high kicks, back bends—had a fluidity about it, and she knew how to hold her head and neck to create a long line. Flinging herself at the brass poles, she managed to get herself practically airborne as she twirled around them as if she were being lifted in a pas de deux.

"She can really dance," said Jane.

"I told you so," said Johnson.

The waitress came over to take away their plates.

"Excuse me," said Jane, as the waitress picked them up. "Could you get a message to Brenda. Stephanie, I mean?"

The waitress looked suspiciously at the two of them. She probably thinks we want her for some kinky threesome, thought Jane. She glanced over at the stage. Brenda was on her knees, leaning back with her eyes closed, in a modern-dance-like attitude of prayerful ecstasy, and tweaking her small brown nipples back up.

Jane knew what Brenda would like. "I'm writing a piece for *Dance Magazine* about really good erotic choreography," she said to the waitress. "I'd like to interview her."

The girl shrugged. "*Dance Magazine,* eh? Is that the stripper magazine that comes out of Vancouver?"

"No," said Jane. "It's a magazine out of New York, about all kinds of dance." She wasn't sure it came out of New York. All she really knew was its name.

"I'll tell her. She keeps a lot to herself, though," sniffed the waitress with disapproval.

"Tell her I think she's a serious artist, and would very much appreciate the chance to talk with her."

The girl rolled her eyes. "A serious artist," she repeated deadpan. "You want some more beers?"

"*Dance Magazine,*" said Johnson thoughtfully after he

had paid her, smiling nicely, and overtipped her by a blue five-dollar bill, and she left. "She'll talk to you. But she probably would have talked to that stripper magazine out of Vancouver too."

Jane wasn't looking forward to breaking it to Brenda that she really wanted to talk about the Cox Pharmacy, but she had to make sure she got the interview. "If I told her her life was in danger she'd think I was nuts," said Jane.

"That's right. You did the right thing. Sometimes, the truth just doesn't work."

"I've discovered I'm a pretty good liar," said Jane.

"You didn't fool me with that Persian miniature stuff," he said. "But you're pretty good. It's a matter of finding the right button to push. With her, it's probably art."

Brenda had shed her second garment and was now down to her shoes and earrings. She was bent over at the waist, tossing her thick, Scottish-looking mane of black hair around. Her skin was very white with a tracing of blue veins on her breasts. Jane suddenly felt very sorry for her.

Apparently, crawling around on all fours and pelvic floor work were part of the standard finale. Brenda enhanced it all with some balletic splits, then cartwheeled over to her clothes.

She slipped back into the dress, flung the Lycra number over one shoulder and clicked her way back through the bar on the spikes. Jane marveled at how she moved around in them. They must be glued to her feet.

She avoided any eye contact as she left. The guys gave her furtive looks. Melanie had smiled at the customers on her way out, and a few of them had said hello to her.

At the door out of the room, the waitress, a tray on her shoulder, leaned over and whispered to Brenda. She looked over at their table. Jane gave a little nod.

Brenda whispered something back to the waitress and went through the door.

The waitress took her time coming back to their table. When she did, she said, "You can go up and talk to her if you want. I'll show you the way in a sec." She looked over at Johnson. "You'll have to stay, though. We just changed the rules. No guys in the rooms. We had a bad experience last week."

"And now," boomed the DJ, "we've got a talented amateur, dying to show you gentlemen just what she's got. Remember, Lorraine St. James, last year's Rookie of the Year, started out at an amateur night right here in Victoria. Do you think this young lady's got what it takes? Give Sylvia a real warm Tip Top welcome."

Thankfully, the waitress came and got Jane just then. She didn't think she could stand to see Sylvia strut her stuff. She came on to the strains of "Shake That Body," wearing a short, cheap red negligee and a terrified smile.

An unprepossessing young man with a scrofulous complexion, presumably her boyfriend, was egging her on from gynecology row. "Just like we practiced, babe," he said, foreseeing, Jane imagined, years of sitting around drinking beers and watching his meal ticket shake her tits and grab her crotch.

The waitress pulled a key from her apron. As she unlocked the door she said a little defensively, "I clean up after them. It doesn't look clean but it is, it's just old."

"What are they like to clean up after?" said Jane.

The girl clicked her tongue. "I had to clean vomit out of the tub yesterday. They're just filthy. There's no point having it nice up there, they'd just wreck it."

She stepped aside and gestured up some narrow wooden stairs. "She's in the room on the right."

Jane believed the girl tried to keep it clean. There was a strong Lysol smell on the painted wooden stairs.

The hall was papered in ancient smudged yellowed wallpaper veined with silver. There were three wooden doors, one of which looked original. Jane knocked on the door to her right. She looked down at the worn seventies red and black tweed shag carpeting at her feet, which looked like it had been recycled from somebody's rec room.

On the wall, written in a schoolgirlish hand and framed neatly like a diploma, were the house rules. Jane read the first four.

1. Be on time for your dance. You will be docked if you are late.
2. Treat staff with respect.
3. No overnight visitors.
4. Door to the bar to be kept locked at all times.

Jane wondered if the Tip Top was in violation of Canadian laws on bilingualism, seeing as the rules didn't appear in French as well.

Brenda opened the door. She was now wearing faded denim cut-offs, a T-shirt and sneakers. She looked completely devoid of any glamour and pleased to see Jane.

"Hi. I'm Jane da Silva."

"I'm Brenda. Stephanie Chantal is just a stage name. We have to have 'em in this business. Come in."

She slapped one hip and gestured expansively with the other hand. "Sorry about the surroundings. I guess they figure we have to suffer for our art," she said with bravado. She was small and young-looking. Jane had a maternal impulse to help her pack everything up in her suitcase and yank her right out of here.

The old hotel room was worse than anything Jane had ever seen outside of a documentary about slum life. There was a chewed-up carpet, a narrow iron bed, unmade, with rumpled white sheets and an army blanket, a dingy, spongy tomato red sofa that looked as if animals had gnawed off all the corners, and a Formica coffee table of fake blond wood with cigarette burns all over the surface.

The wallpaper was the same filthy yellow stuff as in the hall, but in here it was used as a scratch pad. There were a few phone numbers written on it, and some arithmetic. The floor was covered with thin coconut matting, and there was an old radiator, presumably an original fixture, painted in metallic silver. A mirror, the kind usually attached to the inside of a closet, with one corner broken off, was leaning against a wall. Through an open door she saw a dismal bathroom with a big claw-footed tub. There were some wet towels on the floor.

On the opposite wall hung a very bad sepia-colored tourist painting of Venice. An old sash window was partly open, but the place still smelled of must, Canadian cigarettes and Lysol. An old cracked manila window shade hung at half mast. Outside, there was a view of a brick wall, framed by a fire escape.

"Not real glamorous," said Jane. "I kind of expected a dressing room with big mirrors surrounded by lights, like in the movies."

"Ha!" said Brenda. "It's a very sleazy business. But I can make fourteen hundred a week, eh." She was trying to sound tough and brave, but she had the same genteel accent and well-enunciated, ladylike tones Jane had come to associate with Canadian women. "Still, I'm dancing, right? I'm really interested in your article. Is it about strippers?"

"Erotic choreography," said Jane. "I could tell you were a real dancer. Do you like the work?"

Brenda eagerly indicated the hideous sofa and sat herself down on the bed. She produced a red pack of

Craven A's and lit the stubby little Canadian cigarette with a disposable lighter. "Like I said. It's fourteen hundred a week, and you just do three or four fifteen-minute sets a shift. I don't want to do it forever. I'm saving to go to Toronto and study there. And I get to dance. I'm trained for that."

She took on a look of pinched dignity. "It's not like in the States. They pay us every week in cash. Of course, they tell Revenue Canada how much they pay us, which is a real pain, but we get decent money.

"I'd never do this in the States. There, they tuck money in your G-string and you have to do gross stuff—table dancing and sticking out your tongue and stuff." She wrinkled up her nose. "That's why the American girls with some class put up with dodging Immigration to work here. A lot of them down there are hookers. Which is ironic, isn't it, seeing as they make them keep their underwear and that on?"

Brenda seemed eager to explain. "These guys aren't allowed to touch us. They make a move across those blinking lights and they get chucked right out. All they can do is blow on you. I hate that. They blow on you, all beery and that, but they can't touch you."

"Is there anything you can't do onstage?" said Jane.

Brenda laughed. "A few things. We can't insert anything. And we can't get too graphic in the duos—you know, two girls. We can't both be nude at the same time."

"Who are these guys? Do you ever go out with them?"

Brenda snorted. "Are you kidding? They're total jerks. Take a look at them. They're pretty stupid too. They ask you if you get turned on when you're out there. I'm so sure! We're basically thinking about our shopping list or something, eh." She cocked an eyebrow.

"You're a very good dancer," said Jane.

"Thank you," said Brenda rather primly. "A lot of them do appreciate someone who can actually dance."

Brenda leaned forward. "But I'm good at it. I really am. And I'm growing as an artist. I try out a lot of stuff on these jerks—not that they'd appreciate it. I mean, the fact is, what they really mostly want is to look at my cunt. But there really is a lot to be learned out there."

"I'm not from *Dance Magazine*," said Jane. "I'm sorry. But I had to find a way to talk to you."

Brenda stiffened and started to say something, but Jane rolled right over her. "I had to come and warn you. Someone's killed Jennifer, your old roommate in Seattle. And he's probably after you."

"Oh my God,'" said Brenda. She let her cigarette fall to the floor and put one hand against her cheek. She looked like a little child.

Jane picked up the cigarette and handed it back to her.

"I know you used her insurance. And when you did, you went to the Cox Pharmacy. You saw something, Brenda."

"No I didn't. I didn't see anything."

"You were reading a magazine, and a guy came in with a gun."

"That's right. And the lady took out another gun and fired. I think she fired in the air. The guy ran out and I ran out after him. You Americans are crazy, always shooting guns. I was scared."

"And you were scared that if you stuck around they'd find out about the insurance."

"Well naturally. If there was an inquiry or something. But tell me about Jennifer. What happened?"

"She was strangled. Someone came into her apartment, your old apartment in the University District, and strangled her."

"Oh my God," said Brenda again. She crushed out her

smoke in a glass ashtray and then held her stomach and bent over. After a moment she said, "I'm not sorry about the insurance, okay. I mean Jennifer never used it, and I needed it. It's terrible in the States if you haven't got insurance. I'm a diabetic, eh, and I had to cut down my insulin to make it last longer. I went into shock. I was in hospital, and Jennifer said I could use her name and Social Security number."

"Did he drop the gun?" said Jane. She reached out a hand and touched Brenda's shoulder.

"Yes. Nobody got hurt, so I figured it didn't matter. Just a bunch of crazy Americans pulling guns on each other. But the whole thing shook me up so much I just came home."

"I think," said Jane, "that the lady's husband came in from the back room and shot her with the gun the kid dropped. And now he thinks you might have seen something."

"But I didn't. I just saw the guy, a skinny kid he was, drop the damn gun and run out. And I dropped the magazine and ran away."

Brenda began to cry. "Jennifer wasn't a bad person. She didn't even want to do the switch. She just felt sorry for me when I was in hospital. Of course, she thought anything could be cured with thoughts and that, but she still felt sorry for me. We weren't really that close or anything, but I feel so bad.

"Jennifer was kind of lonely. She thought I was a better friend than I was. I guess I used her."

She looked back up and talked through her tears. "We had a fight about it. I came back and told her what I saw and she said we had to stop lying. But no one got hurt. I explained that to her, and she was so religious and all. She said we had to admit I wasn't her. It wasn't just the insulin and the hospital bill. I had surgery on my foot too.

It was a lot of money. I just took off. She got upset, but what could I do? I just wanted to get back home where you're allowed to get sick."

She sniffed. "I could use a drink."

"Want me to go down and get something at the bar?" said Jane.

Brenda went over to a beat-up dresser and picked up some keys with a big antique brass hotel tag on them. "There's a bottle of tequila behind the bar. It's my bottle. Bring it up, okay? The little key's for the door at the bottom of the stairs. Gosh, I don't know what to do."

Jane wanted to help her decide what to do. And if the tequila helped, fine.

"You won't take off or anything, will you?" Jane said.

"No, I've got another dance in an hour," Brenda answered. Then she said, "Damn, I can't believe this. I didn't see anything."

"In this case," said Jane, "what you didn't see can clear an innocent man—and maybe convict a guilty one."

Chapter 35

Jane went down the stairs. They squeaked. She locked the door to the bar after her. She noticed Melanie and another young woman sitting by themselves in a corner, underneath a booth where the disc jockey held forth. The two girls were drinking and giggling. Melanie had her hair tied up in a ponytail and wore a sweatshirt. All the glamour in this business was reserved for the tiny area surrounded by blinking lights.

She looked over at the table where she'd been sitting. Johnson wasn't there. She'd thought of going over and giving him a progress report, but she was glad she didn't have to. Brenda was at a vulnerable point right now. Jane thought she could convince her to come away with her to Seattle and tell her story.

Jane was even willing to try and keep Johnson out of it. If the consequences of Brenda's insurance scam would keep her from coming back to the States to testify, she'd have to find a way to call off Johnson. If she couldn't, she realized she'd have to find a way to get Brenda there without him knowing.

She leaned across the bar. "Stephanie's tequila, please," she said. "And a couple of glasses."

The bartender handed it all over. "She better not

overdo it," he said snidely. "She's got another dance coming up."

Walking back up the stairs, she realized ditching Johnson now would require finesse and nerves of steel. He'd helped her a lot. In fact, he was financing her, now that she was separated from her purse and belongings, which were still, presumably, in Cox's camper.

She bit her lip. It wasn't going to be easy. But she couldn't give up now. She'd work out some kind of deal with Johnson. There had to be a way to do it. It seemed pretty cheesy to nail someone who went into the hospital because she was trying to save money on a drug she needed to stay alive. American medicine, Jane decided, was barbaric. It had made people lie, and because of it, Cox got away with murder. Almost.

She knocked on Brenda's door. There wasn't any answer. Damn, she thought. Maybe she'd bolted. Jane pushed open the door.

Brenda was lying on the bed. On top of her, one leg across her knees to stop her from kicking, was a man, with his hands wrapped around her throat. Brenda was limp, and her face was beet red.

"No!" shouted Jane. She rushed at him, and he turned to look at her. It was George Cox. He let go of Brenda.

Jane dropped the glasses and held the tequila bottle with two hands over her head.

He jumped off the bed and stood looking at her for a second, then, with a quick movement into the pocket of his windbreaker, he produced the knife.

He stood there in a half crouch with the knife in his hand, a burly old man standing there like a teenage street fighter. But he didn't come any closer.

She knew he had her. The tequila bottle wasn't any match for the knife. Even if she managed to bring it down on his head, she was sure she wouldn't be able to knock him out like in the movies.

"Keep quiet," he said. "Or I'll cut you up like I cut up your tires."

She should have screamed by now. But would anyone hear her? From downstairs the rock music bounced. They wouldn't hear a thing down there. And the walls in these old buildings were so thick.

"You thought I drowned, didn't you?" she said, taking a step backward. It was the wrong move. He stepped forward.

From the corner of her eye, she saw a movement on the bed. Brenda had raised one knee. She was alive. Jane didn't dare take her eyes off Cox, though.

Then Brenda sputtered and coughed.

He turned to look at her and Jane rushed forward with the bottle. She wasn't tall enough to hit him on the top of the head. She brought it down with all her force right above his ear.

He let out a yowl and staggered away a little.

Brenda started to scream as loud as she could. She was a terrific screamer. He jumped back on top of her with the knife in his hand and slammed his elbow into her chest, as if to brace himself. Then he laid the blade against her throat.

She wriggled and got her teeth around his hand and bit so hard she drew blood.

"Hang on, Brenda," Jane said. "Keep biting."

Jane prepared to lay into him with the bottle, but the knife was still too close to Brenda's throat. She dropped the bottle and picked up one of Brenda's turquoise spike-heeled shoes in her left hand. She wanted her right hand free.

She used it to grab the collar of his jacket and climbed up on his back, getting the leverage she needed to bring the spiked heel down hard on his hand. Now there were three of them, bundled up on the bed together, Brenda at the very bottom. He screamed a little and his fingers loosened.

She worked on the gash on his forehead with the spike while she peeled off his fingers from the knife. Brenda was still biting.

"I got it, I got it," she said between breaths. All three of them were huffing and puffing with exertion. She kept the shoe in one hand and she had the knife firmly in her other one. She knew she could do it. She could cut him with that knife. She had to find the right spot. It had to hurt him. If she sliced his arm it wouldn't work. And it had to be fast.

She sliced at his neck, trying to find the soft spot at the base of his throat. She saw a line of blood appear in the blade's wake on his sunburned, crepey neck with its sheen of white stubble.

With a huge roar he pulled himself away from Brenda and threw Jane off him. Clutching his throat, he staggered away.

Brenda started screaming again.

"Keep screaming," shouted Jane. It was a horrible, raspy scream. He'd probably damaged her throat throttling her.

He lurched toward the window and fell over the ledge onto the fire escape.

Jane gave him a final push, then slashed at his hands with the knife.

She heard him half falling, half climbing down the metal rungs. It reminded her of her own descent down the wall of the Devil's Bath.

"We've got to get help," she said to Brenda, who had now swung her legs off the bed. Her face was less red. Now it was pink. She was rubbing her throat and spitting.

"I got his damn blood in my mouth," she said. "Jesus. I'm coming with you. I can't stay here alone."

They clattered down the stairs, Brenda leaning on her and sobbing gently. Halfway down, they met the bartender with the black ponytail. He looked stern. "What's all the screaming? What the hell are you guys doing? Is this some kind of a cat fight or what?" he said.

"She's been attacked," said Jane. "The guy got away, out the fire escape."

She handed Brenda over to him and ran through the bar. Johnson was still gone. "Call the police," she shouted to the waitress. "Someone tried to kill Brenda—Stephanie. He went down the fire escape."

The waitress dropped her tray and Jane kept going, outside the door, into the sunshine, around the building and into an alley.

She hoped to find him collapsed at the bottom of the steps. She'd jump up and down on him until the police came. Too bad she wasn't wearing five-inch spikes, but she still had, she realized, one shoe and the knife in her hands.

What she saw there made her hysterical with happiness.

Steven Johnson had Cox slammed up toward his camper. He was kicking his feet back, and he had him in some kind of hold.

He wasn't struggling at all, but Johnson had him clamped down hard, his face, chin up, smashed against the camper.

"The Mounties are on their way," said Jane. She heard sirens in the distance.

"That amateur act was so pathetic, I decided to take a look around here for Cox's vehicle. It was right here in the alley. I was about to slice up his tires for him, when he fell down here at my feet."

"I'm bleeding," whimpered Cox.

Johnson smiled at Jane and gave Cox's arm an extra

little wrench. "Did you do all that damage?" said Johnson. He looked down at her hands. "With a fish knife and a hooker pump? Nice work."

Jane fell backward against a brick wall in the alley and caught her breath. "I used a tequila bottle too," she said.

Chapter 36

There they sat. On the seventieth floor of a large black glass tower in Seattle, in the conference room of the law firm of Carlson, Throckmorton, Osgood, Stubbins and Montcrieff, arranged around a long rosewood table. Six white-haired gentlemen who rose courteously as she entered the room.

The Bishop smiled his encouragement, and Commander Kincaid, the retired navy man, twinkled at her. But the lawyer, Montcrieff, Judge Potter and Professor Gruenwald all looked scrupulously neutral. Franklin Glendinning, the retired banker, looked slightly hostile, but that seemed to be his habitual expression.

"Thank you for waiting outside," said Mr. Montcrieff, "while we discussed your report." He touched the document in front of him, which she had scrupulously typed up at an all-night Kinko's copier store and had Xeroxed on high-quality rag paper. "Your verbal presentation was also very concise, and we think we have all the facts in our possession."

It had been humiliating to sit there in the lobby while Montcrieff's unctuous and overperfumed nephew Bucky had chatted her up. She couldn't imagine they ever kept Uncle Harold cooling his heels. If they didn't come through for her this time, she was going to sue them. First she'd threaten to expose how flaky Uncle Harold's whole foundation was in the first place. It wasn't for nothing they kept hammering at her to avoid publicity.

"We just had a few questions, my dear. More for curiosity's sake than anything else, and to make sure we all—"

"Get it?" she finished impatiently. Horrified at her impertinence, she smiled and added, "I hope I've made myself clear."

"Yes, yes," said the Bishop. "Now as we understand it, Mr. Shea is now a free man."

"That's right," she said. "There was no need for a new trial." How many times did they have to hear it? "Mr. Cox confessed when confronted with the fact that he had in his possession two items taken from Jennifer Gilbert's apartment: a photograph of Brenda MacPherson and an address book with an out-of-date address for her in Victoria. They were found in the room he rented under a false name above the Tip Top Club. It was an old fleabag hotel, and he rented a room down the hall. But they kept the strippers' section locked up, so he had to come around the fire escape.

"In addition," she added, "Brenda MacPherson was able to come up with the corroborating evidence that cleared Kevin. She saw him drop the gun and leave."

"And you got the powder burn thing sorted out?" said the Judge.

"Mr. Nguyen, the present owner of the pharmacy, remembered that Mr. Cox had been working with a harsh chemical used in cancer therapy in the back room." Just to impress them with her thoroughness, she threw in the name. "It is called doxorubicin. He was wearing gloves when he rushed into the front."

"So your work resulted in an innocent man's being freed,

and a guilty one placed behind bars," said Commander Kincaid with just a trace of impatience. "It's clear to me."

"What I want to know," said Professor Grunewald, "is what Cox said about killing his wife. What went through his mind?"

"He was very frank about it," said Jane. "He said when he stood there in front of her, holding a weapon, a good suspect conveniently vanished out the door, and wearing gloves, the temptation was too much for him. He said he hadn't realized until just that moment that he wanted her dead. He'd only known he hated his life and she wouldn't let them retire or spend any money and enjoy themselves. He had the nerve to kill her, but he'd never have the nerve to stand up to her."

"What I want to know," said Kincaid, "is whether this striptease artist is in any kind of trouble because of what she did. With the insurance company, I mean."

Jane cleared her throat. "I omitted that from my report, because I didn't think it was strictly relevant. The fact is, I was able to negotiate a deal with the insurance company. It turns out the parent company held the life insurance policy on Mrs. Cox. They were willing to forget about the fraud perpetrated by Jennifer Gilbert, who is, in any case, deceased, and Brenda MacPherson in exchange for Miss MacPherson's cooperation."

Glendinning nodded his head. "Makes sense. Getting the money back on the life insurance payoff more than canceled out the medical insurance fraud."

"Well young lady," said Mr. Montcrieff, "I guess you pulled it off. Uncle Harold was right about you. We had our doubts," he said waggishly. "A nice young lady like you. We weren't sure you had it in you."

"I am," said Jane with dignity, "my uncle's niece."

"And," said the Bishop, "the work suits you."

"Yes," she said. "It does. It is hard, but as Uncle Harold

so wisely said, 'There is no real satisfaction in anything that is too easy.' " Did this mean she had the money? He'd said I pulled it off, she thought.

"You have brought yourself," said the Bishop thoughtfully, "very close to evil."

"I've thought about that," she said. "It strikes me that a minor evil, something a lot of people would consider victimless, like cheating the insurance company, led to greater evil. If Jennifer and Brenda hadn't lied, a lot of this wouldn't have happened." She kept to herself the fact that she had lied plenty during her pursuit of the case. She'd managed to keep all her own lies out of her report. Another lie, perhaps?

"Cheating the insurance carrier is not a victimless crime," snapped Glendinning. "Everyone's premiums go up when people cheat."

She'd had enough. It was time for the close. "I take it," she said, "you are satisfied with my work, and I can expect the income that goes with the trust."

"Yes of course," said Montcrieff vaguely. "Come by tomorrow and we'll have the first check for you. Six months' worth of income."

"What are your plans now?" said Commander Kincaid.

"I'm going to start looking for another case," she said. Actually, she planned to go shopping—somewhere decent this time—do some major redecorating, get her Jaguar out of storage and get herself a really good haircut.

"Thank you very much for everything," she said, rising. Thanks for nothing, and see you old darlings in six months, she added silently. And I won't be wearing this fifteen-year-old Chanel suit, either.

As she left the conference room, Bucky came up to her. "Well?" he said.

"They gave it to me," she said, allowing a smile to pull up one corner of her mouth.

"All right!" he said, folding her into his Armani'd arms. "Let's celebrate. I want to hear all about how you're going to spend it."

"Oh, that would be terrific, but it'll have to be some other time. I've got lunch plans," she said, trying to look disappointed. After all, Bucky, as George Montcrieff's nephew and a member of the firm that administered the trust, could screw her over sometime in the future. She had better be as nice to him as she could.

He walked her to the elevator. "I'll call you. I'd like to show you around town. You need to meet some quality people."

"Well I already know you, Bucky, that's a start," she said as the elevator doors glided together in front of his handsome face. Crass old Bucky. What he meant was "You need to meet some quality people now that you're rich."

Calvin was waiting for her in the lobby polishing his glasses and examining a large modern sculpture.

She touched him on the shoulder and he turned around. "Well?" he said, replacing his glasses. "Where's lunch? Do we read the menu on the wall and take a number, or do we wait to be seated by someone with an expensive haircut?"

She smiled. "I got it. Help me celebrate. I want you to pick the best place in walking distance from this spot."

He smiled back. "Let's try Fuller's. About six blocks. I made a reservation just in case. Cutting-edge cuisine and great Northwest art."

"That's more than they've got in the art museum in this town," said Jane. "It seems to be full of totem poles."

"Don't be a snob about your hometown. Sounds like you'll be here for a while," he said. "And remember, the coffee here in Seattle is superb. And that's something you use every day."

"I'm glad I'll be able to pay you back," she said.

He cleared his throat. "I've got an invoice all prepared.

I gave you a pretty good rate. I figure you'll be using me a lot and you get a quantity discount."

They walked out into the street.

"I called juror number ten. Miss Marquardt is thrilled. And she's even more thrilled you're going to have lunch with her and tell her all about it."

"I'm kind of numb," said Jane. "I worked so hard, and I still can't quite believe it's real. I get the check tomorrow. Then I'm going shopping. And I think I'll forget about rescuing that old klunker of Uncle Harold's."

"Hope you'll remember the little people who helped you on the way up," he said.

She stopped in the street and embraced him, kissing him on the cheek. "You've been wonderful. Make sure there's a finder's fee in that invoice. For this case, and for the last one that didn't turn out so well."

"I'll throw that one in for free," he said.

Later, after a fabulous lunch in a little niche decorated with a painting by Mark Tobey, and a few glasses of wine, Calvin leaned across the table. "There's one thing I wondered," he said. "That deal you were able to cook up with the insurance company? Was it because of any personal—" He pulled himself back. "Never mind. It's none of my business."

She laughed. "No it's not, but what the hell. I'll tell you anyway. We had a little romantic interlude there before he went back to San Francisco."

She told him, she thought, because she thought he saw her as someone alone, and she didn't want him to feel sorry for her. But she wasn't telling him anything. She made it sound low-key and civilized.

It had begun with a long kiss in the room at the Empress Hotel—a wonderful long kiss of relief after all those hours with the RCMP, after everything that had happened over the past days, after days of driving and adrenaline flooding her body. It felt wonderful to surrender completely to mindless pleasure and stop thinking.

She remembered it in flickers—his hands reaching under her shirt while the kiss went on, and his saying, "I want my clothes back right now." He took them off slowly, kissing her skin softly as it appeared, inch by inch.

They came up for air the next day, Jane in a semi-passion-drugged state, long enough to take the float plane back from Victoria Harbor and a taxi to Uncle Harold's house, where they went right back to bed and talked in low voices and made noisy love in the big quiet house for two more days.

He'd called since, and she still ached for him physically, but she figured the longing would clear up in two or three rough weeks.

"I don't think it'll develop into anything major," she told Calvin. Their frenzy seemed based mostly on the exhilaration of having struggled together.

Calvin looked engagingly sympathetic. "I'm sorry," he said. She felt very fond of him just now.

"Don't be," she said. "I think it goes with the job." After all, they had started out by lying to each other. Could they trust each other again? "Only amateurs at this can fall in love, and as soon as I get that check tomorrow, I'll be entering the ranks of a very peculiar profession."

"What are you doing after you spend some money?" he said. "You're staying in Seattle, right?"

"I think so. Close to those old men on the board who control my fate. And I'll have to start scratching around for another wrong to right. After all, you're only as good as your last hopeless case."